SNATCH!

SNATCH!

RENNIE AIRTH

THE
COMPANION BOOK CLUB
LONDON

© 1969 by Rennie Airth

This edition is published by
The Hamlyn Publishing Group Ltd.
and is issued by arrangement with
Jonathan Cape Ltd.

*Made and printed in Great Britain
for the Companion Book Club
by Odhams (Watford) Ltd.*
SBN.600771180.

Chapter One

THE MOMENT I saw Morland step into the Beauregard I hit the floor and started crawling for the back door. I almost made it too. Another six feet and I wouldn't be sitting here today, staring at this wall, trying to remember how it all happened. Sometimes I wonder how it is that such a little thing like seventy-two inches can make such a big difference in the end. I mean if the smallest things in your life can turn out to be the most important, then what's the use of trying? You can't be on your toes all the time. Maybe the answer is lie back and enjoy it because it's going to happen anyway. But that's a gruesome thought.

I'd almost reached the door of the Ladies, which as the regulars know is the quickest way out of the Beau, when he spotted me.

'Found it, Harry?'

I got up slowly with this cold feeling in my gut. 'No,' I said. 'It must have rolled under the door.'

'Bad luck.' He gave me his special smile—all teeth and sincerity. 'Nice to see you again, Harry.'

'You too, Morland. How's it going?'

'Fine, Harry. Just fine.'

I wasn't fooled by the smile because he was watching me like a snake and he knows that makes me nervous. In fact, I might as well admit it, just being around Morland makes me nervous.

'What are you drinking?' I said. There was nothing else to say.

'Tea, Harry. Just tea.'

I'd forgotten. It was always tea. We sat down and Morland went on gazing at me in this hungry way he has, eyes all shining and fanatical. He's a big fellow, but thin and bony so you can see he needs a good feed. And he's got this white bony face and long beaky nose which make you think of a vulture down on its luck—and I hope he reads that.

'I hear you're in the ticket business these days, Harry.'

'That's right,' I said. 'A couple of years now.'

It didn't seem like two years since I'd seen Morland. It seemed more like two minutes.

I had to say, 'How about you?'—but I want to make it clear right from the start that this was sheer politeness and I had no wish whatsoever to know what Morland was doing and even less to get involved in it.

Morland grinned like a skull and said, 'I've really found it this time, Harry. Something really big.'

'That's great, Morland. Great.' As soon as he said it I was hunting for the waiter to pay and eyeing the door of the Ladies. I reckoned I could reach it in three steps.

'Oh, Harry, you can't imagine what a perfect set-up.'

Couldn't I? 'That's wonderful,' I said. 'I'm happy for you. But keep it to yourself. You can't trust anyone these days.'

'Except you, Harry'—he leaned across the table and started squeezing my arm like he was testing it for meat—'except you.'

'Especially me, Morland,' I said. Never mind the waiter, if I could just get to the Ladies.

'Harry, I'm going to tell you about it.'

'Morland,' I begged him, 'please don't.' I tried to get up but he had his claws dug into my arm. I couldn't move.

'Harry, you know I wouldn't think of leaving you out of something like this. If you'll just listen—'

'Morland,' I said, very calm, very reasonable, 'if I count the times I've listened to you, I'm counting disasters. For once,' I said, 'you listen to *me*. I have a nice business going in tickets and it took a lot of work to get it that way. The money's not big but it's enough—for one. It's a quiet life, Morland, and I like it,' I said, 'so for the love of God and in the name of sweet Jesus, leave me alone.'

You'd think he'd be moved by that!

Not Morland. He just shook his head slowly, dug in another inch or two and said, 'Harry, I'm deeply hurt.'

Deeply hurt! What a nerve! It was time to get tough. I gave him the clenched teeth bit and said, 'Morland, let go.' But he just went on shaking his head and mangling my arm.

'Morland!'—I was getting nervous again, I could feel it.

Suddenly he looked at me, all cold and businesslike, and said, 'Harry, you owe me. You owe me for Tangiers.'

Well that did it. That really did it.

'Owe *you* for Tangiers,' I said. 'Why, you ought to have your body hairs extracted singly at five-minute intervals over an open fire for what you did to me at Tangiers.'

'You always did have a nasty tongue, Harry.'

He let go of my arm then but I didn't move. I was thinking about Tangiers and the other times before that and I was so angry I wasn't sure I could get up without clocking him one.

'That Moroccan prison was no picnic, Harry.'

'You cannot know, Morland, how happy I am to hear that.'

'You're a vindictive man, Harry Brighton.'

I let that one pass.

'But you still owe me.'

He had this dogged look about him and I could see I'd have to be brutal.

'Morland,' I said, 'I certainly owe you, but it's how I'm going to pay you that I can't decide.' I let the menace hang there, cold and unmistakable, but Morland didn't seem to notice it. He waved to the waiter for more tea. I could see he was settling in for a long stay and that meant it was time for

7

me to leave, but quick. I'd been at my usual table in the Beau since ten that morning and anyone who hadn't got to me by then didn't deserve a ticket. Besides, the sight of Morland hanging over the table like a big black buzzard would certainly frighten off any customers who did show up late. I took another look at him and decided it wasn't only the Beau I ought to leave: it was time to blow Geneva too. He must have seen it in my eyes because suddenly he moved his chair around the table and brought his face up close to mine.

'Harry, what does two hundred and fifty thousand dollars say to you?'

'I don't hear a thing,' I said.

'*Two hundred and fifty thousand!*' He breathed the words into my ear in hot little puffs. 'A quarter of a million, Harry.'

He looked really starved and I hated to have to say it.

'Morland,' I said, 'do you know what two hundred and fifty thousand dollars says to me? It says, "Harry Brighton, you've been in some trouble before in your young life but nothing to the trouble you're going to be in if you sit listening to this lunatic any longer." ' Then I stood up quickly and said, 'Well, Morland, nice to see you again—' and that's as far as I got because all at once without any warning he said in a loud voice, 'This ticket business of yours, Harry, is highly illegal.'

'So tell the world,' I hissed.

'You owe me, Harry,' he said in this same loud voice. He wasn't smiling any longer.

With dignity, I asked, 'Am I to understand, Morland, that you are threatening me with the fuzz?'

'I never said it, Harry,'

I sat down stunned. 'I don't believe it,' I whispered.

I did though. Morland is absolutely without moral scruples.

'If you screw me,' I said, 'I'll screw you.'

'You don't know what I'm doing, Harry.'

'You bastard.'

8

'Now Harry'—he grabbed my arm again—'don't look at it that way. I'm not threatening you. I'm offering you sixty thousand dollars.'

'I thought you said a quarter of a million.'

'Split four ways, Harry, and ten thousand for expenses.'

He was serious, too. I could see that. A quarter of a million! Split four ways, Harry! Ten thousand for expenses! It was like an old familiar nightmare which you know from experience has this horrible ending, only you can't wake up. I sat there staring at him, wondering whether I could make a run for it. My hotel was only ten minutes away and I could check out and reach the frontier at Annemasse in half an hour. Then what? Morland knew where to look for me. London, Paris, Berlin, Geneva, Rome. If you're in the ticket trade you've got to be in one or other of those places. It wouldn't take him long to find me again and then he'd drop the law on my neck, or maybe he wouldn't, but how would I know? That was it. I'd never *know*. I'd be expecting the old tap on the shoulder every day, any day, nerves in shreds, business gone to hell . . . It really *was* a nightmare, what with the smoke hanging in the air and the old guy in the corner squeezing 'Petite Fleur' out of the accordion, and Morland's face floating before my eyes like something risen from the grave.

'All right,' I said with a sigh. 'Tell me.'

'I knew you wouldn't let me down, Harry.'

'Cut the crap. Just tell me what it is.'

Morland put his mouth right next to my ear and said, 'A snatch.'

'A *what*?'

'I said a—'

'I heard you,' I said. 'You're mad. You're stark raving mad. A snatch! I've never done anything like that in my life. You want to put the coppers on me? Go ahead. But I'm not getting mixed up in any snatch.'

9

'But it's a perfect set-up, Harry.'

'Perfect set-up! Morland, you've flipped. It must have been that Arab nick. Forget it.'

'You're damned right it was that Arab nick, and I'm not forgetting anything.' There were little red spots in his cheeks and he was giving his tea-bag a hell of a work-out, squashing and jabbing it around the bottom of his glass.

'Mashed beans and water for eighteen months is no picnic, Harry.'

'I thought they gave you two years,' I said.

I suppose it wasn't the most tactful thing to say under the circumstances. Anyway, Morland sort of exploded, punching my leg under the table and hissing like a leaky boiler.

'Never mind what they gave me, Harry Brighton. Just get this into your head. I'm going to pull that snatch and you're going to help me or I'll see you in prison, I swear it.' He was in a fair old froth and the tea-bag was a real mess. I didn't say a word and after a few seconds he calmed down. 'I'm forty-five years old, Harry. I've been on or around the bread-line all my life and I'm sick to death of it. I'm going to pull a big one, Harry, or go under for good.'

That's Morland for you. Always thinking of himself. Go under for good! What about me? I was a long way from forty-five and the bread-line was just a word to me.

But he was in this dangerous mood, so all I said was, 'I don't like this talk of going under.'

'No one's going under, Harry. We're going to be rich.' He was all sugar and smiles again but I wasn't fooled.

'And just who are you proposing to snatch?' I asked, playing for time.

'A baby.'

'Just any baby, Morland?'

'A certain baby, Harry. A certain very rich baby.'

'Do you know what happens to people who snatch babies?' I

said. 'They get put in prison for a long time, sometimes for ever.'

'Providing they're caught, Harry.'

'And you won't be, I suppose.'

'*We* won't be,' he said with a very nasty smile.

I ordered a whisky then. I needed it. Morland sat watching me, elbows on the table, shoulders hunched up around his neck, looking more than ever like a scabby old vulture waiting to take the first bite.

'Snatching babies,' I said, 'is immoral.'

He sneered. 'What was that, Harry?'

'But a kid, Morland.'

'Who better? It won't know a thing and what it doesn't know won't hurt it.'

I said, 'If I refuse and you put the law on me I'll get two, maybe three years for what I'm doing in tickets. If we're caught on a snatch it'll be twenty years for sure.'

'But we won't be caught, Harry. We'll just collect sixty thousand apiece and go our several ways. It's a perfect plan. It can't go wrong. Believe me.'

'I'll think about it,' I said. I was thinking all right.

He shook his head. 'You're coming in, Harry,' he said. Just like that.

'I've got to know more about the job,' I said, still playing for time.

'A snatch is a snatch, Harry. What do you need to know?'

'Don't you trust me?' I asked.

He put his arm around my shoulders, gave me a smile and a big warm squeeze and said, 'No.'

'That's funny,' I responded with cool humour, 'I don't trust you either.'

We sat there grinning at each other, him thinking he'd got me by the short and curly, me thinking all I needed was a little room to manoeuvre and I'd be off.

'Mutual distrust,' Morland said, 'is the ideal basis for any partnership. We can leave right away.'

'Leave? Where are we going?' I didn't like the way he was rushing things.

'Rome, Harry. It's all set.'

'How do you know it's all set?'

'Because I was there yesterday.'

I got this clammy feeling again, only worse than before. I said, 'Do you mean to tell me, Morland, that you came all the way to Geneva just to get *me*?'

'That's right, Harry.'

And that's when I really got scared. I know Morland, you see. He's got this fanatical streak and you just can't fight it. I paid the bill and we walked to the door, Morland breathing down my neck, ready to grab me if I made a run for it. I turned at the door and waved to Louis behind the bar and he waved back, which is something he never does for anyone. Then Georgette, who is his wife or something, came down from the cash-desk to give me forty francs which someone had left with her for me and said, 'Adieu Harry.' Just like that. And then a few other people I knew also waved to me and suddenly I got the feeling that none of them expected to see me again. Maybe they thought Morland was a copper, but whatever it was it scared me even more and by the time we got outside I had the shakes.

'Just tell me, Morland,' I said, 'why is it always me?'

He knew what I meant.

'Harry,' he said, 'I'm not superstitious but ever since we met I've known that one day we were going to make it big together.'

I couldn't believe my ears.

'But Morland,' I said, 'experience has surely taught you better.'

'Oh, I don't get discouraged so easily. And anyway, there's always the law of averages.'

'If there is one thing I don't want to bet twenty years of my life on it's the law of averages.'

'Then bet it on me, Harry. Bet it on me.'

In the half-darkness of the street I could see his eyes gleaming with this mad fanatical light. It didn't do my shakes any good.

'Morland,' I began—but what could I say?

When we got back to the hotel he said, 'There's one more thing, Harry.'

With Morland there always is.

'I'm having some passport trouble. I think I'd better have a new one. British, of course.'

'Now just a minute,' I said, and I was really mad. 'I don't give tickets away. I sell them, Morland, and they cost twelve hundred dollars and up.'

'Of course, Harry,' he said soothingly. 'I'll pay you when we collect.'

'Collect what?'

'The ransom, Harry. The ransom.'

Chapter Two

A BIRD ONCE ASKED ME what life was all about and I said, 'It's a numbers game, dear, and I've got yours,' which wasn't a bad off-the-cuff answer, given the conditions of the moment. What I meant was that it was all in the luck of the draw. Like in those auctions which that Roman Emperor held hundreds of years ago. They were just like any other auctions except for one thing: no one knew what was being sold. Of course the courtiers were too smart to let a little thing like that stop them and they kept the bids rolling in. When it was over one of them would find he'd won a box of jewels, say, or a seaside villa, while the geezer next to him would get a royal sandal, neatly wrapped. Well, that's how I see life, and I suppose it's a fair enough system providing you're not the one who ends up with the shoe.

I met Morland in Athens ten years ago, only 'met' is the wrong word. He found me, I should say, sitting in Zonar's one fine summer morning, waiting to take my daily quota of old birds up the Acropolis. I had this job as a guide then and I was starting in business on my own as well with a cigarette concession from the local U.S. Post Exchange. All in all it wasn't a bad life. The daily bit on the rock-pile could get you down, but I was also running a ruins-by-moonlight tour for the younger birds in the evening which was very relaxing. Anyway, there I was, checking last Saturday's home and away draws, when I heard a voice say, 'Harry Brighton?'

I looked up and saw this weird creature standing by the

table. Black suit, chalky face, long thin beak and rolling eye-balls.

'Harry Brighton,' it says again, 'they tell me you're a likely lad.'

Likely lad!

I let a few cool seconds slip by, then I said, 'The last geezer who called me a likely lad is still walking bandy-legged.'

He laughed and sat down and I was ready to lay one on him, only he didn't seem to notice.

'No offence, Harry. Let me buy you a cup of tea.'

I said, 'I don't drink tea and I don't talk to strangers.' I was giving him the freeze, see, and I thought it wouldn't take him more than a second or two to see he wasn't wanted. I was wrong.

He stuck his elbows on the table, looked at me in this hungry way and said, 'Harry, I'm going to make you rich.'

'Oh, that's nice,' I said.

'Very rich, Harry, and very famous.' His eyes were burning holes in mine.

'Rich *and* famous?' I said, sort of swallowing.

He nodded slowly, grinned, and said, 'Now what about that cup of tea?'

'Could I make mine a beer?' I said.

Now I know what you're thinking. How could I get taken in by that? Well, I wasn't, see. I knew he was trying to con me, the question was, could I con him? When you're young and just getting started you can't afford to let these opportunities slip by. And Morland was opportunity with bells on. So I listened while he trotted out his line and almost immediately I spotted just the chance I'd been waiting for. I've never been one to hesitate, so I resigned from the guide business then and there, except for the evening bit, and told my naval associates to step up the cigarette consignments.

Morland's plan—and now you'll laugh—was to buy a boat

15

and sail up the coast past Sounion to hunt for sunken statues. That's right, *statues*. According to him there were hundreds of them lying about the sea bed waiting to be picked up. Not only would we make a pile, he said, but we'd be doing a service to archaeology. That last part tickled me.

My plan was to get the boat.

The one thing I needed to put my cigarette business on a sound financial basis was a boat, Greece being full of islands and all. I was having to sell most of my stock in Athens and it burned me up to think how much I was losing to the boys who had their own boats. The way I planned it was to let Morland chase after his statues for a few weeks, then put the squeeze on him. Once I was running smokes—and maybe a little hair-spray and deodorant on the side—instead of fart-arsing around after statues, I'd sort of ease Morland out. And keep the boat.

We bought a thirty-footer with a diesel engine for three hundred quid, half shares, and then Morland said we had to buy diving tackle and a winch for all these statues we were going to haul out of the sea, and that was another hundred quid each. We also hired two Greek boys to do the crewing and diving because, as I told Morland, I wasn't getting into any monkey suit to go crawling around the bottom of the sea looking for lumps of marble. What with the cost of stores and fuel I was about cleaned out when we sailed from Piraeus. But I had half a million fags on order in Athens and there was a long summer ahead of us.

I remember that morning well. The sun was bright, the air was cool and the sea had that hard chipped look which you find in Greece. Morland stood in the bow or the prow or whatever you call it shouting things like 'hard-a-starboard' and 'up-your-helm' which kept the Greek boys in fits. I sat at the back under a square of canvas, nice and cool in the shade, sipping retsina and watching Morland perform. He was wearing his nautical gear: pink sweater, blue peaked cap, rope sandals. 'How do I look, Harry?' he asked. 'Like a ponce in the Charing Cross Road,' I said. I'd come to like him in a way. He had this thing about him, innocence, I suppose. He believed in things like fate and good luck.

'We're going to do it, Harry,' he said. 'I've got a feeling in my bones.' Poor old Morland. Still, as I say, I had a soft spot for him then, though it didn't last. We sailed up past Sounion that day and all I remember is that everything was beautiful and peaceful. The sky was this soft pale blue, and the sea was calm and there was nothing to do except eat and drink and kip in the sun. Morland tried to tell me about the temples and things that we passed on the way, but I just said, 'Yes, Morland—sure, Morland,' to keep him happy because I didn't want to spoil the day. Besides, listening to Morland can be dangerous. A lot of people think he's really sharp because he knows so much. And not just about temples and statues either. Mention a subject, any subject, and Morland will give you five minutes on it. Naturally, people assume that with all that information he must have a brain to go with it. They're wrong. Morland is just a sponge.

I'd rather not go into what happened next, not in detail, anyway, because even after all these years it still hurts. What I will say though is if you ever get the idea of going to Greece to hunt for sunken statues, bear one small detail in mind: it's illegal. Morland claimed he didn't know, but with a shifty bastard like that you can never be sure. Anyway, it turned out the Greeks have a law about people coming and lifting their old statues and the only thing that saved us when they nicked us was that in three weeks we hadn't found so much as a finger. But they still fined us, don't ask me why, hunting statues out of season maybe, and when we couldn't pay they took the boat and tackle.

To my dying day I'll remember that morning I stood

17

outside the court-room in Athens with eight dracks in my pocket and half a million cigarettes on my conscience and heard Morland say, 'Well, Harry, that certainly taught us a lesson.' I just turned and walked away because I knew I was either going to break down and howl or else bust him in the snoot. It was a lesson all right: a lesson to keep a lot of distance between me and Morland. A continent, say.

But of course he found me again, in London, two years later. I'd moved into the contemporary antique trade by then and was doing quite nicely, so I knew that nothing Morland could suggest would have the slightest appeal for me. But that business in Greece was still sticking in my gullet. I mean, I'd been had. So I thought I'd let Morland trot out his line just once more in case there was something in it for me. That was a mistake. I spotted a couple of angles right away and decided to branch out from the antique business. It was a clear case of reason overriding instinct. Morland, needless to say, was tickled. 'And it's legal, Harry, it's legal,' he kept repeating, like he couldn't believe it himself.

It was legal all right. In fact, legal was about all you could say for Samarkand Tours—'Your Magic Carpet to the Orient' —'Twelve and a Half Days of Sun-drenched Bliss (demi-pension)' 'Five Quid Down, the Rest in Easy Stages'. When the court declared us bankrupt we had a party of Irish nuns stranded in Jeddah—and God alone knows how they got *there*, never mind how they got back—two groups from Scunthorpe on public relief in Nicosia and warrants out for our arrest in three Middle Eastern countries. The warrants bit was due to a misunderstanding about a party of showgirls travelling to Beirut by stages, incognito. Since it was something I'd arranged personally Morland took it very hard that the warrants included his name and accused me of conduct unbecoming a business partner and some other things of a coarser nature which I'll not repeat.

'Odious bloodsuckers' was what the *News of the World* called us both, and while Morland was negotiating to sell them his life story in four instalments, I quietly faded. I had to get away from Morland. He was becoming an obsession. I'd got this crazy idea into my head that he was some sort of jinx. And then there was this dream I kept having of a big black bird that flew round and round in circles above me. I'd lie there watching the bird flap-flapping its black wings and snapping its dirty great beak. I knew that one night it would turn into Morland.

So I took the boat train to Paris and sent Morland a card saying, 'See you in Hongkong.' Then I flew to Tangiers.

It took him four years to find me that time and when he saw how nicely I was doing with this export business he got all choked. 'I always knew you had it in you, Harry,' he said.

'Thanks,' I said.

'What we have to do now is expand,' he said.

I told him where he could do his expanding and he seemed quite hurt. 'You've no faith, Harry,' he said. 'But sooner or later you're going to need me, so I'll just wait around until you do.'

I said, 'You could grow wings waiting for that.'

I wish I hadn't said that. After I'd watched him sitting at the same table in the same café across the square from my office every day for a month I began to think he *had* grown wings: nasty great vulture's wings. It was my dream all over again. With his black suit and his long thin beak he was like some horrible bird of prey, squatting in the sun, waiting for dinner. He was there when I arrived in the morning; when I went to lunch he was there; and in the evening when I locked up, there he was again giving me a smile and a nod and sort of ruffling his feathers. I knew I'd have to do something drastic. There were two alternatives, and one of them was to have him dumped in the harbour. I gave it serious thought. But I'm soft, see, so I walked over the road and said, 'I can give you a job if you like.'

He said, 'Harry, I wouldn't take money from you without sharing the risk. We'll be partners, just like before.'

'That's what I'm afraid of,' I said.

Morland was very anxious to make some contribution to the business and right away he said we ought to buy two more boats. The suggestion was his contribution, the boats were mine. 'Think big, Harry. Think big.' Then he started checking the cargoes I was running and shaking his head. 'Cognac, cigarettes, porn—small-time, Harry, small-time. We've got to move into the big money.'

So we moved into the big money. It was a success. It was a great success. In fact, by the time I left Tangiers one evening, lying in two inches of stinking water under a pile of stinking nets, we had twenty thousand dollars stashed in the safe at the office. It was one of the things Morland had to explain to the constabulary, along with the six cases of Browning fifty calibre machine-guns and the ten bales of untreated hemp which they found in the back room. I hated leaving all that money but when I heard they'd given Morland two years it seemed worth it. Twenty thousand dollars worth it!

Still, if it hadn't been for the comfort of knowing that Morland was in the nick, I might have thrown in then. Gone back to being a guide maybe or opened a caff. I was sick of building up things just so Morland could come along and tear them down. What I wanted was a business where the profits were high, the risks low and the assets liquid. In other words, a fairy godmother. Well, Ziggy Ziggendorp, bless his fine old Belgian heart, is no fairy, or godmother either. But he did the trick for me, and no matter what happens from now on, I'd like to say that my gratitude to him remains pure and unaffected.

I ran across Ziggy in Majorca, after I left Tangiers, and it was lucky I did because with my departure being so sudden and all I'd had to leave my passport behind. Ziggy had been running a ticket business for longer than anyone could remember, and everyone who knew him trusted him, which, in the circles I move in, is very rare, if not altogether unknown. So I was happy to see him, and after he'd fixed me up with a nice six-month-old British job, good for another four and a half years, I said what about a drink. We ended up spending the evening together, and though Ziggy was his usual charming self, I could see he had something on his mind. It wasn't until quite late—when he ran out of puff and I had to help him to bed—that he came clean. It was old age, see, he was past it. He knew he'd have to retire soon and there was no one to take over the business. One son was in a bank in Brussels, he said, the other was studying law. 'What am I going to do, Harry?' he said. 'I've got clients in five capitals who depend on me.' That was Ziggy for you. He may have been a crook, but he ran his business like a gentleman. With most people it's the opposite.

'Ziggy,' I said, 'if there's anything I can do to help just say the word.'

He shook my hand and I could see he was touched because he was crying. 'Harry,' he said, 'I want you to keep the business going. I want you to take over from me.'

I was choked. Ziggy choosing *me*. I couldn't believe it. It was one of those moments when you take a long hard look at yourself to see what you missed.

But of course I accepted. You don't refuse a man like Ziggy.

He stayed on for six months to teach me the ropes. When the time came for me to take over we discussed price and agreed that five thousand quid was a fair figure. This included a small but select stock of tickets—Ziggy sold only the best, no London-issued Lithuanians for him—and of course his goodwill, which was the prime asset so to speak. It was a very fair price but still a problem. The only way I could pay it was to draw the fifteen thousand dollars which Morland and I had paid into a joint account in Geneva with the idea of purchasing certain goods which, as things turned out, were never purchased. Of course I recognized that a question of ethics was involved in drawing the money but I reckoned that the twenty thousand dollars in the office safe at Tangiers represented more than Morland's fair share and at any rate was enough to meet his legal expenses. It wasn't until much later that I heard the money had been confiscated in part payment of a fine. And by that time of course the question of Morland's legal expenses had become purely academic.

So I paid Ziggy. And as a farewell present I gave him an 1812 French diplomatic, signed by the Emperor himself, a beautiful job, all tooled green leather and fancy script. I can remember like it was yesterday, the tears streaming down his worn old face as he waved goodbye from the train that took him to what I sincerely hope is proving to be a long and happy retirement at Knokke-le-Zoute.

And that about brings us up to date. I had nearly two years in the business before Morland showed up. It was a happy time, the happiest of my life I'd say. Interesting work, a steady financial return, plenty of travel and the satisfaction of doing a public service. I began to understand why Ziggy had felt so strongly about it. To him a passport was more than just a permit to travel. It was part of a man's personality, a second skin if you like. 'These days,' he used to say, 'we all have this problem with identity. Nobody knows who he is any more. But having a passport helps. At least you've got something there in black and white. At least you can open your ticket and look at your picture and say, "That's me—Joe Blow." ' Nicely put, I thought, though in the case of most of our clients, the name in the passport wasn't theirs anyway, so as far as their identity

22

was concerned they must have been more confused than ever. Still, I was sure Ziggy had a point, even if it wasn't entirely clear to me. As far as I was concerned it was enough to be helping people and getting paid for it too. I reckoned I'd found my spot. Until Morland showed up.

Chapter Three

WHEN WE GOT UP to my room in the hotel I set about fixing a new ticket for Morland. I usually travel with a stock of a dozen or so, but at that moment I was running low. I'd sold five already in Geneva including two British, which are generally my best line, and had only picked up one Liberian in return. I did consider trying to palm it off on Morland but I knew he wouldn't take it. Morland can pass for a lot of things but Liberian isn't one of them. I had only one British left with only six months to run. Of course you can alter the dates or forge the renewal but that's a long tricky job which needs an expert pen and stamp man. I usually have my alterations done in London and in fact I was taking this particular ticket back home for just that purpose. I explained all this to Morland and he said he'd take the six-monther as it stood and have it doctored later.

If you're doing a thorough job on a ticket you have to start by changing the name and serial number because both are circulated as soon as the passport is reported nicked. Then you have to switch photos and fix the signature which is often the trickiest part. For a rush job though, like I was doing for Morland, all that's necessary is to change photos. That would get him across the frontier into Italy where he could have the rest done later. Of course the Italian police would know sooner or later by checking the circulated lists that a stolen ticket had entered the country, but Morland would have plenty of time to do the necessary before they caught up with him.

He gave me a photo of himself and I got down to work. First I made a rubbing on tracing paper of the official seal stamped

24

into the picture that was already in the passport. It came up, 'British Consulate-Gen . . .', which meant I had to use my consulate seal, not the Foreign Office one. When I'd got the rubbing done I cut out the half-moon of the seal showing up on the tracing paper and laid it on Morland's photo. Then, fitting my own seal to the rubbing, making sure that the 'British Consulate-General' part coincided, I stamped Morland's photo, leaning hard on the block so that the seal pressed through the paper into the surface of the print. Morland's photo now had the same half-moon stamp on it as the one in the passport. After tracing the outline of the old photo I lifted it with a razor blade, taking care not to damage the paper beneath which carried the same imprint of the seal. Next I spread a thin paste on the back of Morland's photo and fitted it to the traced outline. The seal on Morland's photo fell exactly on the imprint left by the stamp on the old picture. If you looked at the back of the page the picture was pasted on you'd have thought that the stamp on Morland's photo and the one that had come through the page were one and the same. That's the kind of thing your nosy immigration official looks for.

It took me all of half an hour and I was sweating by the time I finished. But I knew I'd done a good job and that's what counts. There's a lot of sloppy work done in this business just like in any other. I know people who'd sell you a third-hand ticket, two years expired, forged with rotten ink and stamped with some seal that could be Cambodian, Congolese or I don't know what. And when you're nicked with it they'll just shrug and say you ought to be more careful what you buy.

Feeling good, I tossed the ticket over to Morland on the bed and said, 'There you are. From now on you're Trumpington Fanhurst.'

'No, really?'—you wouldn't believe it but he actually had a peep to see. 'Oh, Robert Brown,' he said, looking very cut-up.

Sitting there on the bed, sort of slumped over his knees and nodding slightly, he looked older than I remembered and thinner too. His coat was a couple of sizes too big for him and there were loose threads hanging at the ends of the sleeves. Two of the buttons were missing. He looked a mess, like something that had been used once too often, or maybe twice. I wondered when he'd had his last meal.

'How about a sandwich or something?'

He shook his head.

'You don't look too good.'

'I've had a spot of heart trouble.'

'What do you mean, heart trouble?' Right away I was on my guard.

'Oh, one of those things, you know. It comes and goes.'

'Which is it doing now?' I asked.

He shook his head and sighed. 'I might have known I'd get no sympathy from you, Harry Brighton.'

'Now just a minute,' I said hotly. 'Are you sick or not, just tell me.'

'I'm fine, Harry, fine.' He gave me a misty sort of a smile. I'd love to have planted one in his gut just to see how sick he really was, but instead I said, 'I don't think a man with heart trouble should do what you're planning to do.'

'That's just it, Harry. I must.'

'What do you mean?'

'I've got to make a killing. Something really big. I won't be able to work for too much longer. Not the way things are going.'

By this time he was rubbing his chest and giving the odd cough like he wasn't sure whether to lay his money on his ticker or his lungs.

'If you're putting me on, Morland,' I said, but he held up his hand.

'Harry, I don't want sympathy'—pause for cough—'and no special consideration either. This is business.' Two coughs.

26

'Everyone has to pull his weight.' And then he made his big effort to smile.

Of course I didn't believe a word of it, though I knew Morland would do almost anything for sympathy. Even croak. But to keep him quiet I told him he could lie down on my bed till it was time to leave. Later, when I was packing, he told me he'd got two sleepers on the night train to Rome.

'We'll be there by lunch-time,' he said. 'Then you'll meet the others.'

'Who are they?'

'You don't know them.'

'Amateurs?'

'Harry, in this we're all amateurs.'

'What a lovely thought,' I said.

It *was* shaping up beautifully, no question of that. In fact, on the basis of past experience, I was ready to start selling tickets for what was clearly going to be Morland's Final Fiasco. Only this time there'd be a slight change in the advertised programme. This time Harry Brighton wasn't going to be there when the roof came in.

Just before we left Ilona came up to the room. She'd heard I was leaving and hurried over from the Ba-Ta-Clan between shows to say goodbye. She's a sweet kid, Hungarian actually. I'd fixed her up with a Nansen paper soon after we met for which she was very grateful.

'Do you mind?' I said to Morland, who was goggling at us like he'd never seen a couple kissing before.

'Well, don't be too long,' he said. 'I'll wait outside.'

I wouldn't have minded if he'd stayed. I hate saying goodbye to birds. They're too clever at giving you this feeling that you're running off with something that belongs to them. But Ilona's a good kid and all she said was could I get her a passport some time instead of the Nansen. I said I'd try, but now I suppose she'll have to manage without.

Morland said, 'Don't worry about leaving the girl. I've got something arranged for you in Rome.'

'You turning pander, Morland?' I asked coldly.

'Wait and see,' he said, looking very smug all of a sudden. I didn't like it. I didn't like it at all.

It was a long night and I didn't sleep much. I remember staring at this little blue lamp over my bunk and wondering how I could ditch him. On the one hand I didn't fancy spending a couple of years inside just to satisfy Morland's petty spite. But on the other, the thought of twenty years in the nick was like slow paralysis. The only thing to do, I thought, was to play it by ear. When things turned really nasty—and I knew they would—I could always pull out and hope that Morland would be so far up to his neck in the old *merde* that he wouldn't have time even to think about getting back at me. But even that pleasant picture couldn't wash out this other feeling I had that things weren't going to turn out very well, no matter what I did. It's the same feeling I always have when I come within spitting distance of Morland.

Chapter Four

I SAID POLITELY, 'Is this your first visit to Rome?'

I had to say something. We'd been sitting there for ten minutes waiting for Morland to come back and she hadn't made a sound. I don't know what she thought of me but I certainly didn't fancy her. For snatching babies, that is. For a bird she was all right. Red-haired and quite pretty, though sort of tough-looking.

So, as I say, to make conversation, I said, 'Is this your first visit to Rome?'

She didn't answer. Just gave me this green-eyed stare like I'd popped out from under a stone. Right, I said to myself, if that's the way you feel, and I went back to the *Playboy* I'd picked up at the station when we arrived.

Her name was Paula. That was all I knew. Morland had introduced us when we got to this *pensione* off Via Margutta. We were in her room. Through an open door I could see a pair of stockings drying on the bath tap. Some of her clothes were draped over a chair, and the dressing-table was all covered with pots and tubes and pencils, and bits of this and that. There was face powder on the floor and cream on the mirror, and the air was full of the smell of soap and scent and drying clothes. It's always the same, the mess women make. But when it's not there you miss it. I looked at her again, trying to decide what my best line would be. She looked like the kind of bird who'd heard a lot of lines in her time. A real hard trick, I mean. At the moment she was half-lying on the bed, reading some women's magazine, smoking. All I could see was the top of her head, her fingers—no nail polish, I liked that—and her legs. She was wearing capris, green and tight, very fetching, specially as she had those long straight legs you find on dancers. Very nice, I said to myself, very nice indeed. And not too young either, which is also nice. Morland had gone out as soon as he'd introduced us, muttering something about coming back in a minute. That was ten minutes ago. All he'd said was, 'Paula, this is Harry. Harry—Paula. You'd better get to know each other.' And then he'd gone out. She'd looked at me for a few seconds with those cool green eyes, then picked up the magazine and started reading it. I wondered what Morland had been telling her about me. I could guess.

The door opened and Morland came in. He had a copy of *Time* magazine. 'How are you two getting on?' he asked with a smile.

The girl got up, walked into the bathroom and shut the door.

'Now, Harry, what have you been saying to her?'

'Can't you guess?'

He got flushed and said, 'I don't care whether you like her or not but you'd better find a way of getting on with her. I mean it. It'll be better for both of you.'

'Where did you find her, anyway?' I asked.

'Oh, around,' he said vaguely and started leafing through the magazine.

'*Around?*' I said. 'What do you mean, *around?* You're not rolling drunks for a fiver on Poland Street. You're planning a snatch, Morland, a *snatch*—'

'Shhh.' He jumped out of his chair, shot over to the door, opened it, looked both ways quickly, then shut it again. 'For God's sake, Harry.' I could see he was really scared.

'All right,' I said. 'But just tell me, why the bird?'

He stood there, squinting down his beak at me for a few seconds. Then he leaned over a little and said softly, 'Harry,

I've given a lot of thought to this job. Six months, maybe more, I've spent thinking about it. I've gone over the whole thing step by step. There isn't an angle I haven't thought of, believe me. The girl is necessary. She has a job to do. So have you, so have I and so has Hermann.'

Hermann?

'Who the hell is Hermann?' I said.

'Be patient, Harry.' He looked at the bathroom door and said, 'You must have said *something* to upset her.'

'Sure, I asked if it was her first time in Rome.'

He looked worried. 'There must be something about you she doesn't like.'

'There probably is,' I said, 'after what you've told her.'

'Now, Harry—' he began, but the door opened and she came back in. She'd changed the pants for a blue skirt cut above the knee. Her legs were stunning. Morland was right. No sense in starting off on the wrong foot. So I gave her a big smile and said, 'Oh, there you are. We were just waiting for you to begin.'

She sat down on the bed, crossed her legs, took out a cigarette tapped it on her knee, lit it, blew a big cloud of smoke in my face and said, 'So let's begin.'

Morland coughed. You'd have thought it was him who'd got the faceful of smoke. He said, 'Hermann will be here any moment but we can start without him because he knows most of it.' He was speaking softly and we had to lean forward to hear—Paula on one bed, me on the other. Morland was sitting with his back to the dressing-table and I could see our faces in the mirror—Paula's and mine—and the bald spot at the back of Morland's head. Paula had her eyes narrowed like she wasn't sure of the company she was keeping: smart girl. My face looked hurt and distrustful which is not surprising since that's how I felt.

'You both know what we're going to do,' Morland went on in this same quiet voice. 'We're going to kidnap a baby.' He stopped there and let the word sink in. Kidnap! I could swear I felt a cold hand take my heart and squeeze it. Paula's face had gone pale, I noticed, and then I saw *mine*. Morland glanced at us both, nodded like he was satisfied and said, 'The baby in question is a boy, aged thirteen months.' He paused again. 'This is its father.' He held up the copy of *Time* with the cover facing us. 'Yusuf Rifai.'

Yusuf Rifai!

The cold hand gave an extra squeeze.

'Rifai?' I said—only my throat was so dry, it came out in a sort of croak. I swallowed and said again, 'Rifai?'

Morland nodded. He watched me for a moment, then glanced at Paula. She was pulling at a thread on her skirt like she hadn't even heard him. I held out my hand for the maga-zine and Morland passed it over. I didn't need to read *Time* to know about Rifai. I just wanted to see if they'd got it right. The face on the cover was fat and brown with a thin moustache and an oily smile. That was Rifai all right, I'd seen his picture enough times in the newspapers. I'd never seen him in the flesh, but that wasn't surprising since guys like Rifai can afford to keep the sweaty throngs at a distance. What is strange though is that to this very day I've still never set eyes on him. The closest I got was seeing his shadow on a gravel drive—but that comes later.

I started reading the article and right away I saw that *Time* was not being entirely frank. Either that or someone had taken them for a ride. '. . . extensive banking interests . . . huge tanker fleet . . . bulging oil concessions . . .' I read. '. . . financial genius . . . legendary manipulator . . . investment whizz . . .' Friend of kings, it said, adviser to governments, and I don't know what else. Well, I'm not saying that isn't true, all I'm saying is that in a good many establishments around the Med., starting with the Green Blind in Beirut all the way to the Friendly Rooster in Gib, the name of Yusuf Rifai is connected with something altogether different. Mediterranean Monarch, this piece in the magazine called him: Prince of the Ponces is more like it. Frenchy Delacroix, who runs a small place in Marrakesh, once told me Rifai owned seventy per cent of the houses in the Med. ports. Frenchy is given to exaggeration, so let's cut that to sixty per cent. It still makes Rifai just about the biggest King Pander out of captivity. And I didn't need Frenchy to tell me he wasn't a man to cross. I'd had some personal experience in that line when I'd tried to go into real estate in Beirut a few years back. I'd made a payment on this place and already had offers for more than half the rooms when a couple of meatballs from the organization called on me with the word that this wasn't the season for independent productions. They said they'd come to buy me out so I asked what they were offering. 'We're offering you a free ride out of town,' they said. 'And you can go in one piece.' Not everyone would think that a generous offer, I know, but generosity, as Morland would say, is relative. Anyway, I took it. Of course I'm not claiming Rifai had a personal hand in it because obviously he wouldn't know I even existed. But it did show he approved of what you might call a policy of generalized brutality towards the competition. And I couldn't help asking myself what a man who was ready to carve up a simple business competitor would do to anyone who knocked off his kid. There was a bit about the kid at the end of the article. This is what it said:

> . . . Syrian-born Rifai was childless until his third marriage to
> lovely Dina Arifa, eighteen-year-old daughter of Lebanese
> banker Suleiman Arifa, who died giving birth to their son,
> Selim. Rifai has told friends he will not marry again, so
> presumably little Selim one day will inherit his father's
> hundred-million-dollar business empire.

Father and son live in a sumptuous penthouse in Beirut, but Rifai usually spends a few months of each year in

Rome where he maintains a palatial villa on the ancient Appian Way. The playboy-millionaire of ten years ago is now a quiet-living widower, absorbed in his business interests and devoted to his only child. The baby, guarded day and night by a squad of tough bodyguards, accompanies his father on his worldwide travels . . .

'I don't want to upset your plans, Morland,' I said, 'but there's a little mention here of bodyguards. Day and night, it says. Day *and* night, Morland.'

'Have you finished?' He took the magazine and gave it to Paula.

'Well?'

'Patience, Harry, patience.' He looked at his watch and then smiled at me in this knowing, fatherly way. I could feel my stomach tying itself in a knot. Paula put the magazine aside without even looking at it.

'Aren't you going to read it?' I asked.

She shrugged and started fiddling with her nails.

I tried to blink away the black spots but it was no use, so I went into the bathroom and dipped my face in cold water. When I'd cooled down I went back and said, 'Morland, I don't like it. I wouldn't steal last week's newspaper from Yusuf Rifai. As for snatching his kid—' I just shook my head like it was beyond belief. It wasn't though. I knew Morland.

He rubbed his hands. 'What about some coffee?' he said brightly.

Paula said, 'There's no room service here. I'll go down and get it.' She smiled at him as she went out. Maybe she likes him, I thought. I couldn't believe it. The whole thing was getting more creepy by the minute.

As soon as she'd gone I said, 'All right, Morland, let's have it.'

'What do you mean, Harry?' he said smiling.

34

'Don't give me that "Harry" bit,' I said. 'If you brought me down here for a joke you've had your laugh. Now the laugh's over. I'm clearing out.'

'Don't be in such a hurry,' he said. 'You haven't met Hermann yet.'

Just then there was a tremendous thumping on the door and a deep voice called out, 'I may enter—yes?'

'Come in, Hermann,' Morland said.

Hermann came in and suddenly the room got smaller. He was one of the biggest krauts I'd ever seen, six foot three or four and a yard wide, with one of those flat squarish heads you find on your kraut, pale-blue eyes and an inch of snow-white hair that stood up like pig bristles. He had dark tanned skin and deep wrinkles round the eyes. It was difficult to guess his age but I'd have said closer to fifty than forty. He wore a pale-blue suit straining at the seams and a bulge under his left armpit which wasn't part of his winter woollies. He looked a very tough meatball.

'Hermann, this is Harry,' Morland said. 'Harry—Hermann.'

We shook hands and mine came back with a different shape.

'I am pleased to meet you, Harry,' he said, spitting the words like nails, but giving me a big toothy grin to show he meant it.

For a moment I was stunned, then it clicked. This is the boss, I thought. He's the one that's running the caper, not Morland. At first I was relieved, but then when I started to think about it I didn't like it at all. I could handle Morland, but Big Hermann was another matter.

'I've been looking forward to meeting you, Hermann,' I said warmly. 'Morland's told me a little about the job but I'm anxious to hear the rest.'

Hermann nodded. 'Soon you will know,' he said and sat on the bed beside me—it sort of whimpered but held up. 'Jonathan will tell you when he is ready.'

35

Jonathan?

'Who the hell is Jonathan?' I said. The boat was getting crowded.

Morland coughed and Hermann looked puzzled.

'Jonathan,' he said, pointing to Morland.

'You never told me your name was Jonathan,' I said coldly.

Morland shrugged and simpered.

Jonathan! You know a geezer for ten years and then find out his name is Jonathan.

'Okay, Jonathan,' I said. 'So you're the boss.' I went back to the bathroom to do some thinking. What I couldn't figure out was how come a very tough kraut like Hermann was taking orders from Morland. It didn't make sense. I looked at myself in the mirror and said, 'Harry, it stinks.' Then I gave my face another rinsing in cold water and went back. Hermann was watching Morland scribbling something in a small black notebook. He sat all tensed up and alert. You could see he was ready to bark, sing, stand on his head, or roll over and play dead. Morland only had to give the word. It scared me. The door opened and Paula came in with a tray. 'Hullo, Hermann,' she says in this nice low voice—nothing like the snake act she'd given me. Hermann gets up and helps her with the tray and she says, 'Thank you, Hermann.' Then Morland looks up and smiles and she smiles back, and I can see that everyone is very chummy with everyone else. Except me.

'Let's get on with it,' I snapped.

Morland shut his notebook sharply and said in his brisk official voice, 'The snatch will take place in approximately one month, that is to say—'

'A month—' I began, but the girl cut in with, 'Can't you let him finish?' and gave me a cold stare.

'—that is to say,' Morland went on, 'in the last week in June. The interval of a month is necessary'—he looked at me—

36

'because of certain preparations which have to be made. You'll know what they are very soon.'

'Why not now?' I said.

'I prefer to deal with each point as it comes up.'

'Well, I don't,' I said. 'And furthermore—'

'NOT NOW.' It came like a blast from a double-barrelled shotgun. And it came from Hermann, right beside me. His neck had turned a nasty shade of red, he was breathing like an old bull seal, his fists were enormous. Well, you can't argue with brute force—not unless you've got a bigger brute to help you—so I shrugged and shut up.

'We start tomorrow,' Morland said. 'Harry, you and Paula are coming for a drive into the country with me. We'll need to hire a car. You and I can do that later. Paula, I'd like you to go over to the apartment this evening and see that everything's in order. And tell the neighbours you're moving in, make a big thing of it. You know, settling into a new home and all that sort of thing. Hermann, you stay at your post and keep your eyes open. I want to know immediately about any changes in the normal pattern.'

'*Ja*, Jonathan,' Hermann said, and I could see he was just dying to click his heels and snap out the old salute.

'May I ask a question?' I said sweetly. Actually there were a whole lot of questions I wanted to ask—car? apartment? drive in the country?—but I was playing it cool.

'Of course, Harry.'

'Just what is Hermann's post?'

Morland smiled. He was so pleased with himself you could almost hear the applause. 'Hermann,' he said, 'is Yusuf Rifai's chief bodyguard.'

I whistled. I couldn't help it.

'Well, what do you say now, Harry?'

I looked at Hermann. He was beaming with pride. You could see this was a big moment in his life.

37

'Well, Harry?'

They were all looking at me—Morland, the girl, Hermann —and suddenly I realized they weren't so sure of themselves after all. I remembered what Morland had said. Each of us had a job to do. I had a pretty good idea that if I didn't do mine the whole damn bubble would burst. Maybe Morland did have me where it hurt over my ticket business, but I was beginning to see that if I waited long enough I'd be able to get him in exactly the same position. It was the nicest thought I'd had all day.

'Morland,' I said, 'I'm impressed. Really impressed.'

'Harry, I've waited ten years to hear you say that.'

Well, for crying out loud, I thought, then I saw the girl sort of sneering at me so I said, 'Big deal,' and drank my coffee, which was cold.

Morland went on grinning and preening himself and I began to wish I hadn't told him I was impressed. Praise goes to Morland's head. He took a quick peek at his notebook, shut it with a snap and said, 'Well, that's it for today.'

I started to get up but he coughed and I saw he wasn't finished.

'I just want to say,' he began, looking embarrassed, which for Morland is practically impossible, 'I just want to say that I'm delighted to be working with the three of you. In fact I consider myself very fortunate to have you as partners.'

I was about to say, 'I'll second that,' when I noticed Hermann beside me grinning like an ape and sort of rumbling with subdued pleasure, so I thought better of it. Paula was smiling too.

'There's nothing else really'—I noticed a funny look in his eye—'except I ought to tell you there'll be one more member joining our little group tomorrow.'

One more? At first I thought it was another surprise cooked up for my benefit. Then I saw Paula looking puzzled and I stole a glance at Hermann. There was no doubt about it. The kraut looked stunned.

Morland glanced at us in turn and I could see he was dying for someone to say, 'Who?'

I said, 'Who?'

'It's a surprise,' he said, chuckling.

'Well, I've got a surprise, too,' I said. 'I came in on a four-way split. One, two, three, four, Morland. I'm not counting up to five.' The other two looked a little shocked, as if the sordid fact of money hadn't entered their heads.

Morland's grin stayed right where it was. He said, 'Oh, I don't think Alberto will require any payment for his services.'

Alberto?

'It is a joke?' Hermann said hopefully.

'Yes, a sort of joke.'

Hermann's relief was huge. He beamed, slapped his thigh like a pistol shot and said, 'Very funny.' Then he slapped my thigh like a pistol shot and said, 'No?'

I didn't reply because frankly I was incapable of speech. The girl giggled. You could see her day had been made.

We left then. Morland, Hermann and I. The girl said, 'Goodbye Jonathan, goodbye Hermann,' and curled her lip at me. The hall was empty and Morland told Hermann to leave first. The kraut gave me a big smile and gripped my arm.

'Harry, we will be friends. Bygone is bygone, *ja*?'

He looked so earnest with his baby-blue eyes and his wrinkled forehead that I said, 'Sure, Hermann, sure.' Besides, he was killing my arm.

We watched him stride away down to the Corso, scattering Ites right and left.

'What's all this bygone stuff?' I asked.

'Hermann is very sensitive about the war.'

'Which war?' I asked, and Morland shrugged. 'Where did you find him anyway?'

'In that Moroccan prison.'

'Look,' I said, 'about that business in Tangiers—'

'Forget it, Harry. As Hermann says, bygone is bygone.'

Which is very generous, I thought, coming as it did from a man who'd screwed up my life three times already and was doing his best to make it four out of four.

Chapter Five

THAT EVENING Morland and I went down to the Piazza Navona. Morland said he wanted to sit in the Tre Scalini for half an hour and 'compose his thoughts.' That was all right with me because I was hoping to see Bruno there. Not in the Tre Scalini of course—Bruno has temporarily surrendered his place in bourgeois society—but maybe cruising round the square in his *carrozza*. For a man who once worked at the desk of the Excelsior driving a horse and cart must have seemed quite a comedown, but Bruno never complained. A few years before he'd been doing very well, and was considered a real comer in the ticket trade. Then he'd had a sudden rush of blood to the head, one of those things you can't explain, and lost his job, and his reputation too. It must have come from standing at the desk every day watching all those tickets passing to and fro across the counter. Like letting a dipso work in a bar. Anyway, one fine day he upped and walked out with a whole bundle of them. Pretty stupid, I know, but you could see his point. With that kind of capital he could have set himself up in business for life. As it was he got three years. But he's a tough kid and when he came out he was ready to start again. That's when he found out the trade had turned against him. You can't have people running off with whole bundles of tickets all at once. For one thing it attracts the attention of the fuzz, and for another it lowers the value of what is and ought to remain a rare commodity. I agreed with the general view but I felt sorry for Bruno, who had to fall back on his father's old business, namely driving this *carrozza*. Whenever I was in town

I'd look him up and we'd have a chat about old times and how things were going in the ticket trade. He was grateful and used to say to me, 'Harry, if ever I get my hands on another ticket, you've got first refusal.' Which just shows that a little kindness is never misplaced.

He wasn't there that evening so I sat with Morland in the cool spring air watching the birds walk by and wishing I had Ilona with me. The trouble with women is that you get used to them, and it's very hard to break the habit. It did seem to me though that if anything could cure me suddenly it would be this new chick Paula. I wondered where Morland had found her.

Sitting there, watching the fountains and the birds and all, sipping my second Campari, I began to think that things weren't as bad as they seemed. I still had my ticket business—for some reason Morland didn't seem to want to get his claws into it—and as far as the snatch was concerned I thought I could safely play it by ear. I wasn't going to do anything as stupid as trying to knock off Yusuf Rifai's kid. That was strictly a Morland fantasy. But the situation did offer certain possibilities. I mean, since Morland was so anxious to dangle the fuzz over my head, I didn't see why I shouldn't return the favour. But not now—later, when it would be worth something. I began to feel so good that I offered to buy Morland dinner. Of course he accepted.

Morland is one of those people who often forget to eat. He can miss a couple of meals without even realizing it unless there's someone there to remind him. So in a way feeding him is a public service. But it has its drawbacks, and the main one is having to watch him while he's at it. Morland is a very messy eater. Knowing this, I waited until he had a bowl of *spaghetti alle vongole* safely tucked away before I started to prod. I wanted to know more about his plan. Not because it would ever come off, but because it wouldn't, and I didn't want it lost to posterity. There's a sort of lunatic brilliance about most of Morland's schemes that makes them real collector's items, the kind of things you want to stick up on a wall to show guests after dinner. I decided to start with this Alberto person. Morland had said it was a joke, but I wasn't so sure.

'Come on, Morland,' I said, giving him the old you-and-I-know smile, 'what about this Alberto?'

He almost choked on his spaghetti and it was quite some time before he could speak. 'Sorry, Harry, it's just that it's so funny.'

'Really?' I said.

'You'll meet him tomorrow. I promise.'

'So tell me about him now.'

Morland shook his head and went on grinning at me. 'It's my little surprise, Harry. I'm not going to spoil it.' He had this smug look again. Like a cat bending over a bowl of cream, only this cat had clam sauce smeared all over its whiskers.

'Well, you're spoiling my dinner,' I said. 'So either tell me the joke or stop grinning.'

He said, "It's just that every time I think about it I want to hug myself. It's so perfect.'

'I'm a little hurt that you don't trust me enough to tell me.'

'Now, Harry, you mustn't think that, please.' It's a funny thing about Morland but there are times when I think that underneath it all he's just another mark. I mean he can be as tough and nasty as you'd wish, a really hard case, and then suddenly turn so soft you practically have to scrape him off the pavement. I don't know what comes over him but whatever it is it's given me some anxious moments in the past. 'Morland,' I'd say to him, really cool and sarcastic, 'either you're a goody or a baddy. You can't be both.' He'd get very huffy and say that a man had to keep in sight what he called 'a certain minimum level of morality.' I'd ask, 'Why?' and when he couldn't answer I'd say, 'Morland, in the circles we move in a minimum level of morality is like bad breath. It's anti-social. And you know where it leads, don't you, Morland?' I'd say. 'It leads to the thin end of the wedge, *the thin end of the wedge*.' Boy, did he get furious. I considered a little needling along these lines now —like how close to the old minimum level of morality was knocking off someone's kid?—but I decided to play it cool.

'Where did you find the bird?' I said.

'Beirut . . . dancer.' He had his mouth full of *bocconcini*, which is what he'd ordered after the spaghetti.

'What makes a dancer want to get mixed up in a job like this?'

'Money,' Morland said, sucking his fingers.

'There are easier ways for a girl like Paula to earn money.'

'She's not that sort of girl.'

'For crying out loud, Morland,' I said. 'All girls are that sort of girl, and especially dancers in Beirut.'

Morland got red in the face. Sex bothers him. He said, 'I don't know how much money girls earn in the manner to which you are alluding but I assume it is not sixty thousand dollars.'

Sixty thousand dollars. I'd forgotten.

'That's a lot of bread,' I said. 'But why not more?'

'More?'

'For Rifai's kid? A quarter million's nothing. His old man can pay ten times that without even sneezing.'

Morland sighed like he was having to tell the same thing over and over to some stupid kid. 'Harry, we could ask a million, or two, or three, or fifty million. But we're going to ask two hundred and fifty thousand because that's the right price. Less than that and we're small-time, more than that and Rifai will dig in his heels. It's not that he values his boy more or less than a quarter million. It's just that in this situation, a quarter million is the *right* price. It's *right*. Got it?'

'No,' I said, 'but never mind.' I watched him soaking up his gravy with a piece of bread. I think the reason he looks so

44

starved is that he really is starved. 'What about Hermann?' I said.

'. . . told you . . . found him in Morocco.'

'How come Rifai employs an ex-con?'

'Well, Hermann is not really the criminal type—' I kept a straight face—'in fact, he wouldn't have been in prison if he hadn't been working for Rifai. Rifai got into some trouble with the Moroccan police, knocked over a pedestrian in his car. Hermann took the rap. Six months.'

'And now he wants his revenge?'

'Sort of.' Morland reached for the toothpicks and I turned away. 'At first he seemed to think it was all right and natural. Servant pays for master's mistakes. All very feudal and Teutonic. But after I'd explained it all to him he began to see things differently.'

'How did you con him?' I said. 'Go on, tell me.'

'I did not *con* him,' Morland said huffily. 'I explained to him in simple philosophic terms how he'd been had. There are certain social contracts written and unwritten which people make with one another, I said. Contracts between equals, between master and servant, between governed and government. When one side breaks the contract, the other is free to act in his own interests. This was a recognized historical process, I said. Hermann is not very bright but he finally grasped my point—that he owed it to himself and to society to extract compensation in some form from Rifai.'

That's what I mean about Morland. He does have this streak of brilliance, you can't deny it. There aren't many who could make snatching a kid look like a recognized historical process.

'How long have you been working on it?'

'Six months. Hermann got out before I did and went back to work for Rifai. When I came out we started making plans. We needed a girl to take care of the kid. That's why Paula's here.'

45

'Hardly the motherly type,' I said. 'But I still don't understand why you chose kidnapping. It's a nasty business.'

Morland didn't reply for a moment because he was busy with his third toothpick, chiselling away like a maniac. The first two were scattered over the tablecloth in about five hundred mangled pieces. He spat out a few more shreds and said, 'Not if you think about it.'

'I'm thinking,' I said.

He gave his mouth a good rinsing with acqua min, swallowed and said, 'There's a lot of sentimental nonsense talked about babies in general and kidnapping in particular. What is a baby after all?'—he spread his hands, like he'd got one right there on the table—'It's a small living organism which spends its time eating, sleeping, crying and occasionally making sounds and gestures which credulous parents take for signs of human awareness. A baby is not human until it's two years old. There's no doubt about it. I've studied them closely. So tell me, Harry, what are you snatching when you snatch a baby?'

'You've got me,' I said.

'A thing,' he said. 'You're snatching a thing, that's all. Granted it's alive, but what else can you say for it? I mean, if all it's going to do for two years is gurgle and belch and mess its pants it might just as well do it in one place as another. I can't see that it does a kid any harm to get snatched, in fact it may even do it some good. Spur its development perhaps. So much for the kid, now for the parents.'

He broke off to order some lemon tea and I could see I was in for a session.

'The parents,' he went on. 'Well, there I agree you have a problem. Obviously no parent is going to like having its kid nicked no matter how well it's looked after. And frankly, Harry, if young Selim's mother had been alive I wouldn't have dreamed of snatching him. One has to keep a certain minimum level—'

'Yes, yes, I remember,' I said. If I let him get on to the morality bit we'd be there all night.

'You do?' He looked surprised. 'Well, there you have it. The only person who gets hurt if we kidnap Selim is his father, and let's face it, Harry, neither you nor I is going to shed a tear for Mr Yusuf Rifai.'

I was curious. 'You feel that strongly about him?' I asked.

'It's my understanding that he finances brothels,' Morland said stiffly. 'I consider that the lowest form of human activity.' Suddenly he gave me a very sharp look. 'I hope that you, Harry, have never indulged in anything like that.'

'What? Me?'

'I've always wondered about that business with Samarkand Tours. What were those showgirls going to Beirut for? And why were they taking so long getting there?'

'They were going to Beirut to be showgirls,' I said. 'And they were taking their own sweet time about it.'

The nerve of it. Trying to put the finger on me. I could see I'd have to get tough.

'What have you got against cat houses anyway?'

Morland flushed. 'I just don't happen to like the idea of getting a lot of young girls and putting them in these places and making them . . . making them—' He couldn't finish so I said, 'Yes, Morland, making them is right.'

He sat there glaring at me, red in the face.

I said, 'Well, now, the way I understand it is that we're going to knock off Rifai's kid because it's a recognized historical process and because his father is a pimp. Morland, this time you've excelled yourself.'

He didn't say a word and it looked as though I'd delivered the old cruncher. In fact I was a little nervous in case I'd gone too far. He was staring at me with these mad monk's eyes, and when he gets like that anything can happen. So to cool things off a bit I said, 'Anyway, when did you decide to include me in all this?'

'Right from the start, Harry,' he said softly. 'You were in right from the start.' He kept up this blistering stare for so long I began to feel uncomfortable.

'I'm asking you again, why me?'

'One reason is that you had it coming to you.'

'Now just a minute,' I said. 'About Tangiers—'

'What about Tangiers?' he said softly.

We sat there staring at each other. Then I shrugged. It obviously wasn't the moment for explanations.

'The other reason—'

'Yes?'

'The other reason is that I still think you've got it in you to do something big, something that really counts. You've got talent, Harry, but you won't use it. Just look at yourself. You're a nit-picker, a crotch-scratcher, you're a parasite living on the soiled linen of society, you're—'

'Now just a minute—'

'—small-time, Harry, that's what you are, small-time. But I'm going to change that. I'm giving you a chance to test yourself against the best. I'm letting you bet twenty years of your life against a fortune. A fortune, Harry. And if you come through a winner you'll know you're a man fit to stand against the best of them.'

Of course I could see he'd gone out of his screaming mind, the only question was what to do about it.

'Relax, Morland,' I said—his eyes were turning cartwheels —'take it easy. Have some tea.'

In the end I got him calmed down, but not for long. Suddenly he reached across the table and gripped my arm. 'The important thing is to believe, Harry. You've got to believe in this. You've got to believe in me.' His eyes were begging me and he went on squeezing my arm which was already in pretty bad shape from Hermann's little gesture of affection. 'You *must* believe,' he said again.

Oh, sure, I thought, trying to remember the last person I'd believed in. I'd almost given up when I remembered Ziggy, but thinking of him made me remember how Morland was screwing up my ticket business and I felt bitter.

Morland must have read my mind because all of a sudden he gave this big sigh and relaxed, letting go my arm. 'All right, Harry,' he said. 'Forget the sermon. I want sixty thousand dollars out of this. So does Paula and so does Hermann. We mean to get it. So don't you screw it up.'

'Who's screwing anything up?'

'Just don't you do it,' he said. Then he smiled like he'd remembered something nice and added, 'Hermann wouldn't like it if you did. He wouldn't like it at all.'

He had a point there.

'What's with Hermann anyway?' I asked. 'All this Jonathan bait. He acts like you popped out of a Christmas cracker.'

Morland shrugged. 'Hermann needs someone to look up to. You know how these Germans are.'

'Sure,' I said, 'and I know how *you* are. You want someone to strike your matches on, someone to snap out the old salute when you go by. You know what your trouble is, Morland? You're an egomaniac.' I hadn't forgotten that crack about soiled linen.

Morland sneered. 'Never mind my ego, Harry Brighton,' he said. 'Just do your job. And if you're thinking of pulling any fancy stuff, remember, Hermann belongs to me. Just think about *that*, Harry Brighton.'

I did. It wasn't a happy thought to end the evening with.

Chapter Six

THE NEXT MORNING we took our drive into the country. It turned out to be the sort of trip you don't forget. After we'd gone about a hundred yards I made Morland stop the car and change places with me.

'What's wrong?' he said.

'If you don't know,' I said, 'then that's what's wrong.'

I backed the car out of this one-way street, ignoring a lot of curses and fist-shaking from the two old bats whom Morland had practically written off on the way up, and snatched the map from him.

'Just tell me where we're going. I'll do the rest.'

'Tivoli,' he said, staring out of the window, sulky as a spanked kid.

It didn't bother me. We weren't on speaking terms anyway. Not since I'd discovered the latest little twist in his scheme. It had started the evening before when we went to hire the car, but I hadn't spotted it right away, not being suspicious by nature. He'd asked me if I minded putting down the deposit for the car as he didn't happen to have any cash on him. Of course I said no and coughed up twenty thousand lire without thinking about it. But that morning at breakfast when he'd said to me, 'By the way, Harry, you'd better bring some cash with you,' I realized he was up to his old tricks. The discussion that followed was, as the saying goes, nasty, short and brutish. It ended with Morland snarling, 'All I want to know, Harry, is are you in or out? In or out?'

'I've told you I'm in.'

'Then you've got to help with expenses. That's the way it's always been with us. Share and share alike. You know that.'

'I know the way it's always been with us,' I said.

He chose to ignore that remark. 'Have a look at this,' he said, waving a piece of paper under my nose.

It was a sort of balance sheet which Morland had drawn up.

Deposit on apartment	60,000 lire
Two months rent in advance	120,000 lire
Baby's cot	25,000 lire
Baby's chair	10,000 lire
Baby's clothes	15,000 lire
Three dozen nappies	10,000 lire
Baby food	5,000 lire
Toys etc.	10,000 lire
	255,000 lire

'Toys et cetera,' I said. 'TOYS ET CETERA.'

'Paula said we had to get them and she's running that side of the caper.'

'Then let her buy them.'

'She's kicked in. So has Hermann. You're the only one that's shy.'

'What about this apartment? If we're paying for it why aren't we living in it?'

'You can move in tonight if you like,' he said with a snigger.

'What's so funny?'

'You'll see.'

Very fortunately for him Paula came in just then to have her breakfast. 'Dear, dear,' she said to no one in particular, 'we're not quite ourself today, are we?'

'No,' I said, 'but give us time.'

A *cinquecento* is no place for three people with nothing to say to each other. In fact a *cinquecento* is no place for three people. Morland was in front with me so he was all right, but Paula had quite a job squeezing herself into the back. She ended up sitting half-sideways with those long legs of hers curled up on the seat. I didn't mind. It gave me something to look at now and then. Each time I glanced over my shoulder she'd tug at her skirt. It didn't do much good.

We'd been batting along the Tiburtina for what seemed like five hundred miles when I said, 'What's going on in Tivoli anyway?'

'We're going to a farm just this side of it,' Morland said, very cold, very polite.

I can be polite too. 'And what is happening at this farm?' I said.

'We're going to collect something.'

'Where'll we put it?' I looked round like I was indicating the cramped situation and managed to get another peep at Paula's pins.

'It won't take up much room.'

'I see,' I said. The politeness bit was becoming a strain already.

'There.' He pointed. 'That dirt road running off to the left.

We could see Tivoli up on the hill a couple of miles ahead. The road we took ran along the base of the hills through olive trees and a field of tomatoes to a wooden gate in a high stone wall. The gate was barred, with a padlock and chain. On the other side was a stretch of mud and straw and rotting vegetables with a few pigs rooting around in it and farther on a farmhouse painted that rusty red colour the Ites like so much.

I said, 'We're not going in there, I hope. I got these suedes new in Geneva.'

Morland got out of the car and went to the gate. For a second I thought he was going to try and climb over it, which would have been foolish but interesting in view of this row of iron spikes along the top. But all he did was check the lock. Then he shouted at the top of his voice, 'Tony . . . Tony.' Dead silence. The shutters were down on all the windows. There wasn't a sign of life. Paula got out too and started picking some little red flowers growing by the road. It was a nice spring day, I noticed.

'Tony,' Morland shouted again. One of the pigs looked up.

'Bull's-eye, Morland. Never mind, we can always go and see the fountains.'

He was turning away when the door of the house opened and a woman came out. You could tell it was a woman because it wore a dress. She came across the yard with long heavy strides. Even the pigs looked jittery. She had on black rubber boots that came up to her knees, a torn black dress and a black handkerchief tied under her chin. When she got near the gate I saw she also had a black moustache. I'd like to be able to state categorically that she was the meanest-looking Italian mamma I'd ever set eyes on, but I can't be that positive. It's a field with lots of competition. She was swinging what looked like a wooden club.

Morland stood his ground, I'll say that for him, and when she reached the gate he started talking to her in Italian. He's quite a linguist, surprisingly. He soaks up foreign languages in this same sponge-like way he does everything else without really having to use his brain, which is just as well. I can't say I've got the gift myself, though I do manage to understand quite a lot, even if what I understand is often more a matter of intuition. Anyway, the conversation between Morland and the woman went something like this:

Morland: I want to speak to Tony.

Woman: Tony?

Morland: Your son.

Woman: What son?

Morland: Your son Tony.

53

Woman: Do you want a crack on the head?

Morland: Madame, I am a friend of your son, Tony. I was here two weeks ago. Don't you remember me?

Woman: Perhaps. Who are your friends?

Morland: We have all come to see Tony. He is expecting us.

Woman: If you are lying I will split your skull.

She walked back to the house. Morland was sweating. I didn't feel too good myself and I was wishing we'd brought Hermann with us though I wouldn't have backed the kraut for more than a bob or two against Big Mamma. After a few minutes she came out of the house again. She was smiling. I can't say it suited her.

'Tony says come in,' she called out in Italian and then went into a long spiel most of which I didn't catch except something about Tony not wanting to get his feet wet. When she saw me starting the car she spoke to Morland and he came to the window.

'She says the car'll stick in the mud. You'll have to walk.'

I took off my suedes, put my socks in my pocket and started rolling up my trousers. Then I saw Paula watching me, giggling. She was wearing the same blue skirt as the day before and high-heeled pumps, which she hadn't taken off.

I swept her a low bow, real sarcastic, and said, 'Does Madame think she's going to be carried across?'

'As a matter of fact she does.'

It's never wrong, you know—the old rule about learning to keep your mouth shut.

After ten yards or so I was panting, partly because of the effort of keeping my footing in the mud, partly because Paula was no Audrey Hepburn.

'You're not the smallest girl I've ever known,' I said.

'You're not the strongest man.'

Halfway across she said to me, 'Stop squeezing my thigh.'

54

Now I swear I wasn't, had no intention and never even thought of doing any such thing. All I wanted was to stay on my feet and not trip over one of those slobbering pigs. But as soon as she said it I realized her face was only an inch or two from mine and I smelled this scent which wasn't pig, far from it. 'I can't help my hand on your leg,' I said. 'You should wear longer skirts.'

She smiled. It was the first time she'd smiled at me. 'I'll make a note, Harry,' she said softly. Then she took one of those red flowers she'd picked and stuck it behind my ear. It was the first time she'd called me Harry, or anything.

Morland was waiting for us at the door of the farmhouse. He'd slopped through in his shoes needless to say, and looked a real mess.

'I'm glad to see you two getting on at last,' he said. He has a gift for putting his foot in it.

We went into the kitchen, which seemed to take up most of the ground floor and had a big brick stove along one white-washed wall, a wooden table and chairs, and a row of heavy iron pots hanging from nails in the wall. The table was covered with flour and traces of dough and I saw that what Mamma was carrying was a rolling pin, not a club after all. It made me feel better, the domestic touch, though Mamma herself didn't look very domesticated what with her black hairy arms and her thick moustache.

A door opened and in came this little runt. He wore a hound's-tooth shirt with button-down collar and a bow tie. There were knife-edge creases in his skin-tight charcoal greys and his shoes were black and pointed.

'Tony,' Morland said, holding out his arms.

'Hi,' said the runt. He had eyes like black marbles and a dark thin face that made me think of a ferret. His hands were white, the nails clean and shiny.

Morland introduced us. Tony rolled his marbles over me like

it wasn't worth the trouble, then he gave Paula the old up and down. He snapped his fingers at Big Mamma. '*Caffè*,' he said. The old girl trotted off to the stove happy as a lark. Mother love is a wonderful thing.

'Siddown,' said Tony. He pulled out a chair for Paula and sat down next to her, giving her a big smile and what looked like a wink. She didn't seem to mind.

'Well, Tony, we're all set. Have you got it?' Morland was starting to tremble with excitement.

'Sure. Let's have coffee first.' Tony pulled out a thin black cigar and lit up. He couldn't take his eyes off Paula who was looking around her in this fascinated way birds have when they get into kitchens, though Paula wasn't exactly that kind of bird. Tony was hard to place. American obviously—Italian-Yank, say—but still I couldn't see what he was doing in a broken-down old farmhouse with a lot of pigs and mud and only Man-Mountain Mamma for company. I could see him on Via Veneto: in Danny's Dive he'd be like part of the wood-work. But down on the farm? Never.

'Tony. Please.' Morland was acting like a junkie who'd missed his fix three days running. It was embarrassing.

Tony grinned and flicked his ash on the floor. 'After coffee, Johnny.'

Johnny! For Christ's sake.

Mamma brought the coffee and we sat around drinking and chatting of this and that, like wasn't the spring weather lovely and was the tomato crop good this year? Morland quietly did his nut. At last Tony killed his cigar and nodded to Mamma. She went out.

'It's in good shape,' Tony said. 'I checked it myself this morning.'

Morland just licked his lips. He was past speaking.

Mamma came back in a couple of minutes carrying a bundle. As soon as I saw it I said to myself, that's funny, that looks like

56

—and then she put it on a clean part of the table, pulled back the wrappings and sure enough it was—a baby.

A *baby*!

'What's this?' I said. 'Is it—?' I couldn't believe my eyes. Had someone made the snatch already?

Morland was bending over it with a drooling look on his face.

'Well?' said Tony.

'Perfect.' Morland stood up straight and beckoned to me 'Harry, come and meet Alberto.'

Alberto! I stared at this kid lying there on the table. It stared right back at me. It wasn't a bad-looking kid, black hair, dark eyes, toasty brown skin. A typical Ite. Nothing wrong with it, nothing special either. Someone pushed me aside. It was Paula. She bent over the baby with the same sort of expression as Morland's, only more dignified.

'He's beautiful.'

'Yeah,' said Tony, sidling up to her. 'Six teeth, I checked them myself this morning. No nappy rash either, I guarantee.'

Paula said, 'May I—?'

'Sure, sure.' Tony bundled up the baby in its wrappings and Paula picked it up. She walked round the kitchen, rocking it in her arms and making noises that sounded like 'coochie-coochie-coo.' Pretty disgusting, I know, but all the same she looked a different bird suddenly, all soft and gentle; I wouldn't have known her.

Morland watched her for a few seconds with a soppy smile on his face. Then he sighed, straightened his shoulders and said to Tony, 'How much?'

How much!

'Now just a minute,' I said. 'Morland, step outside.' He started to argue but I cut him off. 'Outside,' I said.

We left the others in the kitchen and went out to join the pigs.

57

'All I'm saying,' I said, 'is that it had better be good.'

'Now, Harry—'

'Firstly,' I said, 'who is this creep? This Tony?'

'He used to be in the fruit business in Chicago. He got into some trouble with the Federal people and they had him deported. He's all right, Harry. He knows the score.'

'I'll bet he does,' I said, remembering the way he'd eyed Paula. 'But what else does he know?'

'About the snatch, you mean? Nothing—not a thing, Harry, I swear. I told him we needed Alberto for a con job. Playing on the sympathies of a wealthy childless couple.'

'Well?'

'Well what?'

'I'm still waiting.'

'About Alberto, you mean.'

'Yes, Morland. About Alberto.' I watched him closely, wondering why he looked so pleased with himself, so tickled, when he ought to have been ashamed, or at the very least, embarrassed. All I spotted though was this funny bubbly look in his eyes like he'd swallowed a bottle of Alka-Seltzer. I knew what it meant. The old fanaticism was coming up for another run round the track.

'Tell me, Harry, when you make a snatch, what's your biggest problem?'

'You're telling me, Morland.'

'It's the merchandise,' he said. 'It's the kid. What do people start looking for when there's been a kidnapping? Kids, of course. Spare kids. Kids that don't belong, kids lying around loose, so to speak. So what do you have to do? You have to hide the kid you've snatched. But how do you hide it? You can't bury it, you can't stick it in a safe deposit or dump it in the left luggage. How the hell *do* you hide a kid?'

'I wish you'd stop asking yourself questions.'

'There's only one way to hide it, Harry. You put it where everyone can see it.'

'Let's have that again,' I said.

'You don't try to *hide* it. You keep it out in the open where people can see it. Then it's just another baby—and who can tell one baby from another, except maybe the mother?'

'Brilliant,' I said. 'I can't think why everyone isn't snatching kids.'

'No, no, Harry, you've missed the point,' he said impatiently.

'I believe I have.'

'You can't suddenly produce a baby that wasn't there before. It's not natural. People get suspicious. But if—'

'Now just a minute,' I said. 'I think I see. You mean that Alberto will . . . will—'

'That's it, Harry, Alberto will play the part of Rifai's kid Selim until we snatch him. Then everyone will think Selim is Alberto and Alberto is Selim, if you see what I mean.'

'Not exactly.'

'Look,' he said with this oh-you-silly-little-boy expression which really gets me, 'in the next few weeks Alberto will become an accepted member of society, a familiar figure in his own milieu. A baby that belongs. When we snatch Selim he'll take Alberto's place and everyone will think he's Alberto.'

'That's great,' I said, 'except for Alberto.'

'Don't worry, I've got plans for him too.'

'I'll bet you have,' I said. But all the same, it wasn't bad, not bad at all. Of course only a lunatic could have dreamed it up, but that was the beautiful part about it. The coppers would be tearing around looking for babies where there shouldn't be babies: they'd never think of checking cribs. Only a monster would make one kid impersonate another. Impersonate?

'Look,' I said, 'I'm not claiming to be an expert, but are you sure all babies look alike?'

'Well, not exactly, obviously. But near enough. I asked for a

59

dark-haired, olive-skinned kid at least a year old. That's what we've got. And anyway, who's going to argue with the mother?'

The mother? I knew there was something worrying me.

'This milieu bit,' I said. 'This accepted member of society lark. How do we pull that?'

He gave me a funny look. 'That's the easiest part,' he said. 'Alberto will simply move into his new home with his mummy and his daddy and everyone will accept him.'

'Well, I can see that Paula is mummy,' I said. 'Lucky old Alberto. But who—? Oh, no,' I said. 'Oh, God. Oh, Morland. You wouldn't—'

'Now, Harry, let's look on the bright side—'

'I'll never forgive you,' I said quietly. 'I'll get you, Morland. I'll fix you good and proper if it's the last thing I ever do.' I know—melodramatic. But I just couldn't find the words I wanted, I was that choked.

'Harry, please. It's only for a few weeks. There's no one else who can do it. I mean honestly, Harry, can you see *me* posing as anyone's father?'

I looked him up and down slowly. What could I say?

'Does she know?'

'Of course.'

Of course! I was really burning. Harry Brighton, everyone's favourite fall-guy. If Ziggy could have seen me then he'd have wondered what he ever saw in me. I sometimes wonder myself.

'It's not that I don't trust you, Harry. It's just that if I'd thrown it at you all at once you'd have run a mile.'

'You underestimate me,' I said. 'I'd have been in orbit by now. However, it's not too late—'

'Oh yes it is.' He thrust his face close to mine and suddenly it wasn't the same Morland. This one had a really nasty snarl on its lips and a mean, mean look in its eye. 'You're in, Harry,' it said. 'You agreed and you're in. Don't you go backing out now.

Just remember, there's your ticket business and there's Hermann, and if I put my mind to it I don't doubt I could come up with something else too.'

I didn't doubt it either.

Well, there you have it. If you've been wondering why I have this thing about Morland, now you know. Sneaky isn't the word for him.

I stood there, watching the pigs snuffling around in the mud, asking myself what the hell I could do. Once I'd moved into that flat with Paula and the kid I'd be in it up to my neck. Conspiracy to kidnap, accessory before the fact, never mind what else. He'd really got me nailed down this time.

The door opened and Tony stuck his head out. 'So what's keeping you?' he said.

We went back into the kitchen. Mamma and Paula were twittering round the kid, feeding it from a bowl of mush. Each time it took a spoonful Paula said, 'There's a good boy,' and Mamma rumbled with approval. I thought the kid looked pretty bored with the whole production.

Tony lit another cigar, put his legs on the table and said, 'I figure two hundred a week.'

Of course I knew he was joking, but I'd had about enough humour for one day.

'Come on, Morland,' I said. 'Let's pay up and get out.' I took a fifty-dollar note from my pocket and slapped it on the table in front of Tony. 'And don't forget the change,' I said.

Tony took his feet off the table. He picked up the fifty, held it to the light for a few moments, sniffed it, put his ear to it, rubbed it between his fingers a couple of times, then put it back on the table carefully.

He said to Morland, 'This guy has got to be a comedian.'

Morland coughed and looked embarrassed. He said, 'Sure Tony, but two hundred does seem a little steep. How about one-fifty?'

'Two hundred's the price, Johnny. Kids don't rent cheap these days.'

Rent!

'What do you mean rent?' I said. I pushed the fifty back to Tony's side of the table. 'That fifty *buys* the kid. Got it? And the clothes it stands up in too. And if you ask me,' I said to Morland, 'that's about forty-nine dollars too much.'

'What is this?' Tony socked the table with his fist—it didn't do the table any harm. 'Who is this joker? Just tell me, Morland, you wanna deal or not? Tell me now, right now. Do I get the two hundred or do I take the kid someplace where he's appreciated?'

'Take it easy, Tony, relax.' Morland was getting into a panic. 'Harry, will you please be quiet. Just leave it to me.'

'But you're out of your mind,' I said. 'Two hundred a week for a *baby*.'

'He's worth it, Harry.'

'You're kidding.'

'Oh, kidding, is he? Kidding, is he? What kind of a wise guy are you anyway?' This Tony creature had suddenly gone out of his tiny mind, prancing around in front of me, shaking his fist in my face and baring his blunt little ferret's teeth like he was just begging for one smack in the kisser, which I was only too ready to provide and would have if Mamma hadn't walked back to the table just then and picked up the rolling pin. Tony sneered. 'So he's not worth it, is he? You can find one cheaper maybe. So go find one, wise guy. Check the parks. Maybe they left one lying around there. And keep an eye on the want ads, you never know what people will be selling next. Have you tried the department stores? They got a sale in babies this week maybe. Go ahead, wise guy. Check the yellow pages. Find yourself a kid.' He sat down again and put his feet back on the table. Mamma beamed at him and said something in Italian which sounded like, 'That's my boy.' She started edging round the table with this rolling pin and I could see the moment had come to cut my losses.

I shrugged and said, 'Okay, Morland. It's your money.' Except it wasn't—it was mine.

Morland heaved a big sigh of relief. 'Thank you, Harry,' he said. 'All right, Tony. Two hundred it is. In advance, I suppose.'

'For two weeks,' Tony said, flicking those black marbles in my direction. 'That'll be four hundred.'

'Right,' Morland said quickly before I could get a word in. 'We can go then. Is Alberto ready?'

Paula had the kid in her arms again and was patting its back. After a couple of seconds it burped. She nodded. 'We can go now.'

'Just a moment,' Tony said. 'You gotta check it first.'

Paula brought the kid to the table and they unwrapped it except for its nappy and its little woollen socks.

'It's in good shape, right?'

Morland nodded.

'Well, make sure it stays that way. Any damage you pay for. And just remember, this kid is no ordinary baby.'

I couldn't help it. 'What's so special about it?' I asked.

'He wants to know what's special about it,' Tony said, like there was someone around who was deaf and needed things said twice. 'Wise guy wants to know what's special about it.' He strutted right up to me, five foot two of naked menace. 'I'll tell you what's special,' he said. 'This kid is a professional. That's what. Morland said he wanted a kid that didn't cry or get sick or need its tonsils taken out or catch the measles—or anything. Well, this is it. This kid eats, sleeps, craps and minds its own business. Just you do it the same favour.'

Oh Tony-baby, I said to myself, one day when Mamma's not around you're going to catch it a treat.

I looked at the kid lying there on the table. It was awake all

63

right, it wasn't missing a thing, looking around with this real cool gaze like it knew what was what and wasn't about to give the secret away. All the same, it didn't look *special*, though as I said before I'm no expert.

'Who are its parents?' I asked.

'It's an orphan if you want to know,' Tony said. 'But don't let that give you any ideas. I'm the one that owns it now.'

'Lucky old Alberto,' I said.

'Come on,' Morland said quickly. 'Let's go. You've got the money have you, Harry?'

I could have said no, I suppose, but what the hell. They were all against me, including Paula, who obviously wasn't going to let go of this baby now that she'd got her hands on it. And there was always the chance that Mamma would cut up rough if her Tony didn't get his four hundred green ones. To be frank, I didn't fancy having to make a quick break across the mud, particularly as I'd got my suedes back on. But more than anything was the fact that Morland still had me where it hurt while I hadn't been able to get a thing on him yet. I mean, renting babies is not illegal that I know of. So there was nothing to do but count out another three fifty on the table. But don't think it came easy.

Mamma watched her boy pocket his money, then went out to open the gate. Tony turned very sweet all of a sudden and said Paula couldn't possibly walk back across the mud and he'd have to carry her. That gave me my first laugh of the day.

'The only thing you could carry, short-arse, is a disease,' I said.

Tony spat something in Italian, went into a crouch and whipped his hand into his hip pocket.

'Oh, very good,' I said. 'Very Chicago.'

When you wear skin-tights you're not hiding a thing and I knew that all he had in that pocket was my four hundred. I could have flattened him then and there but I knew Mamma was outside at the gate which made the line of retreat a little tricky.

'For God's sake, Harry'—Morland stepped between us—'there's nothing to fight about.'

'Just let me at him,' Tony hissed, now that he'd got Morland between us.

Paula, who'd been standing by the door watching this little comedy, said, 'I'm going, anyway.'

I followed her out. 'Don't you want a lift?' I asked.

'And who's going to carry Alberto?' she said, hugging this little bundle like she thought I might drag it away from her. 'You could take my shoes though.' And cool as you please she lifts up one foot, then the other. Watching her picking her way across the mud, I remember thinking that even dirty her legs weren't half bad. Behind me Tony was saying, 'Just let me at him, just let me at him' like the needle had stuck.

I stripped off my suedes and socks, rolled up my pants and followed Paula to the car. Mamma gave me a suspicious look as I went by. Maybe she sensed all was not kosher back at the ranch. To be on the safe side I gave her a sweet smile and said, 'Up yours too.'

Morland came after me panting and as he got in the car I heard Tony shouting something from the house. Of course the little bastard didn't want to get his feet wet.

Mamma called back something like, 'What is it, my son?'

By the time she'd got her answer I had the *cinquecento* turned around and was making a fast getaway through the tomatoes. She must have had a good arm though because she caught us with a lump of rock that left a fair-sized dent in the back mudguard.

'Think of Alberto, can't you,' Paula said angrily.

When we reached the main road I asked Morland, what next?

'Back to Rome. You and Paula must move in right away.'

He said it in a funny gaspy way like he couldn't get his breath back. He was really quite pale.

'You all right, Morland?'

'Fine, Harry, fine. Let's get back to Rome.'

Of course it could have been his heart, but more likely it was just sheer fright. Morland is a shocking coward.

Chapter Seven

MORLAND AND PAULA had both been to the apartment before so they both knew the way. 'Turn right here, Harry, no not here, the next one, didn't you hear me say left?—What's that, Paula?—No, I'm sure it's right, I mean left, come on Harry, I said left.'

After an hour of this I stopped the car. 'I'm going into that bar to have a Campari,' I said, 'and when I come back one of you had better know the way. And I mean *one*.'

'But it's not on the map,' Morland said, sulking. 'Via dello Scorpione—it's not here.' He looked really furious like he thought someone was playing a sneaky trick on him. We'd already asked about ten people who'd all said, sure, they knew the way to Via dello Scorpione and then given us all kinds of directions, mostly with their hands. The trouble was we were right in the middle of Trastevere, and finding your way around there is about as easy as picking a winner at the White City on needle night. The streets all look exactly the same—short, crooked and cobbled. And the buildings are all painted this same gold colour which is supposed to be so romantic. At least that's what the guide books say though I notice they don't talk about the kids and the cats and the garbage and the decrepit old bats which is what these streets are mostly full of. And they don't mention the smell either.

Paula said, 'Can't you *do* something?' It's the kind of useless remark you get from a bird on these occasions. Still, I felt sorry for her. She'd had the worst of it, squeezed in the back with Alberto on her lap all the way from Tivoli. He'd kipped for most of the way, but now he was awake and looking pretty restless too.

I went into the bar. It wasn't only a Campari I wanted. I'd suddenly remembered they have this special street directory in Rome, this *Stradale*, and I thought I might as well check it. It was there in the *Stradale* all right—Via dello Scorpione—and the nearest main square was given as Piazza di Santa Maria in Trastevere. I went back to the car.

'I've remembered now,' Morland said. 'If you turn left at this next corner—'

I held up my hand. 'Please,' I said.

When we got to the Piazza di Santa Maria I went into Galeassi's where the waiters speak English and came out two minutes later with a nice neat map drawn for me by the *maître d'* himself. The atmosphere in the *cinquecento* was getting pretty tense. They didn't say it of course but I knew they were just dying for me to fall on my face. Morland said, 'We've been this way before, three times.'

'It's a pity you didn't recognize it.'

Paula shouted, 'Left here.'

'Yes, dear,' I said, turning right, and right again. Then I stopped the car. 'Via dello Scorpione, I believe.'

Neither of them said a word, for a while, then Morland muttered, 'A bit farther.'

I drove on slowly so as not to run over the cats and the kids and the old bats. Maybe it was my imagination but I felt there were more of them in this street than any other we'd been through—and we'd been through a fair number. It seemed narrower too, or maybe it was just the garbage cans moving in closer. The farther we went, the noisier it got. Kids screaming, transistors playing, women yelling across the street from their windows, young studs tuning up their Hondas. I recognized the locale immediately from my days in the travel business. It was what we used to call a rich slice of Roman life.

68

I was just beginning to hope I'd made a mistake—there are worse things than being wrong—when Morland and Paula said together, 'Here.'

We got out and I took a good sniff.

'No smog hazard, anyway. It wouldn't stand a chance.'

Suddenly there was this scream, louder than the rest, and a fat little bird came barrelling across the road towards us. '*Bambino, bambino,*' she yelled, or something like that—it's tough picking up these Roman dialects—and made a grab at Alberto. For a second I thought someone was trying to snatch *our* kid, then I saw Paula smiling and introducing Signora something-or-other to Morland, so obviously they knew each other. The cause of all the excitement, needless to say, was Alberto. The poor little sod was given a real work-out, poked and patted and called *bravo* this and *bello* that.

'Charming,' said Morland. 'One of the neighbours, I gather. She certainly seems impressed with Alberto.'

'Let's hope she feels the same way about Selim,' I said sweetly. 'And let's hope she has a bad memory for faces.'

'Oh my God,' said Morland. He rushed forward and dragged Paula away. 'Come on. We're going up.'

We went into this doorway next to the car and started up a flight of stone steps with the fat little bird in hot pursuit. Morland called out something in Italian to her and said to me, 'I've told her you're the father. See if you can stop her.'

I whipped round and said, '*Buon giorno, Signora, felice di conoscerla,*' which is one of the phrases I've mastered.

Of course that set her off. One thing you can say for the Ites. They never use a couple of words where a hundred and fifty will do. I have to confess I didn't really get the drift of it either except that she kept calling me *professore*, which was a little puzzling, and there was also a lot of chat about a bar. I kept saying '*si*' till she stopped for breath, then I slipped in an '*arrivederci*' and beat it up the stairs after the others.

The apartment was four flights up, on the top floor, and I must say I was quite pleasantly surprised after the mess down below. There were a couple of big rooms, newly painted, bathroom and kitchen, a small balcony overlooking the street and up on the roof a nice big terrace with flower pots and a few garden chairs.

'You should thank Paula,' Morland said. 'She's been over here nearly every day for the past fortnight putting the place in order. We took it furnished but there was still a lot of stuff we had to buy. This, for example'—he thumped the couch he was sitting on, one of those long, fold-out affairs—'and of course all the kid's stuff. Officially, you and Paula and Alberto have been staying in a *pensione* until the place was ready. Now you're moving in—one big happy family. And I mean that, Harry. A happy family. Got it?'

'Now what makes you think—?'

'I want Paula treated properly, Harry. She's a fine girl and she's going to have quite enough to do looking after Alberto without fighting a guerilla war on the side with you.'

'What's all this guerilla stuff?' I snapped. 'Watch your language, Morland. And I'll thank you to keep your nose out of my domestic affairs.'

My domestic affairs! All I could hope was that Ziggy never got to hear of it.

Paula came out of the bedroom. 'Alberto's asleep,' she said. 'Please don't wake him up.' She smiled at me. 'How do you like it?'

'It'll do,' I said. I suppose I could have thought of something nicer to say but frankly it had been a trying day and from what I could see tomorrow wasn't going to be any better.

'Well, don't strain yourself,' she spat and stamped off into the kitchen.

Morland sighed. 'When it comes to making trouble for yourself, Harry, you're all genius.'

70

That may very well be true. But as sure as hell I've never run short of help. I don't understand it either because I'm not what you'd call a trouble-maker, far from it. In fact I'm about the most peace-loving anti-imperialist, anti-communist, anti-anything you like that I know. You name it, I'm against it. Or for it, if you prefer. You can't be more reasonable than that. But it doesn't help, it just seems to goad people on, makes them think of you as a target that no one's ever hit before—and boy, are they dying to be the first!

Morland, who'd been looking at me in this wistful fatherly way—real creepy in fact—said, 'I'm going downstairs to phone Hermann.'

Paula must have heard him because she looked out of the kitchen and said, 'Ask Hermann to come round if he can. I'm going to give you all dinner tonight. A sort of celebration to start us off.' She smiled at Morland and made a big thing of pretending I wasn't there. She had rubber gloves on and her hair was pinned up any old way on top of her head.

'Very fetching,' I said, but with a smile to show I was kidding and we were going to be friends. I should have saved my breath. She didn't even look at me. Just whipped back into the kitchen.

Morland shook his head. 'You're going to have to try harder, Harry. Women need careful handling.'

What Morland knows about handling women would fit on the point of a pin with room to spare.

'I'd give it serious thought,' I said, 'if I didn't have to think of everything else around here.'

'Such as?'

'Such as are you really going to invite Hermann around?'

'Why not?'

'Because he ties us in with Rifai. That's why not.'

'Oh, once won't matter, Harry.'

'Once is all it takes, Morland.'

71

'Anyway, I want him to see Alberto so we'll know if the two kids look alike.'

'And if they don't?'

'They can't look *too* different, can they? Same colour hair, same colour skin, what more do you want? One kid is much like another.'

I gave up. What did it matter? There wasn't going to be a snatch anyway. I'd definitely made up my mind about *that*. And especially now that I'd seen how Morland had the whole thing worked out so if anything went wrong I'd be the one to catch it.

When he'd gone I went into the bedroom. Alberto was asleep in a cot next to the bed. All I could see was this little brown face and one hand. I'd never really looked at a baby before, not close up, so I gave this one a good going over. Right off I was struck by something interesting, and I thought if this was what people saw in babies I could understand it. I mean they're perfect. No, really. Take the skin for instance: so soft and smooth, not a mark on it, no scars, no pimples, no lines, not a scribble: it's like a clean sheet of paper. And then there's the hair, fine and thin, more like silk, you'd never think that one day it'd be all greasy and dripping dandruff like the rest of us. Kids *are* perfect, useless maybe but perfect.

'Don't touch him.' She'd come in quietly and was standing right behind me.

'I was just looking—'

'Shhh. I told you not to wake him. What are you doing in here anyway? Get out.'

I walked past her without a word and went straight out on to the balcony. For a few minutes I stood there, leaning over the wall, blinking away the black spots. I couldn't see too much of the street from up there what with all the washing strung across it. But I could hear it all right, and I could smell it. It could have been quite a pretty street, I thought, with the buildings this gold and red colour and the flowers in the window pots, if it wasn't for the mess people made of it. I heard a noise behind me and looked round. It was Paula.

'I'm sorry,' she said, straight out, just like that. 'I didn't mean to be rude. It's just that I was upset from before. Don't be angry, please.' She was smiling in this nervous little-girl way and half blushing, or maybe it was only the sun on her cheek. The thing that gets me about certain people, is that just when you're ready to write them off, bang, finish, they come up with something new and you're back where you started. You can't depend on anyone.

'Forget it,' I said.

She came out on to the balcony and looked up and down the street. An old bat in a black dress waved from a window across the way. 'I like it here, don't you?'

I shrugged.

'Come and talk to me in the kitchen.'

Well, as I've said before, I'm soft, so I thought, why not?— and of course I end up stringing beans.

'Why are you doing this?' she asked—I looked at the beans —'No, silly, the kidnapping.'

Why am I doing it? *Why am I doing it?* I was speechless, struck dumb, only I had to say, listen, Paula sweetheart, in one little word, the reason I'm doing it is that your friend, brother Jonathan, has got me by the old pigeon-eggs, that's why. Well, not quite so crudely perhaps. But I let her have it all from start to finish—the threats, the blackmail, the extortion, the lot.

'Why, that's terrible,' she said.

'Yes.'

'And you mean to say if you refuse he'll—'

'Yes.'

Those green eyes of hers started flashing. It's lucky for Morland he didn't walk in just then or he might have got the bread-knife in his kidneys. But then she started thinking it over.

'He must have a reason. What have you done to him?'

73

'What have I *done* to him? Supported him for half his adult life, that's what.'

'Oh, come on, Harry.'

Oh come on, Harry!

'Now you're sulking.'

Women!

I strung the last bean carefully. 'Will there be anything else?' I said, cool and polite.

She was busy on the potatoes and had this funny look on her face, half screwing up her eyes so I wasn't sure whether it was concentration or whether she was laughing at me.

'You could finish these for me.'

'By all means.'

That time I definitely heard her giggle.

Still, it's hard to keep up the freeze bit when you're squashed in a two by four kitchen with a dish like Paula. She didn't say anything, just went busily along banging pots and opening cupboards, and every now and then she'd bump me, not hard, just glancing sort of bumps, the kind you pick up in a kitchen. And then there were a couple of times when she reached over to get something and actually leaned on me, continuously, so to speak. It was very upsetting.

'What about you, anyway?' I said. 'Why are you in this?'

'I need the money.'

'You need sixty thousand dollars?'

'Do you really think we'll get that much? I just can't believe it.'

'That's the right attitude. Stick to it.'

She giggled again. 'It really started with me wanting my plane fare back to London.'

'*Your plane fare?*'

'From Beirut. Jonathan said he'd pay my way to Rome if I helped him with this. After I'd got my share, he said, I'd have enough to go anywhere I wanted.'

74

And Morland has the nerve to talk about this minimum level of morality.

But I still couldn't make her out. 'Doesn't the idea of a snatch seem to you, well, a bit brutal?' I asked.

'It did at first. Then Jonathan explained it to me. You know, about the mother being dead and it not doing the baby any harm. It certainly sounded logical.'

How dirty can you get? Using logic on a bird!

'What about the father?' I said.

She slammed down a pot. 'I know about him.'

'You know Rifai?'

'I said I know *about* him.'

All of a sudden I got this queasy feeling. Beirut-Rifai-Cat House. I was really furious, about this queasy feeling, I mean.

'You worked for him?'

She was round on me, quick as a whip. She had the pot in her hand. I had an idea it wasn't the table that was going to get socked next time.

'Just what do you mean by that?'

'You worked in clubs, didn't you?'

'Well?'

'Well, Rifai owns clubs, doesn't he? And in Beirut, too.'

'That's not all he owns.'

'Oh?' I said.

Her eyes were shooting sparks, no mistake, but she still wasn't sure what I was up to.

'I worked in a club called the Red Petal.'

'The old Petal,' I said. 'I know it well.' I also knew it was owned by Rifai. 'Stripper?' I said.

'Dancer,' she snapped. Then she blushed and gave me this little-girl smile again. 'Well, it's true I was a stripper once.'

'Some of my best friends are strippers,' I said, which happens to be true.

She was turning back to the stove when I added, 'Rifai owns the Petal, doesn't he?'

She faced me slowly and I was surprised to see she wasn't angry any longer. 'Harry, if you want to ask me something ask it.'

I picked up the last potato.

'If you know the Petal you must know there are rooms upstairs. Do you want to know if I used them?'

Did I want to know if—? Who the hell did she think she was, anyway. What the hell did I care?

'Well, I didn't, Harry, and that's why I only kept my job three weeks, and you can believe it or not, I don't give a damn, but if you don't take that dirty look off your face I'm going to take it off myself, with this.' I hadn't noticed, she'd got hold of that pot again.

'Look,' I said, 'it never crossed my mind. And even if it had I wouldn't have given it a thought. Why,' I said, 'some of my best friends are—'

Bong!—and suddenly I was sitting on the floor. She'd hit me! She'd actually hit me! And what's more it hurt! I just couldn't believe it, except there she was, standing over me, waving this dirty great pot around, getting ready for another crack. The situation called for some quick action. I groaned and rolled over.

'Harry, are you all right? Oh my God—' She was down on her knees in a flash and the next thing I knew my head was in her lap. That was more like it. I groaned again and gave the old eyeballs a spin around the track. 'Oh, no.' She started rubbing my forehead, which wasn't where she'd socked me but was pleasant enough, so I sighed to show it was appreciated.

'What on earth—?'

Trust Morland to choose that moment to come back.

'Hold his head'—no more lap, just Morland's grubby fingers—'I'll get some water.'

76

It was time to come round. I opened my eyes and looked straight into Morland's beady little pair.

'He's awake, Paula.'

'Knock it off,' I said.

'What happened?'

'She socked me. Surprised?'

'She *hit* you?' My head landed on the floor with a thud. 'Harry, I don't know about you, I just don't know. Fifteen minutes, a quarter of an hour I leave you two together and when I get back, what do I find? She's had to slug you. Harry, I don't *understand* you.'

'You and the world,' I said. I got up. My head hurt like hell.

'Are you all right?' It was Paula. She was back with a bowl of water and a cloth.

'There's no blood, if that's what you're hoping for.'

'I'm sorry. I have a terrible temper.'

Now she tells me. Still, she really did look sorry, but to make sure I let her see how shaky my pins were. She took my arm and helped me out of the kitchen. Morland sneered.

I said, 'I'd better lie down for a few minutes.'

'Over here.' She pulled me towards the couch.

'No, over here.' I pulled her towards the bedroom.

Being the injured party, I won, but I could see she didn't like it, me lying down on the bed and stretching out comfortably like I was staking out a claim. Morland came in.

'I bought some wine, Harry. Would you like a glass?'

'It'd help.'

Paula made this funny noise—it sounded like a snort—and went out. Morland brought me the wine.

'Hermann's on his way over. I told him to look inconspicuous.'

I wanted to ask him how a six-three kraut with a white crew-cut could look inconspicuous in Rome, or anywhere, but I knew if I did, he'd tell me. He sat on the bed, which wasn't

77

quite the way I'd planned the scene, and he rolled up his sleeves. His arms were very thin and white with little red blotches all over them. I shut my eyes and tried to picture myself winning the pools. It was no problem, no problem at all. I'm rather given to day-dreams as a matter of fact. I know it's nothing to boast about, but how else can you get a break from the daily grind? Like the next one I started having which involved me and Paula and this big bed I was lying on. To tell the truth that bed had been on my mind for some time. For one thing it was the only bed in the place, for another it was in the only bedroom. Morland wanted us to be one big happy family, did he? Well, Mrs Brighton's boy was ready to do his bit. I gave a little bounce to test the terrain. Springs nice and firm, no squeaking. There's nothing like a rusty spring to bring a bird to her senses. I gave a few more bounces just to make sure. Motion smooth and even, no trace of sag. I liked the brass bedstead too, all polished and golden, and the dark-blue spread. It was the sort of bed you could easily grow attached to.

'Goo goo goo'—there was this funny sound, I couldn't place it—'goo goo goo'—I looked round and saw Morland bending over the cot—'goo goo goo'—

'What's all this goo stuff?' I said.

'He's awake. Alberto. Giddy giddy goo'—I swear, that's exactly how it sounded—'Giddy giddy goo . . .'

I was feeling pretty queasy as it was, so went out on to the balcony again. It was cooler than before and maybe even a little quieter. The street was in the shadow but the sun was still hitting the top floors of the houses across the way, which had this warm biscuit look you get in Rome at sunset. Down below the street was full of young birds in bright colours tripping home from a day at the office or whatever. Paula was right, it wasn't a bad place. I even waved to the old bat opposite but the sun must have been in her eyes because she just went on staring out at nothing, which is something old bats spend a lot of time doing.

Suddenly I spotted this figure marching down the street in a straight—but a dead straight—line. It was Hermann. He was stepping it out, shoulders back, arms swinging. Cats and kids and young birds were scattering on all sides. It did make me wonder what Hermann thought inconspicuous meant. From where I stood, watching his white crew-cut bouncing along, he looked about as inconspicuous as a ten-foot toothbrush.

Chapter Eight

THE DINNER was quite a success. Paula dished up steaks which weren't half bad, though I only got one, and a small one at that, while Morland and Hermann went through the rest like a couple of hungry bears. I could understand Hermann, who was a big guy and needed it, but with Morland it was just sheer greed. I suppose it comes from a lifetime of not knowing when your next meal will be. Whatever it was, it was certainly no spectator sport. Still, as I say, the dinner went off well enough with lots of the old chianti flowing and Paula playing the little housewife to the hilt. '*Do* have some more salad, Hermann'—'Jonathan, you've hardly touched a thing' (a gross distortion of the truth). I didn't come in for any of this and I could see from the looks she was giving me that she'd been thinking over what had happened earlier and had decided that her first impression was right after all: I *was* a creep. It looked like I'd have to call on the old Brighton charm, and pretty damn quick.

Hermann had given us the okay on Alberto, though I for one wasn't entirely convinced he knew what he was talking about. For a start Morland had had to explain the whole thing to him about twenty-three times while Hermann sat there scratching his head. Each time he finished Hermann would say '*Ja*, Jonathan, I understand, but tell me, why do we need *this* baby?' Well, in the end he got it, or said he did, I wasn't too sure, and then Morland asked him if Alberto and Selim looked alike. That really set old Hermann scratching. He stared at Alberto for a long time, then made us turn him over on his stomach, and stared at him a bit longer. Then we had to turn him back again. Finally Hermann said, '*Ja*, I suppose so,' which was very reassuring.

We ate on the terrace with the sun slowly sinking. Paula had got Hermann to bring up a table from below and we sat around it with Alberto next to Paula in a high chair. Alberto himself was pretty quiet, though you could see he wasn't missing much. His little black eyes kept darting around and now and then he'd give a sort of gurgle, quiet and restrained like, as if he'd spotted something that needed comment, Morland's table manners for example.

Besides doing most of the eating Morland was also doing most of the talking, which may sound like a neat trick but is very rough on those who happen to be within range at the time. I remember he was going on about this café he wanted to open in London one day. A caff! How's that for ambition? I didn't hear what sort of café he had in mind because, as I've said before, I make a habit of not listening too closely to Morland. But I did pick up something about a place 'where kindred spirits can gather' so I guess the Savoy can sleep easy.

It was just getting dark when Morland gave one last belch, stretched his arms, and said, 'A lovely party, Paula my dear. But I'm afraid this is the last time we can get together like this, be ourselves, I mean, be natural. From now on we've all got parts to play, you and Harry particularly. I know it won't be easy'—he shot me a quick glance which I shot right back—'but it's absolutely essential that you do a good job. In fact, the whole thing really depends on you. You and Harry are the key elements. If things go wrong here, we can kiss it all goodbye. From now on you're Mr and Mrs Brighton and son. Remember that. The neighbours must get to know you, but not too well. And they must see Alberto, but not too closely. It won't be easy, I know. But I'm counting on you.'

'Don't worry, Jonathan, we won't let you down.' She was

practically howling. Old Morland is a fiend when it comes to con.

'Harry?'

'Paula's said it.'

Morland frowned, like he was trying to work out whether I'd actually answered his question. I remembered something I'd been meaning to ask him. 'What am I supposed to be doing here?' I asked. 'Me—the head of the family, the breadwinner.'

He grinned. 'Come downstairs and I'll show you.' We all went down to the living-room. Morland dug around in a cupboard and came out with a portable Olivetti which he put on a table near the window. Then he took a stack of foolscap and half a dozen pencils from a drawer and put them next to the typewriter.

'There it is, Harry.'

'What?'

'Your new trade. You're a writer. What do you think of that?'

'Lovely,' I said. 'Are you telling me I have to sit pecking at that thing all day long?'

'Of course not, it's only a front. Just stick a piece of paper in, wait, I'll do it.' He took a sheet from the pile of foolscap and slipped it in. 'Now anyone who calls will take your word for it you're writing a book. Tell them you gave up your job—any job, it doesn't matter what—to come to Rome and write the great novel. They may think you're mad but they'll believe you. Artists can get away with practically anything.'

I made a mental note of that. If it was such a good racket I might try it myself some day.

'In fact, you don't even have to pretend to be working,' Morland said. 'If anyone asks, tell them you're thinking. It's bound to impress them. It's a fact that a lot of writers spend so much time thinking they never get around to actually writing.'

Now I knew I was going to try it one day.

I drove Morland and Hermann back across the river. After I'd dropped Morland at the *pensione*, Hermann asked me to take him out to Rifai's villa. He was in pretty good spirits, humming these old kraut marching songs and beating out the time with his fist on the door which is okay with me except that your *cinquecento* isn't really designed to take that sort of punishment.

'Harry, we are going to biff Mister Rifai.'

'Come again.'

'I said we are going to biff Mister Rifai. "*Biff*"—' he gave the door a tremendous sock—'it is an English word, no?'

'It must be,' I said, anxious to please.

'I thought so. I remember from the old days, in the desert, when we biffed the British. Biff'—the car sort of shuddered. 'They were good days, Biff, biff, biff—'

'Take it easy, Hermann,' I said nervously. I'd remembered the car was in my name.

'And you, Harry? You were biffing?'

'I was too young to serve.'

'Of course. It is good we are friends now. The war is over, Harry.'

'That's what they say.'

'I like you, Harry. You are my friend. Bygone is bygone. All is forgiven.'

'Thanks, Hermann,' I said.

We'd reached the Appia Antica. I said, 'Hermann, I don't think I ought to drive you right up to Rifai's front door.'

'It is not far from here. I will walk.' But he sat there not moving, grunting and grumbling to himself in kraut, which is not a language I understand even by intuition. Not that I needed an interpreter to tell the old boy had suddenly lost his bounce. These war memories can play hell with the nervous system.

'I was an officer, Harry.'

'That's nice,' I said.

'For twenty-five minutes.'

'Oh.'

'At Alamein. You know Alamein?'

'Before my time, Hermann,' I assured him.

'It was not good at Alamein. The *Oberst* said to me, "Schmidt, your officers are dead, you are the senior sergeant, I promote you *Leutnant*." It was—how do you say it, Harry?'

'A battlefield commission?'

'*Ja*, that is right. A battlefield commission.' Hermann said it a couple of times like it tasted good. He sighed. 'Then the *Oberst* was killed and when I said he had promoted me *Leutnant* they laughed and said, "Schmidt, go and sit in the shade. The sun is bad for your head." They did not promote me again.'

'War is hell,' I said.

Back in Via dello Scorpione I dropped in at a bar under the flat for a nightcap. The fat little bird we'd seen earlier was sitting behind the cash-desk and of course she went into a long routine the minute she spotted me. I noticed she was giving me this *professore* bit again and I wondered what it was all about. Then a guy with a big moustache came out of the back and the bird said something to him, pointing at me.

'Professor Breeton, welcome.'

It turned out he spoke English, he owned the bar, his name was Giorgio and the fat little bird was his wife.

'It is a wonderful thing to be a writer, an artist. We Italians are all artists at heart, but we are lazy. We spend our time sitting in the sun drinking coffee and watching girls. It is a terrible way to live.'

'Terrible.'

'But you, *professore*, are a true artist. You give up your job, your home, your security. You sacrifice all for art.'

'Call me Harry,' I said.

It was a nice little bar. Not much bigger than a fair-sized bathroom, but with all the usual trimmings: a shiny metal counter which Giorgio kept rubbing with a damp cloth, glass display cases full of cakes and sweets and biscuits, and right at the end of the bar, the old espresso machine with its row of handles standing at attention. Just like a thousand other Roman bars, in fact. But I did notice a couple of small differences, artistic touches you might say. Instead of the usual plastic strips hanging in the doorway, Giorgio had strings of coloured beads which made soft clicking sounds as you walked in and out. Nice and soothing. And at one end of the counter was a big bowl of flowers, which is something I've never seen in any other bar in Rome, or anywhere else. I liked the place and I liked Giorgio. I could see myself spending a lot of time there.

'The Signora Breeton is well?'

'Who?—oh, yes, fine.'

That's what I call coming back to earth with a bump. I finished my cognac and said goodnight. It was after midnight, later than I thought, though to tell the truth I had been hanging back a little, simply because I wasn't sure how I ought to play the next bit. On the one hand I could act cool, real cool, just breeze in and take it all for granted. It's the kind of line that works with a stupid bird who thinks if you're so sure you're going to bed with her you must know something she doesn't and that makes her feel comfortable because it's a situation which is all too familiar. Paula wasn't that sort of bird. Then there was the old straightforward assault, the passion-run-rampant bit which often works with your cool bird but which can be physically dangerous, particularly if the bird fights back. I'm no coward, let me tell you, but frankly I didn't fancy taking on Paula. I mean these dancers are trained and all. Well, anyway, it ended with me not being able to make up my mind, which is worse than anything, and going upstairs in this somewhat nervous condition.

The lights were out but it wasn't too dark to see that the couch had been made up into a bed. That damn Morland must have known when he bought it. I switched on a light and found a note on the pillow. 'Just leave my suitcase in the living-room. I'll unpack tomorrow.' It was a nice try. I went into the bedroom.

'Harry?'

'Yes.'

'What do you want?'

'A chat.'

'It's late.' She was curled up on one side of this big bed with Alberto's cot next to her. I could see her hair spread all over the pillow and the room was full of this same scent I remembered from the *pensione*. I sat on the bed.

'I wanted to say I was sorry for this afternoon.' It was true. I'd never really believed she was one of Rifai's hustlers.

'I shouldn't have hit you.' She giggled. 'You looked so surprised.'

'How's the kid?'

'Sleeping, I think. He's so good, I almost wish he'd cry sometimes.'

'The first time he does I'm getting back that four hundred from Tony.'

'You do work at it, don't you, Harry?'

'At what?'

'Being tough.'

That kind of remark gets no one anywhere and I wanted to tell her so, only she looked such a dish lying there with her hair over the pillow and her arms all long and white on the dark spread that it slipped my mind. After a second or two she said, 'No, Harry.' All I'd done was take her hand.

'No?'

86

'No.'

'Look,' I said, 'we're going to be stuck together for a month, maybe more. We could at least get to know each other.'

She smiled, at least I think she did, it was hard to be sure in the dark. 'Oh, I know you, Harry.'

'You never met me till yesterday.'

'That's true, but I know you all the same.'

'You've really been around, haven't you?'

'Don't be nasty, Harry.'

What did she expect? If there's one thing I don't like it's the kind of girl that puts you down and then has to step on your face to prove it.

I got up and took a peep into the cot. Alberto was flat on his stomach, out like a light, not a care in the world. Lucky little bugger, I thought, enjoy it while you can, they'll be at you sooner than you think.

'Goodnight, Harry.'

I went to the door.

'Harry, I didn't mean—'

'Sure,' I said. 'No one ever does.' I shut the door behind me quickly because I damn well wasn't going to lose the last word on top of everything else.

The couch wasn't too bad and right away I found myself popping off. Then I had to go and remember that she hadn't had her suitcase, couldn't have had any night things, and must have been in the raw all the time we were talking. Hermann was lucky he only had war memories to screw up *his* nervous system.

Chapter Nine

WHAT I'M ABOUT TO SAY now is bound to cause a certain amount of comment. There'll be those, I know, who'll claim I'm not qualified to say it, not being a father and all. To which I can only reply that I've been the nearest damn thing to it: in fact, I'd go even further and say I've had just about all the headaches of fatherhood and not one bit of the pleasure. But to get back, what I was about to say is this:

Babies are a pain in the neck.

And now, if the shouting's over, I'll explain.

Babies are born trouble-makers. I mean when *people* want to stir up things they have to work at it. Babies don't. Babies *are* trouble. It's as simple as that. On the other hand, there's trouble and trouble. There's the kind you have with the fuzz, with your bird's husband, with the mark you've sold a ticket to: with other people, that is. Nasty, noisy, violent trouble. That's not the kind babies cause. Their kind is all in the head —your head. It's the trouble you're always waiting for and which never happens—maybe. It's electric switches and hot water taps, flights of steps and heavy ashtrays, knives and forks and screws and nails and pins and pencils. It's everything that a baby can eat, drink, drop, pull, crawl into, fall out of, or just lie around it. It's the world.

That's one thing.

Then there's the question of who's giving the orders, who's running things around the home. I found out about that on the very first morning when I was woken up by this crash from the kitchen. It was still dark.

'What's going on?' I called out.

'I'm feeding Alberto.'

'But it's not even six yet.'

'Well, he's hungry.'

'How do you know he's hungry?'

'Don't be ridiculous.'

I went back to sleep, or tried to, thinking I'd sort it all out later and get a little order and discipline into the way the operation was run. I should have saved myself the bother. Nobody runs babies. They go their own sweet way. All you can do is try and keep close enough to pick up the pieces. I've often wondered since how long normal parents can stand it without cracking. Paula and I lasted about a week. And then we had this nasty scene. It started with me sticking a safety-pin into Alberto's gut—quite by accident and not very deep—when I was doing up his nappy one day as a favour. He may not have been a crying baby, like Tony claimed, but he certainly let out a yell that time. Paula burst out of the kitchen, red hair flying, and tore Alberto out of my hands.

'Blood,' she screamed. 'Blood.'

There were about two drops.

'What did you expect?' I said. 'Paraffin?'

Luckily Morland turned up just then and after we'd got her calmed down he explained about this 'anxiety neurosis' which he said a lot of parents have because of their kids. They got so worked up imagining all the things that might go wrong, he said, that when something did, they flipped. It seemed to make sense. Paula was certainly worried stiff day and night about Alberto. And even I found myself getting a little nervous on occasion. After all, I had four hundred dollars tied up in him.

Quite apart from the normal wear and tear of looking after a kid, we also had Morland on our backs right from the start wanting to know if Alberto was 'doing his bit.' He had to be seen by all the neighbours, Morland said, though not close up.

Everyone had to know we had a baby, but no one should know what he looked like. I pointed out that the street was always jammed and you couldn't take two steps without running into Giorgio and his wife or half a dozen other people we'd got to know. Morland agreed, and suggested we should wait until the siesta hour, when everyone would be either asleep or on their balconies and terraces, and then wheel Alberto up and down the street a couple of times. That way we'd be giving him a little air and also showing him off to anyone who happened to be looking into the street at the time. Brilliant! So the very next day, after an early lunch, Paula took Alberto downstairs, stuck him on this little trolley which doubled as a pram and a shopping cart—a piece of Morland economizing—and started up the old Scorpion.

I'd decided to stay behind, not feeling up to a stroll in the sun after two plates of *spaghetti alla carbonara*, but I did go out on to the balcony to watch them. At first the street was empty, not a soul in it except Paula and Alberto, and maybe a cat or two. She walked along slowly, pushing the trolley in front of her with Alberto sitting propped up, legs sticking out in front, arms hanging over the side of the wire cage. It was like a bit out of *High Noon*—you know—the empty street, the sun beating down, the lonely figures. And then bang!—like an ambush, all these women suddenly appeared out of dark doorways. They were round Paula in a couple of seconds and the next thing I saw was poor old Alberto being passed from hand to hand like the club mascot on Saturday night. Mrs Giorgio was there in the thick of it and one or two others I recognized too. I could have gone down to help, I suppose, but what was the point? They weren't doing any harm. All they wanted was a good look at Alberto, and that's what they got. I can't say they actually stripped him, but short of that there wasn't much they missed. Paula tried to stop them at first but then she joined in too, laughing and pointing at bits of Alberto like he was a prize peke or something. She was still laughing, when she got back upstairs. 'Did you see that, Harry?' She fetched a rag from the kitchen and started wiping off these bits of jam and cheese and salami and I don't know what else that were stuck all over him. 'We never had a chance. They all know what he looks like now. What are we going to do?'

'Don't worry. I'll think of something.'

I meant it. I was going to think how the hell I could escape from the whole terrifying scene. My problem was roughly as follows: to pull out without either Morland or Hermann or both landing on my neck. Why didn't I just disappear? The answer is that in the circles I move in disappearing is not that easy, not unless you have the more permanent variety in mind. The trouble was I was known all over, for one reason or another, but mainly because of the ticket business I'd inherited from Ziggy. Ticket men are rare, like the goods they peddle. And though most of us do a lot of travelling in the line of business we're not hard to find because there are so few of us. Even *you* could find Harry Brighton—if you knew where to ask. Morland knew where to ask.

And so for the moment I stayed, spending a lot of good money and getting sweet fanny in return, unless you count the actual experience of living with a bird *and* a baby which I won't go into now except to say that it's very educational. And one thing I'd have to admit is that under certain circumstances a baby can do a lot to improve a bird. Take Alberto and Paula. Right from the start he softened her up and you could almost see this tough look of hers melting away. At first she was snapping at me morning and night, ready for a fight any time, but after a few days she got so wrapped up in the baby she almost forgot I was there. Well, not entirely, because I made a point to keep the issue of me moving off that couch and into the bedroom a live one, so to speak. It made Paula pretty mad.

'Don't you ever give up?'

'No.'

'If you do that again I'll hit you.'

'I'll hit you back.'

'You would, too.'

'Not hard though. Like this—'

'Oh, Harry, can't you buy yourself a *Playboy* or something?'

We did have one nearly nice evening together, though, and it all started with Alberto having his bath. I'd gone into the bathroom to find out what all this splashing and screaming was about and found Alberto in a plastic tub, rolling around like a little pink ham and laughing his head off. I'd never seen him actually laugh before so I stayed to watch, and before I knew it Paula had me holding his head up while she soaped and sponged and splashed away and Alberto giggled and gurgled and carried on till he almost choked.

'There, that was fun, wasn't it?'

'Yes,' I said, wringing out the sleeve of my cashmere sweater.

'And now we're going to have our rice pudding, aren't we?'

'We sincerely hope not.'

'He says he doesn't want rice pudding, Alberto. What shall we give him? Something special?—Something really special? —Yes?—All right.'

I left them to it. Something really special! She knew what I wanted really special and it wasn't *cannelloni*.

But a couple of hours later, when I came up from having a drink with Giorgio, I found she'd made this lobster thermidor and done the table up with candles and flowers and a bowl of fruit.

'It's your birthday,' I said. Birds are great ones for dropping hints.

'No, it's not. We're having a party.'

92

'Why?'

'Why not?'

Watch it now, Harry, I told myself. This could be the night.

We had a bottle of Soave Bolla, chilled, with the lobster and fresh fruit and cheese to follow. Over coffee on the terrace I said, 'You're a great cook, Paula. Where did you learn?'

'At home.' She was sewing something of Alberto's. All I could see was this curtain of red hair and a bit of her cheek. I'd kept an eye on that hair ever since we'd moved in and I had to admit it was natural.

'Where's home?'

'Liverpool.'

'A scouse. Fancy that. I'm from London myself, the Battersea High Street.'

'I know. Jonathan told me. I asked him if you were American.'

'What do you mean, American?'

'The funny way you talk.'

'What's wrong with the way I talk?'

'Nothing. It's funny, that's all.' She glanced up from her sewing with this wicked little smile and I saw the evening sort of collapsing around me. Then she started laughing—a tight squeezed-in laugh, like she was trying not to let it show.

'Well?' I said, turning on the freeze.

'It was something Jonathan said about you.'

I got a queer feeling in my gut.

'What,' I asked, 'did Morland say about me?'

'He said you were a cultural hybrid.'

'A *what*?' It sounded like some sort of insect.

'He said you were the sort of person things stuck to. You know, films and comics and telly and fashions, things like that, different accents, ways of eating, anything new. He said some people never changed, you could stick them in the middle of the desert with a lot of Arabs for twenty years and they'd still be themselves. But you, he said, you'd be wrapped in a robe and flogging camels in less than a week.'

I could see she was putting me on. Still, it made me think. Maybe I do sound like an American sometimes but that's because there's more American stuff around these days than anything else, and it does rub off on people who don't resist. I don't resist, and for a very simple reason: because it doesn't touch me—not *me*. It's all part of being a friendly mixer which is good for business and also stops people from getting too chummy, too intense like. Besides, things that rub on easily rub off the same way. The way I see it I'm just plain cosmopolitan.

I left her to finish her sewing and went downstairs. There was something I'd promised to do for Morland, though after that cultural hybrid crack I wasn't so sure I ought to. What it was was to fix his ticket, the one he hadn't paid me for. He hadn't been able to find a good pen and stamp man in Rome and he was getting pretty nervous about the name and number on this ticket not having been changed yet. What with the *pensioni* having to report all passports to the police, he'd moved three times already and was getting pretty sick of it. So he'd asked me to do it for him, even though he knew it wasn't really my line.

I got out my suitcase and opened the secret compartment at the back where I keep my kit. This compartment, half an inch deep and running the length of the suitcase, was a very neat trick. To open it you had to slide a tiny zipper all the way round, using a knife point or maybe your fingernail. The inside of the case was lined in felt, so if you didn't know the zipper was there you'd never have spotted it.

I'd just set myself up at the table under a good bright light when Paula came down from the terrace. Of course she wanted to know all about it, so I spent the next half hour showing her everything: the compartment, the inks and pens

94

and stamps, the tickets I still had—the lot. She seemed really interested.

'How much are these worth?' she asked, pointing at the four tickets which were all the stock I had left.

'It depends,' I said. 'Take these two for instance, French, both of them. They're a very nice line. In fact, after your British ticket a French is probably about the best you can hope for these days. I wouldn't sell a French ticket for under twelve hundred bucks.'

'What about these?'

I shook my head. 'This one, Liberian, nothing the matter with it really except you can only flog it to a spade.'

'And this other one? It's Egyptian isn't it? What's wrong with it?'

'You may well ask.' That gyppo ticket was a real sore point with me. I'd bought it off a barman in Rotterdam six months ago—and if I ever meet him again there'll be a new soprano on the old Zuider Zee. 'See this?' I said. 'This stamp?'

'What is it?'

'An official government stamp. All passports have them.'

'I can't read it. It looks like Arabic or something.'

'Yes, doesn't it. But it happens to be Hebrew.'

'Hebrew? But—' She began to shake with laughter. 'I'm surprised you didn't sell it to Jonathan.'

Don't think it hadn't crossed my mind. The only trouble is that damn Morland speaks Arabic. And Hebrew too, for all I know.

She shut up then and let me get on with the job. It took me all of an hour and by the time I'd finished my hands were shaking from the strain. But I was pleased with the job I'd done. Morland now had a new number on his ticket and a new name too—Browning, instead of Brown. I'd taken a lot of trouble matching the inks and I was pretty sure it would need an expert to tell that the ticket had been doctored.

I showed it to Paula. 'Morland had better be grateful,' I said.

'I'm sure he will be, now that he's Robert Browning.'

'Don't be too sure. He'll find something to complain about.'

'You're really very clever, Harry.'

I looked at her. She wasn't kidding me for once.

'It's just something you pick up,' I said. 'Like dancing.'

She held the ticket under the light and looked at it for a long time.

'Harry, why are you a crook?'

'Why am I a *what*?' I was speechless.

'I mean, you could do almost anything you wanted to.'

'I know,' I said. 'That's why I'm doing this.' The nerve of it. 'Anyway,' I said, 'who are you to talk, dancing in flea-bitten knock-shops like the Red Petal? And stripping. You used to be a stripper, remember.'

When she didn't bite I asked, 'How did you get into the business anyway?'

She smiled, not at me, at something she was remembering. 'I met a boy called Lenny who said, "Let me take you away from all this"—all this was a shipping office in Liverpool. I made the tea when the boss wasn't trying to pinch my bottom. So I went with him to London, and one thing led to another and I found myself needing a job, and someone said, "Why not try stripping?" So I thought, why not?'

'And what did Lenny say to that?'

'Lenny? Oh, he'd gone by then.'

'And one thing just went on leading to another, I suppose.

'Yes.' She gave me this long, slow, green-eyed look. 'I haven't been very clever with my life, Harry. I've done all sorts of stupid things.'

I shrugged. 'I'm not pointing any fingers. Who was it who let himself get conned into a snatch? A *snatch*!'

She smiled, but only for a second. 'I'm worried, Harry.'

'What about?'

'This whole business—the kidnapping.'

'Well for crying out loud, why did you agree in the first place?'

'It seemed a joke at first. I really didn't take Jonathan seriously. But he was so sweet about it I thought, well, I'll go to Rome and look after their baby for a few weeks and maybe something else will turn up. You see I'm not clever at all. I don't think about things. I just do them. And then I'm sorry later.'

I wanted to ask her whether she'd been sorry later for going to London with this Lenny creep, but it would have sounded too soppy. Instead I blew a big sigh to show her that she'd handed me a real problem, though in fact I was thinking that if the two of us were against the snatch we ought to be able to screw Morland a treat.

'Well, no one's been kidnapped yet,' I said.

'But he's serious, Harry. Jonathan really means it. I just never thought—'

She was getting scared, poor bird, I could see it. Morland had been round at the flat that afternoon saying things were nearly ready and we'd pull the snatch in a week or so. And then besides the kidnapping she was also worried about Alberto, about losing him. People just never seem to learn that you shouldn't grow too attached to things because things change.

'Don't worry about it.'

'I can't help it.' She was on the couch now, curled up and looking very small and weak all of a sudden.

'Listen,' I said, 'nothing Morland does ever works. Ten to one this whole thing'll collapse before we even set eyes on Rifai's kid. You don't know Morland. He's the all-time loser. You can count on it.'

'Poor Jonathan.'

Poor Jonathan! What about poor Harry?

I went over to the couch, but she looked so depressed that all I did was take her hand.

'I'll see that everything's all right. I promise. Don't you worry.'

'Oh, Harry, will you really?'

'Of course,' I said. What else could I say?

She smiled and suddenly leaned over, kissed me on the cheek, ran her hand through my hair and said, 'You're really not so bad, are you?'

Well, thanks, I thought, thanks very much.

She stood up. 'I'm going to bed, Harry.'

'Now just a minute.' That hand in the hair bit had fooled me.

'Goodnight, Harry.'

I made a grab and missed—that's what happens when you get rattled.

She laughed at me from the bedroom door. 'Tell me, Harry, is there ever a time when you're *not* thinking about it?'

'Yes,' I said. 'When I'm getting it.'

Chapter Ten

A COUPLE OF DAYS LATER I got a very nasty shock. Coming upstairs from a literary chat with Giorgio, and finding I'd left my key in the flat, I rang the bell. The door opened—and there stood King Kong. At least that's what I thought, I swear, until I looked closer and saw it was only Big Mamma. Only!

I nipped past her like a flash, bobbing and weaving just in case. The living-room was empty but I heard voices from the bedroom.

'Look how much weight he's put on.'

'Yeah, but I don't want him going soft now.'

They were bending over the cot. Tony was right up close to Paula, touching her. Well, damn nearly, anyway. Morland was sitting on the bed fanning himself with a newspaper. I was surprised to see him. We'd had words that same morning, a nasty little scene, and all because of the way I'd fixed his ticket for him. 'Robert Browning,' he'd said. '*Robert Browning*—is this meant to be a joke?' I could only assume he'd developed some sort of persecution mania to go with his other peculiarities. So I said so. That's when we started to have words.

Tony looked round and saw me. 'Look who's back,' he sneered. 'How were things at the zoo today?' He was wearing a white Palm Beach suit and a striped shirt with fancy cuffs. A mauve silk handkerchief hung out of his breast pocket. It looked like a chewed-up orchid.

Morland stood up quickly. 'Tony was just passing,' he said. 'He thought he'd check up on Alberto.'

'Passing, shit,' Tony said. 'I came for the rent.'

I laughed, good and loud. 'I hope you've got your bus fare back to that stinking pig-sty of yours,' I said, 'because you're not going to get a penny of it here.'

'Now Harry,' Morland shouted, louder than Tony who also shouted something, which I didn't catch, and it was probably just as well for him that I didn't.

'Don't "now Harry" me,' I said. 'We've got the kid, haven't we? This little runt can go blow bubbles.'

I'd got so angry I'd forgotten about Big Mamma, which wasn't very smart. She walked in just then to see what all the fuss was about and that sort of cooled me off. But not Tony.

'Are you gonna get yours,' he hissed. 'Boy, are you gonna get yours. Just wait, just wait—' It was the same as before, saying everything twice like he had to make up for his pint size. He started round the bed towards me and Mamma moved in from the door. I was just thinking, Hermann, where are you? when Morland stepped forward and said, 'Now everybody calm down, calm down. Let's talk about this. There's no point in getting excited.'

'Who's excited?' I said, though I knew one who was—Big Mamma. She was breathing down my neck.

'We made a deal, Harry,' Morland said. 'Fair is fair.'

'Morland,' I said quietly, 'the kid is here, we've *got* him. This creep is not Alberto's father and she's not his mother. What makes you think they can take him back short of using'—I took a quick step forward—'physical violence?'

'That's not the point, Harry—'

'Screw that goddam point,' Tony shouted. 'This is what says we can take the kid back any time we like—any time.' He shot his hand in and out of his pocket so quick I thought he was really going to do the whole Chicago bit. But all he came out with was a piece of paper. 'In case you can't read Italian,' he said, waving the paper in my face, 'it says that this kid, this Alberto, is the legally adopted son of Antonio Bellone, that's me, and Claudia Bellone, who doesn't happen to be around right now but who can easily be dug up if she's needed. So just tell me, wise guy, do I get the rent or do I take the kid?'

Well, there was an easy answer to that one and I was about to give it when I saw Paula looking at me in this soppy way and sort of crouching over the cot. It took my mind off what I was going to say and before I knew it Morland had jumped in.

'You'll get your rent, Tony. We'll pay.'

'Who'll pay?' I said.

'Harry!' Paula sounded like she couldn't believe it. '*Harry!*'—This time it was more accusing. 'HARRY—'

'All right, all right.'

Tony laughed out loud. Morland sniggered. Paula gave me a nice smile—but don't think that made up for anything.

I peeled off four fifties. There wasn't much left on the roll.

'This is only two hundred,' Tony said. 'I want two weeks in advance, like before.'

'You're getting one week,' I said. 'And you're lucky that's all you're getting.' I turned to Morland. 'Your friends can leave any time. Just be sure you open the windows when they've gone.'

Then I turned and walked out: out of the bedroom, out of the flat and downstairs to Giorgio's where I told him to set up a double because I could feel the flushes coming on and that's when I know I'm really upset.

'Ah, I see the writing is not going well, Harry. *Coraggio!* An artist is born to suffer. It is the price he pays for his art. Posterity will reward you.'

I was still seeing these black spots and things when Morland came in.

'Harry—' he began, then took a closer look at me and shut up.

I had another brandy while Giorgio gave Morland a big

hullo. I'd noticed before how well they got on together. Giorgio was very hot on this art bit and I think he found his chats with me on the subject not altogether satisfying. He was always going on about how he was really a poet at heart— aren't we all? I said—and wanting to show me his work. Fortunately I was able to say I couldn't read a word of Italian, which wasn't strictly true but saved me a lot of trouble. Morland had looked at them once though and said they were great which sent Giorgio approximately into orbit. Since then they'd been very thick, always chattering away, though usually in Italian so I didn't know whether it was art or what they were talking about.

After about ten minutes Morland sneaked another glance at me and apparently decided he could risk it. He came over carrying a cup of tea Mrs Giorgio had brought him.

'You shouldn't get so worked up, Harry. If only—'

'Worked up?' I said. 'Who's worked up? Look—steady as a rock.' And I was too. I'd suddenly realized what I was going to do. I was going to leave, pull out, drop it right there. I wasn't worried about Morland any more, or Hermann either, *If* they came after me, *then* I'd start worrying. For now though it was finish—no more Alberto, no more Tony, no more Morland: and no more lying awake on that damn couch listening to noises and making pictures and never getting any sleep.

Morland coughed, which is usually a sign that he has something important to say. He was looking at me in this funny way, sideways, eyes all screwed up. 'I know what you're thinking, Harry,' he said, soft and friendly.

'You do?'

He nodded. 'You're thinking, how the hell am I going to get out of this thing and do old Morland at the same time. That's what you're thinking, isn't it?'

I didn't say a word.

'Well, let's have a look at your problem. You can't go to the police, obviously, and you don't dare just walk out on me because you know I'll get you one way or another. Or maybe Hermann will. So what do you do? Shall I tell you? You ring up Rifai. You tell him his son's going to be snatched. You tell him there's this fellow Morland and his own bodyguard, Hermann, who are planning to kidnap young Selim. And after you've told him that you say that all *you* want in return is protection—the rest you leave to his generosity. What do you think of that, Harry?'

'Bloody brilliant,' I said, and it was too. Why hadn't I thought if it myself? 'Why are you telling me all this?' I asked.

'Because I don't know whether you've thought of it yourself,' he said. 'If you have, you probably think it's a stroke of genius.'—Well, wasn't it? 'I just want you to know that I've thought of it too—a long time ago—so forget it.' Suddenly he wasn't friendly any longer.

As coolly as I could, I said, 'Suppose I do call Rifai? What are you going to do about it?'

'I'm not going to do anything, Harry. Tony is.'

'Tony!' I started laughing. '*Tony!* The boy gangster? The Chicago drop-out? Morland, you're not serious. What's he going to go? Get Big Mamma to fill me in?'

Morland shook his head, he was grinning too. 'Nothing like that. You know I don't approve of violence.'

'Well, what's he going to do then? Go on, Morland, tell me.'

'All right, Harry. I'll tell you. He's going to charge you with kidnapping, that's what.'

I felt my stomach turn. 'Look,' I said, 'he can't—'

'Oh yes he can.'

'But I've paid him.'

'I hope you've got your receipt.'

'You bastard. The two of you. You had it set up all along.'

'Don't be silly, Harry. Tony doesn't know a thing about it. Not yet.'

103

'Then what's all this kidnapping stuff? Tony doesn't want to charge me with snatching Alberto. He just wants to go on getting his two hundred a week.'

'That's true. He's not very imaginative. But if I were in his shoes do you know what I'd do? I'd put the squeeze on you now for a lot more than two hundred a week by threatening to charge you with kidnapping Alberto. And if you didn't pay up I'd go ahead and charge you anyway because I hate your guts, being Tony, that is.' His eyes had gone very cold all of a sudden and I didn't need two guesses to know who was going to put this charming idea into Tony's head.

I managed a shrug. 'It wouldn't work,' I said. 'We've had the kid for more than a fortnight. Why hasn't he reported it missing?'

'Because he's afraid of getting involved with the police of course. A man like Tony, deported from the States, what do you expect? But his love for Alberto is stronger than his fear of the fuzz—that's a nice touch, I think—and he comes forward and lays the charge. Says you offered to take the kid to the seaside for him two weeks ago and that's the last he's seen of either of you. As stories go it has a lot of possibilities.'

'Yes,' I said. 'And there's a part in it for you too.'

Morland shook his head. 'I'm afraid not, Harry. You and I know each other of course, but Tony will say he's never set eyes on me. And as far as I'm concerned this new family of yours is something you've acquired since I last saw you two years ago. Of course I'd be happy to come forward as a character witness though I doubt if it would help. Let's face it, Harry, in the eyes of most courts the complete undesirability of your character would be hard to challenge.'

'Don't be too sure,' I said. 'Paula and I together can knock down any story you and Tony cook up.'

Morland groaned: the sort of groan you hear when someone is trying to get something through someone else's thick skull and is not making a very good job of it. 'Harry, just stop and think for a moment. Here you are, living with a woman who you say is your wife but isn't, with a child which you claim is yours but in fact belongs to neither of you. And to cap it all— what are you doing here? You're writing a book. *You* are writing a *book*. Please, Harry. If you tell the fuzz now that the real reason you're doing all this is because you want to snatch some other kid, some millionaire's son, the only problem they'll have is whether to send you to prison for life or stick you in the nut-house and forget about you.'

The flushes were coming back again. And the black spots too.

'Come on, Harry. I told you I'd been planning this thing for months. Do you think I didn't take into account the possibility that you'd try and weasel out?

'What about Paula?'

'What about her?'

'If Tony hits me with a kidnapping charge, she'll get it too.'

'That's right.'

'But Morland, you can't do that to a bird—'

'Not me, Harry. *You*. You agreed to come in. Remember that. If she gets hurt now because you're trying to back out then you're the one who's to blame. And anyway,' he said, looking very prunish all of a sudden, 'she's your responsibility now.'

'What do you mean, my responsibility?'

Morland sneered. 'Don't try to fool me, Harry Brighton. I've had my eye on you. You like playing house with her, don't you? You like the fun and games and the . . . the slap and tickle and the . . . the . . .'

'Please,' I said. 'The word is—'

'Never mind the word,' he shouted. 'Just try to feel a sense of responsibility towards someone. If not to me, then at least to Paula.'

'Gentlemen, gentlemen.' Giorgio came trotting over. 'What is the trouble?'

I didn't reply, just slammed a thousand lire down on the bar and walked out. As I brushed through the string beads I heard Giorgio say, 'It is the creative fury.'

Morland caught up with me at the bottom of the stairs.

'Just one more thing, Harry, if you're thinking of taking Alberto back to the farm on the quiet, save yourself the trouble. Tony and his mother have gone to Naples for a fortnight. By the time they get back, it won't matter any longer.'

'What do you mean?'

'I mean it won't matter.'

'The snatch?' I said.

He nodded.

'When?'

'Tomorrow.'

'It's too quick,' I said. 'You're rushing me. I want more time to think about it.'

'There's no more time, Harry.' He'd been standing in the doorway, looking like a thin, black scarecrow against the bright sunlight. Now he stepped forward and I saw his white face and the big black eyes gleaming. 'This is it, Harry. The big one. The last one. If this doesn't work, I'm finished. I only hope you're not the one who stops it working. For your sake, that is.'

I didn't say a word, just stood there looking down at him. I had this funny feeling, half tired, half sick, which comes when I've put a lot of effort into something, really worked at it like, and then seen it all come tumbling down.

'Come on,' he said, and we went upstairs.

Paula had Alberto up on the terrace in the sun. He was messing around in a broken flower pot, getting his hands and face filthy and spraying dirt and stuff all over the shop. 'You want to watch him,' I said to Paula who was stretched out in a deck-chair. 'He could cut himself on those broken pieces.'

She just smiled and shook her head at me.

Morland took off his coat and leaned over the side of the terrace, looking down into the street. He wasn't so sure of himself any more, not with Paula and Alberto there.

I said, 'We're snatching Rifai's kid tomorrow.' Then I looked away because I didn't want to see her eyes saying I'd promised it would all be all right.

After a while she said quietly, 'What happens to Alberto?'

Morland started coughing. Anyone who didn't know him would have said he looked unhappy.

'I said what happens to Alberto?'

Morland almost choked. Then he said, 'I'm sorry, Paula, really sorry. You're not going to like this, I'm afraid, but this is how we're going to do it . . .'

Chapter Eleven

MORLAND was getting worried. I could see him across the square wiping his face with a handkerchief and looking at his watch again. They were late: twenty minutes already. Just enough to make me hope they weren't coming at all.

It was after three and the sun was beating down on the square turning the tar on the cobbles all soft and sticky. I'd stood with Morland for about ten minutes and then crossed the road to get into the shade where the trees hung over the park wall.

'Harry, we're supposed to be tourists,' Morland hissed after me.

'This tourist's going to get himself an ice-cream.'

There was an old boy selling ices near the park gates and I bought a chocolate and vanilla from him. Then I stood in the shade and watched Morland trying to look like a tourist, walking up and down in front of this old church, which was across the square from the gates, pretending to study the guide-book which he'd bought specially for the occasion. He'd also bought a walking stick, a pair of dark glasses and a floppy linen hat. 'How do I look, Harry?' he'd asked, just like that day years ago when we'd sailed up the Aegean together. This time I didn't answer, though it was my personal opinion that any copper who spotted him in the full rig would arrest him purely on reflex.

I glanced through the gates. Halfway up a long straight path running between two hedges Paula was sitting on a bench with the pram beside her, waiting. She was thinking about Alberto, that was for sure. Or if she was thinking of me it couldn't be anything I'd want to know about.

A car was coming slowly up the hill under the chain of arches and for a moment I thought it was them. It went straight through the square without stopping. Morland shut his guide-book and looked at his watch again. Mine said three twenty-five. The ice-cream man started his motor and went put-putting down the hill. The square was empty now except for Morland and me and our *cinquecento* which I'd parked in the shade near the gates. The new aluminium luggage-rack on top shone like silver. It was very quiet. The only noise came from the traffic down on Via di San Gregorio: it sounded a long way off. Morland took off his hat, wiped his face, put the handker-chief back in his pocket and started walking slowly towards me. He'd given up.

Then I saw it, turning the corner at the bottom of the Clivo di Scauro, coming up the hill, big and black. It had to be a Rolls. And at half past three on a Tuesday afternoon in Piazza dei Santi Giovanni e Paolo outside Villa Celimontana, it had to be Yusuf Rifai's. Morland saw it too and stopped. He looked at me across the square and I could feel him asking the ques-tion, asking if I really was with him this time. I took a last long suck on my cone, just to keep him guessing. Then I tossed it away and walked across the road. The Rolls came whispering into the square behind me and stopped in the shade next to the *cinquecento*.

'It's them, it's them.' Morland hadn't even set eyes on the kid yet and already he was having kittens.

'Stop goggling,' I said. 'We're supposed to be tourists, remember.' I pulled him round so we were facing the church. 'Open your guide-book.'

We heard the doors opening and shutting. I took a quick peep over my shoulder. They were getting the pram ready, pulling up the hood to keep the sun out. I turned around.

'Careful, Harry—'

'It's all right. They're not watching us.'

The woman opened the back door of the Rolls and leaned in. She came out carrying this bundle of white drapes which she put in the pram and then spread a white veil over the top. The guy held the pram to stop it running off down the hill. When she'd got the veil tucked in neatly she said something to him and he laughed. He was a nice-looking Ite with dark curly hair and white teeth, so you couldn't really blame her. She wasn't bad-looking herself from what I could see through this blue nurse's uniform, though not in Paula's class, say.

'What are they doing? What are they doing?' Morland was still staring at the church like he'd been struck with paralysis.

I watched them push the pram through the gates into the park.

'It's all right,' I said. 'Everything's just the way you said it would be.'

It would be dead simple, Morland had said, a piece of cake.

'And even if something goes wrong, they can't touch you. It'll look like an honest mistake.'

Paula said for the third time, 'What happens to Alberto?' You could see this time she meant it.

'I'll tell you,' Morland said. 'But let me tell it all, just the way I've planned it. Then you'll see why—why things have to be done this way.' He was sitting in front of Paula, elbows on knees, staring into her eyes. It was the old Svengali bit—the thing he was always trying on me. It didn't work on Paula either. She stared right back at him with the kind of look in her green eyes that made me glad it wasn't me sitting in the line of fire.

'First,' Morland said, 'the situation. Every Tuesday and Thursday afternoon Rifai's son Selim is taken to the park at the Villa Celimontana by his English nurse, Helen. They are always accompanied by the same bodyguard, Silvio, an Italian. Helen and Silvio are in love. On each of their visits to the park our lovers follow a strict routine. Silvio parks the car outside the gates in the Piazza dei Santi Giovanni e Paolo and helps Helen put Selim in his pram. Then together they walk through the park, past the villa, right to the end of the gardens, always to the same spot: a bench at the corner of a terrace—no doubt it has some romantic significance for them. There they spend at least an hour, talking, holding hands, kissing, snogging and so forth. During this time Selim sleeps in his pram under a tree a dozen feet away. A veil is spread over the pram to keep the flies off him. Every quarter of an hour or so Helen remembers her duties to the extent of going over to the pram and glancing at the baby. At the end of the hour—that is to say, at four o'clock—Helen and Silvio wheel the pram back to the car and return to Rifai's villa. I should add that at this hour of the day—between three and four—there are generally very few people in the park, which presumably is why our lovers choose that time to go there. Finally, I can assure you that this account of their actions and behaviour is accurate since I've compiled it myself by personal observation on numerous occasions, in particular—'

'All right, Morland,' I said. 'We're impressed. Get to the point.'

He looked a bit put out. I could see he was starting to enjoy himself, leaning back in his chair, finger-tips touching, trying like hell to look inscrutable.

'I've given you the situation, now for the plan. From what I've told you you can see that any attempt to snatch the baby out of the pram would certainly fail since Silvio and Helen are never more than a few yards away from it. That leaves one other method: taking the baby and pram together. And that's how we're going to do it.'

He paused, waiting for the gasps of amazement. There

weren't any. All that happened was that Paula started tapping one finger-nail on the arm of her chair—tap, tap, tap, tap. Pretty soon Morland got the message.

'Now you're probably wondering how we can walk off with a baby *and* a pram any more than with just a baby. The answer is that we have to make Helen and Silvio think that nothing's happened, that pram and baby are still there. And the only way we can do *that* is by a substitution.'

'Of the pram?' I said.

A very shifty look came over Morland's face.

'*Of the pram?*'

'Not just the pram, Harry. The kid too.'

'*Alberto!*' Paula jumped up. 'You mean put my little Alberto in a pram and leave him and . . . Oohhh, you monster. You'll do no such thing. Just you dare try.' She stood right over him, red hair blazing in the sun. Remembering our little scene in the kitchen, I reckoned there was a good chance of Morland being flattened. He must have thought so too because he stood up quickly and backed away.

'Now, Paula, don't get excited. Just listen. I haven't finished yet.'

'Oh yes you have. I'm going straight to the police.'

Harry, I said to myself, this is where we do a very fast fade. I thought Morland would have the same idea but I have to admit I underestimated him. At the word 'police' he grabbed his chest and let out a terrible groan.

'Jonathan—?'

'It's all right, it's all right. I'm fine.' He groaned again. 'What is it?'

Morland felt his way round the chair and sat down carefully like his backside was marked FRAGILE. He was still holding his chest. He looked just about ready to croak.

'Jonathan—?' She was crying. She didn't know what to do. That Morland really is a bastard.

'Go on, Paula,' he gasped. 'If you want to go to the police, then go. I won't stop you. Nor will Harry. Go on.'

'You must come and lie down. Harry, help me get him downstairs.'

'Please, it's nothing. I'll be all right in a moment. Just a touch of indigestion.'

Indigestion!

I could see Paula was about ready to flip so I pushed her aside and looked into Morland's eyes.

'I've seen him like this before. He'll be all right in a couple of minutes.'

If looks could kill I'd have been mashed potatoes.

Morland started coughing and wheezing.

'I'll get him some water.' She ran downstairs.

'Knock it off, Morland,' I said. 'She's worried out of her mind.'

He made a croaky sound. 'You think I'm putting you on? I've had these attacks before.'

'Well, they certainly come at convenient times.'

Paula came back with the water. She still looked worried, but also angry.

'This settles it,' she said. 'You're in no condition to kidnap anyone. We'll have to call the whole thing off.'

Morland shook his head. 'The only way you can stop me is by going to the police,' he gasped out.

'But Jonathan, you can't—'

'I've been planning this caper for two years, Paula.' So it was two years now! 'It's too late for me to go back. I'm old and I'm tired and I'm sick. It's too late for most things for me. Go to the police if you must. I can't say I won't hold it against you because I will. I'll hold it against you that you broke your word to me. I'll hold that against you, Paula, but only in my heart. I won't try to stop you doing whatever you feel you have to do . . .'

I just stood there speechless. I mean *that* is what I call con, the real article.

Paula didn't stand a chance. When she'd had her little cry she said, 'But you're treating Alberto like—like a thing—'

'You didn't let me finish, Paula. We're going to get him back, I promise. That's part of the plan.'

'How?'

'He'll come back with the ransom. Two hundred and fifty thousand dollars and our baby. That's the price I'll put to Rifai.'

'But something may happen to him—'

'What?'—Morland flung his hands in the air: his ticker was certainly making a good comeback—'He'll be in Rifai's hands for less than a week. In a millionaire's home. What do you think they'll do to him? Starve him? He'll probably have the time of his life.'

I said, 'Why can't we leave an empty pram, or a doll?'

'Yes, why not?' Paula said.

'Because the way I've planned it we're safe right up to the moment that we put the baby in our car and drive off.'

'I don't understand—'

'Listen,' Morland said. He took a couple of big breaths and a gulp of water. 'I'll tell you exactly how we're going to do it and then you'll understand. While Helen and Silvio are busy on the bench and the baby is asleep in the pram, you and Paula will appear pushing a pram identical in every detail to Selim's. With one small difference. Draped over the hood of your pram will be something brightly coloured that catches the eye, a shawl, say, or Paula's red raincoat. When you reach the spot you'll park your pram as close as possible to Selim's under the tree. Helen and Silvio will note your arrival of course but not, we hope, with more than passing interest. When you've got your pram in position you'll take the coat off the hood and go for a short walk together, out of sight of the lovers. When you return they should be absorbed in each other again. If not, wait until they are. According to my observations they seldom allow more than five minutes to go by without kissing. And I've noted that one kiss invariably leads to another. Once they start you can count on them being lost to the world for at least two consecutive minutes, an important point. Once you observe them to be in this state, walk up to the prams, spread your coat over Selim's and walk off with it. What could be safer?'

I said, 'What do we do when the nurse starts screaming?'

'She won't, Harry. She won't even hear you. But supposing she does. Supposing she looks up and sees you pushing away this pram with the coloured coat on it. She'll automatically glance under the tree to check on her own pram. And there it'll be safe and sound. I repeat, what could be safer?'

Paula said, 'But I don't see then why you can't leave an empty pram.'

Morland leaned forward and took her hand. He said, 'Because in spite of all the odds against it, the worst may happen. The nurse may suddenly decide to get up and go to the pram and take off the veil and look inside. If she does that and finds it empty, or with a doll inside, then you and Harry can only be kidnappers. But if she finds another baby in a pram identical to Selim's, then no one can say you haven't simply made an honest mistake. You've walked off with the wrong pram. And that holds good right up to the moment when you reach the car. Only then, when you strip the veil and take the baby out of the pram, can you be expected to know that you've got the wrong one. From that moment on it's a kidnapping. But by then we'll know whether they've discovered the switch because you'll have had to walk a quarter of a mile to get from the end of the park to the car. That's plenty of time for them to sound the alarm. If they do twig it, if they do come running after you, then whatever you do don't try to escape. Just act astonished. Don't you see?—It's the one way of snatching a kid that's absolutely *safe*.'

'And if they do notice the switch and stop us, what then?'

Morland shrugged. 'Then that's it. We've failed. Finish.' From the way he said 'finish' you could see he meant himself too.

'No second shot?'

He shook his head. 'You can't pull that sort of thing twice.' There was a silence. Morland looked at us—first me, then Paula. He'd got a bit of colour back in his cheeks and his eyes were burning. I don't know what Paula was thinking but I was beginning to admit to myself that if you have to do something as crazy as snatching a kid, then Morland's way was as good as any. I was even prepared to admit that it was just about the best way I'd ever heard of. But there was one little point . . .

I said, 'You keep saying Paula and me are going to make the snatch. That's not the way I see it, Morland.'

'It has to be you two, Harry. An ordinary married couple taking their baby for a walk in the park. No one will give you a second glance—no one will remember you. But don't worry, I'll be there, right beside you.'

'And Hermann?'

'He stays at the villa. He's our inside contact. We can't risk giving him away.'

'Supposing it works—what next?'

'We call Rifai immediately. I want to be the one who breaks the news to him. Once we've made contact he won't want to call in the police. He's not the type. He'll want to handle it himself.'

'But the nurse will give the alarm anyway. They're certain to notice the switch when they get back to the car, if not before.'

'I don't think she will,' Morland said. 'And I'll tell you why. The first thing she'll think is that there's been a mistake—she'll remember seeing you with a pram that looked like hers. And the very fact that a baby and a pram have been left behind will tend to point to some kind of mistake. The first thing they'll do is search the park for you, the second is phone Rifai. Only we'll have told him already.'

'I don't know,' I said. 'It all sounds very iffy.'

'That's where you're wrong, Harry. It's all based on predictable human responses. Helen and Silvio won't call the police because they won't want to believe the worst—that Selim has been kidnapped. By leaving them Alberto we provide them with a straw to which their natural optimism will cling. And as far as Rifai is concerned, providing we can tell him about the kidnapping before he learns of it from some other source, I'm confident he won't go to the police. He'll do business with us, Harry, you'll see. It's a matter of elementary psychology, of understanding your opponent.'

'And if this psychology bit doesn't work and he calls in the police after all?'

'Then we've got the perfect hiding place for Selim—*la famille* Brighton. Whichever way he plays it he's going to have to pay to get his kid back. I tell you, Harry, I've thought it all out. Every last detail.'

He had, too. I couldn't find a crack in it anywhere. I tried to imagine what it would be like to have sixty thousand dollars all at once. I hadn't thought about it before. It was something I hadn't believed in. Now suddenly it was looking real.

'Well, Harry?'

I shrugged, meaning, 'Yes, I suppose so'—I didn't want to seem too impressed. As I think I've mentioned before, praise goes to Morland's head.

'Paula?' He was pretty sure he'd got her with that sneaky heart attack bit but he wanted to make sure.

She didn't answer right away. Instead she got up and went over to Alberto, knelt down and started cleaning some of the dirt and stuff from the flower pot off his face with her handkerchief. When she did speak it was so soft I hardly caught it.

'Do you promise to get him back, Jonathan?'

'I promise, Paula.'

'Harry?'

'What?'

'You, too. Do you promise?'

Did I promise—? What the hell did it have to do with me? I mean I had nothing against Alberto, but when it comes to a snatch it's every man for himself and tough luck if you happen to be a kid. I was about to explain this when Morland grabbed my arm and nodded frantically at Paula's back. So to stop him throwing another fit I said, 'Okay. Yes. I promise.'

She looked over her shoulder at me. It wasn't a friendly look, but not nasty either. It was more sort of curious.

Morland ended up by staying the night. He said he was tired after his 'attack' but I think he was just scared to leave us alone for a moment. He must have felt like one of those juggler boys in the circus who gets a whole lot of stuff—cups, plates, balls, brooms and I don't know what—balanced on the end of one finger, and then sees this clown creeping up to tickle him in the ribs. He slept on the other half of the pull-out couch and made a pretty bad night of it, groaning and coughing and carrying on till you'd almost have thought there was really something wrong with him.

In the morning we went up to Villa Celimontana for a dry run. In case you don't know it, the villa is on a hill about half-way between the Colosseum and the Baths of Caracalla. There are two ways of getting to it: from Piazza di Porta Capena or from Via della Navicella. Going from Piazza di Porta Capena, which is the way we took, you drive up this narrow cobbled street—the Clivo di Scauro—overhung with trees and big bushes of pink and yellow flowers. The street winds round a church and then goes straight up the hill under a chain of old brick arches to the Piazza dei Santi Giovanni e Paolo, which is where the park gates are.

The park is really the garden of an old villa which Morland says was built a few hundred years ago by some noble Roman. Now it's open to the public and on summer evenings you'll find it crawling with kids and lovers and so forth. The villa itself isn't much to look at but the gardens are a treat. Lawns and fountains and lots of tall old trees, also flowers. It's the sort of place almost anyone would enjoy a visit to if he didn't have other things on his mind. Like a snatch, for instance.

Morland said he'd show me the exact route that Helen and Silvio would take that afternoon. From the gates we walked up this long asphalt path running straight between high hedges. At the end of it was a rockery, a couple of fountains and some bits of old statues—the sort of thing Morland had wanted to fish out of the sea back in Greece. Seeing them there gave me a nasty turn. Not because I'm superstitious but because they reminded me how Morland's plans always finished up. Just past the rockery was another long asphalt path which led up to the villa itself. It was all shut up and dead-looking. We walked past the villa and then turned right down a gravelled path which ended at a low brick wall. On the other side of the wall was a drop of twenty feet to a lower level of the garden. From where we stood the wall ran to the left with a path beside it hedged in with flowers and bushes and thick shrubs. We walked along this path for maybe fifty yards until we came to the end of the wall. Near the corner was a bench set back in the shrubs and looking out over the wall on to the tops of the trees growing on the terrace below. We sat down. It was dead quiet. There wasn't a soul in sight.

'This is the place,' Morland said.

'Where do they leave the kid?'

He pointed to the left where the path and the wall made a right-angled turn and disappeared behind us.

'Right at the corner. Under that tree.'

The spot wasn't ten feet away.

'It's too close. They'll hear us.'

'Probably. But it doesn't matter so long as they think their pram is safe. You've got to get the prams right up close to each other, Harry. And make sure the nurse sees the coloured coat on your pram when you wheel it past. It's like picking pockets or playing the shell game. The mark must see what *you* want him to see. Just keep cool.'

Oh sure, cool as a slab of marble, with twenty years hanging over my head. I looked around a little more to get every detail fixed in my mind. There wasn't much to see. The only thing that really caught the eye was a statue of this nude Roman gent standing at the corner of the wall. He had a chopper on him that would have made a donkey blink. I could see what Morland meant by romantic significance.

'Now the getaway.'

We went round the corner and Morland pointed. 'If you leave this way you won't have to walk past them with the pram. Take the first path on the left—that gets you into the shrubbery where you can't be seen—then first right and after that first left again. That'll bring you to the main path leading back to the villa. Remember that, Harry—left, right, left. These paths are a bit confusing and you may find yourself going in circles.'

He insisted on taking me over the route though it wasn't really necessary. If there's one thing I have it's a sense of direction. I was surprised though when we got into the shrubbery to find how thick it was, more like a jungle, with bushes and trees and trailing vines. The paths were easy to follow and in a couple of minutes we were back at the villa.

From the park we drove to Morland's *pensione* to collect the pram. I was curious to see it. According to Morland it was only a shade smaller than a Mini and twice as plush. He'd been going on all morning about how much he'd had to pay to have it imported from England and it came as no surprise when he suggested I might like to contribute to the cost. He was still bitter when we got up to his room.

'Just look at it. How can you expect me to pay for that alone?'

I whistled. I'd never seen a pram like it. Gleaming chrome bumpers, independent four-wheel springing, two handbrakes and a royal coat of arms stamped on the chassis. When I pushed it across the floor it purred.

'Do you know what that cost me?' Morland said for the tenth time.

'Sorry,' I said. 'It's just not my style. I hope it's the right kind.'

Morland bent down and read from a small metal tag attached to one wheel: 'Finch and Cromley, Perambulator Manufacturers . . . Blue Marlin model, Mark II. Come on, Harry, a quarter share at least.'

'Not a chance.'

He blew a big sigh and slumped down on the bed. 'You're a hard man, Harry Brighton. Here I am down to my last few pounds, and you're walking around with all that money.'

'All what money? Do you know what it costs to keep a family these days? Not to mention having to *rent* your kid.'

'All right, all right.'

But he looked so down and out that in the end I did offer to buy a luggage-rack for the car which we'd need to cart the pram around and which Morland hadn't even thought of. We went out and bought one and clamped it to the roof of the car and then went back upstairs and fetched the pram. It caused quite a stir on Via Margutta. One geezer with a beard asked me where I was going to exhibit it. I didn't understand till Morland explained about this pop art business in which anything is art if you say it is. What a racket! I was really impressed.

The fuss on Via Margutta was nothing compared to the

small riot that broke out when we came weaving down Via dello Scorpione with the pram strapped on top, looking like some sort of mobile mushroom. Women leaned out of their windows and screamed. Mrs Giorgio shouted '*Fantastico*' and grabbed me in a half-nelson. All the kids gathered around and a couple of old bats started polishing up the chrome before we'd even got it off the car.

The only person who wasn't impressed was Paula. She said, 'Don't bring that thing into my house,' so we had to leave it on the landing.

Alberto gave us a wave as we came in. He was sitting in the sun on the balcony finishing up his lunch. The floor of the living-room was strewn with his gear: wooden blocks and rattles, a couple of fluffy animals and a big rubber duck. Morland almost broke up when he saw the duck since he was the one who'd bought it for Alberto. He picked it up, squeezed it a couple of times and then dropped it quickly when he saw Paula watching him. I think she must have left it there on purpose.

We watched Helen and Silvio disappear round the corner of the villa, pushing the pram ahead of them.

'Give them a few minutes to settle down to their snogging,' Morland said.

I walked back down the path to the bench where Paula was waiting. She hadn't raised the hood of the pram yet and Alberto was lying on his back in the sun getting a good tan. A bottle of milk was tucked away at the end of the pram. Paula said it would remind them to feed him. She'd also wanted to leave a note saying he was partial to caramel custard and liked his carrots minced fine but I'd put my foot down.

'Next thing you know Rifai will be charging *us* a quarter of a million.'

She didn't argue. She'd stopped fighting. In fact, she'd

hardly said a word since the night before. Just 'please' and 'thank you' and 'pass the butter'. I wasn't sure I liked her that way. I wished she'd lose her temper over something so we could have a good punch-up and clear the air.

'We'll move in a couple of minutes,' I said, trying to act nonchalant. Actually I was pissing razor-blades.

Paula pulled up the hood and spread the veil over the pram. I reached inside and gave Alberto's tummy a last tickle: it was something he always appreciated. Then Paula bent down and held him tight for a moment. She was crying as she draped her red raincoat over the hood like Morland had told her to do.

I said, 'When you see him again in a day or two he'll be fatter than ever.'

'Oh, shut up.'

We pushed the pram up to the villa. Morland was sitting in the shade reading his guide-book. He must have heard the pram wheels crunching on the gravel but he didn't look up. As we came level with him he said softly, 'I've had a look—they're all alone.'

We stopped and I bent down, pretending to fix something on the wheel. Paula blew her nose.

'Don't worry now,' Morland said to his guide-book. 'It'll all be over in a few minutes.'

'Where will you be?' I asked.

'In there—' he nodded at the shrubbery—'I'll be watching you. Just remember, if anything goes wrong, don't panic. You're not kidnappers, you're just a young couple taking your baby for a walk.'

Paula said, 'For God's sake let's get on with it.' She looked like she was going to start crying again.

I stood up and had a last look around. Down at Via della Navicella a woman and her child were coming through the gates, but they were still a long way off. The path from the piazza which we'd come up was empty. It was dead quiet except for the splash of water in a fountain and the noise of the crickets.

'Right, let's go.'

We went down the side of the villa to the wall and then turned left along the path skirting the parapet. I spotted them in the distance sitting on the bench. The pram was under the tree. They seemed a long way away but somehow it took us no time at all to reach them. When we got close I saw that something was wrong. They weren't necking, or holding hands, or anything. In fact, from all I could see it was ten to one they weren't even on speaking terms! Silvio was sitting at one end of the bench with his arms folded and his jaw stuck out, Mussostyle. Helen was at the other end, filing her nails. I think they were both quite pleased to see us. It gave them something to look at. They certainly looked hard.

Under my breath I was calling Morland names that even I hadn't thought of before. Lovers! Morland wouldn't know a lover from a baboon's backside. But there was nothing else to do but go on with it, so I ran our pram up close beside the other, which was parked against the tree-trunk, and left them so they were almost touching. As I bent down to fix the brake I saw they were still watching us. Paula took her raincoat off the hood—who needed a raincoat on a blazing summer day?— the whole thing was crazy. I glanced at both prams. At least Morland was right about one thing. They did look the same. And with the shade and the white veils you couldn't see into either of them. I took Paula's arm and we strolled off round the corner.

'He's done it again,' I said. 'He's done it again. Lovers! Snogging! Morland probably thinks they're having it off by remote control.'

'Sshhh.' Paula squeezed my arm. 'Wait.'

'What for? The big moment when she asks him what time it is?'

'It's only a lovers' quarrel. They'll make up in a moment. They were just waiting for us to leave.'

'Are you sure?'

'Of course.'

I didn't argue. Birds are supposed to know about these things. I looked around and spotted the path we had to take on the getaway. It was clear. Thank God for that. Something moved deep in the shrubbery. I caught a glimpse of a white linen hat. Morland was keeping close enough to see what was going on and far enough away so as not to get involved if things turned nasty.

'Listen.' Paula touched my arm again.

Silvio was shouting something in Italian.

'He's jealous—' she smiled faintly—'something about the boy who brings the groceries.' It was amazing how quickly Paula had picked up Italian from Mrs Giorgio and the neighbours.

'He says all English girls are the same.'

'How's that?'

'Fickle.'

Poor old Silvio—welcome to the club!

'Listen,' Paula said again. 'She's crying.' There was this soft whimpering sound. 'She's got him now.'

'Got him?'

'Where she wants him.' Paula smiled again. 'Good for you, Helen.'

Terrifying, isn't it?

We waited a few more minutes. Helen stopped crying and then we heard some murmuring. Then silence. Paula nodded to me.

I whispered, 'Give me your coat. I'll do it.'

She shook her head.

'We don't have to do it,' I said. I don't know why. It just came out. She looked at me and for a moment I thought she

was going to agree. Then she shook her head again—this time
angrily.

'Come on.'

We walked back round the corner arm-in-arm. They were
locked together on the bench like two pieces of a jigsaw.

'Quick, the coat.'

Paula slipped her coat over Selim's pram while I kept an eye
on the action. Silvio was putting up a good show, huffing and
puffing and carrying on, while Helen kept her arms tight
around his neck, giving him a little pat on the back of the head
now and then to keep him keen. Paula touched my shoulder.
The coat was ready. I tried to see through the white blur of
the veil. What a joke, I thought, if this one turns out to be
empty.

I bent down quickly and loosened the brakes on both prams.
Then I tried to push Selim's forward but it jammed against the
side of the tree and I had to back it a few inches and twist the
wheels to get a clear run.

'Come on,' Paula whispered. She was standing at the head
of the pram trying to pull it free.

I twisted the wheels another fraction—it was like trying to
move a rock.

'Now'—I pushed and she pulled and I thought it was clear
until the knob on the push-bar caught in the bark. I didn't
dare look behind but I could hear Silvio starting to growl. Any
moment now she'd push him away and say, 'No, Silvio, no.'
One last twist and a heave and the knob broke free with a
sharp crack, taking a slice of bark with it. I grabbed the bar
of Alberto's pram, pulled it back a couple of feet, twisting the
wheels as I did it, and then ran the pram as close to the tree
as I could. It wasn't in the same spot as Selim's had been but
it was close enough. Paula was already wheeling Selim round
the corner of the shrubbery. I flashed a glance at the bench.
Helen had her hands against Silvio's chest, pushing. Then I

followed Paula round the corner out of sight and damn near threw up.

'Oh, God,' Paula said. 'Never again.'

'We did it,' I said. I couldn't believe it.

And then, like a punch in the gut, this noise suddenly exploded right under our feet. I remember thinking, this is how a burglar alarm must sound when you're caught inside with the stuff on you.

But it wasn't a burglar alarm. It was Master Selim Rifai screaming his little Arab lungs out.

Chapter Twelve

IT's NOT EASY to tell this next part, but, in the interests of what Morland calls objectivity, I suppose I'll have to try.

To put it briefly, I panicked.

With this terrible screaming noise getting louder every second all I could think of was getting away. So I shouted, 'Come on!' to Paula, grabbed the push-bar, put my head down and charged. The only thing I can say for myself is that I remembered to take the right path into the shrubbery. It was a pity I did, as it happened, because Morland was standing in the middle of it waiting for us. He went down without a sound, if you don't count the crunch of the chrome bumpers hitting him head-on. It took a couple of seconds to work the pram free as he'd somehow managed to get one foot tangled in the spokes. Normally I'd have been patient but the screaming in the pram was getting worse every moment.

'Come on, come on!' I said, jerking the pram backwards and forwards.

'Oh, oh, oh, oh'—poor old Morland, it must have been the shock or something.

'Harry . . .'

I heard Paula running up behind me. Then Morland got his foot loose and without waiting I raced off again into the shrubbery.

Now, under normal circumstances, I wouldn't have lost my way for a moment, let me assure you. But the collision with Morland really threw me off and before I knew it I'd missed the path on the right, or was it on the left, I couldn't remember. I stopped. 'Keep cool, Harry,' I whispered to myself. The bushes and vines and things were even thicker than I'd thought, but that wasn't what was worrying me. It was the screaming. I didn't know how to stop it. Alberto had never *screamed*. I gave the pram a couple of hard shakes. 'Knock it off,' I said. I should have saved my breath. It only screamed louder. From that moment I knew I wasn't going to like the little bastard.

At the spot where I'd stopped the path forked. It was a toss-up, and I took the one to the right. Pretty soon it started bending and twisting and splitting into new forks until I'd lost any idea of where I was. I couldn't see the villa, or the wall we'd walked along, or anything: just these bushes and old rotting trees and bits of broken statues. I suppose I could have found my way out quite easily if I'd been able to concentrate but my brain was paralysed by the screaming. All I could think was that any moment I was going to be nicked, and with the stuff on me too. There had to be *some* way of keeping it quiet. I lifted the veil and took a peep inside. It was lying on its back with its eyes screwed up and its little fists waving around, bawling its head off. I was shocked to see what a scrawny little thing it was, being a millionaire's kid and all. That stupid kraut certainly had a nerve saying it looked anything like Alberto. And still the screaming went on. I was getting worried for another reason now. Somewhere I'd read that kids shouldn't be allowed to cry for more than ten minutes—or was it twenty, or thirty? I'd forgotten. After that they choked or something. It seemed like this one had been screaming for ever. I tried poking it in the gut with my finger, which always made Alberto giggle, but it only yelled louder. Then I tried these 'coochie-coo' noises that Paula used but it was making so much row itself it couldn't have even heard them. I was desperate. There were people moving around me in the bushes, I was sure: everyone in the park must be closing in on this spot where

I was standing. And then I remembered something Paula had said about you always having to pick up babies to stop them crying. I hauled it out of the pram on the double and shook it a few times. Right away it went quiet, just like magic. Would you believe it, I thought, there's nothing to it. But when I tried to put it back in the pram it let out another screech and I had to start shaking it all over again. It did this several times, and on purpose too, so I could see it had a nasty streak in it. I'd just about reached the end of my rope and was getting ready to toss it into the nearest bush when suddenly it shut its eyes and seemed to go to sleep. I didn't believe it at first and I went on jogging it gently in my arms for a couple of minutes. Then, very slowly, taking extra care not to bump it against the sides, I bent down and laid it gently in the pram. Its eyes stayed shut, its breathing was nice and regular. I held my breath and waited. Not a move, not a murmur. Bit by bit I spread the veil, tucking it in with the tips of my fingers so as not to rock the pram. I let my breath out. Dead silence. I'd done it! Then as I put my hands on the push-bar to get moving again it let out a bellow that practically blew my head off.

'All right, you little Arab bastard,' I shouted—I was quite hysterical. 'Go ahead and choke, scream your lungs out, yell your bloody head off—'

'Harry, what are you doing?' It was Paula's voice, near by.

'Help,' I shouted. 'Help.'

'Where are you?'

'Here.'

'Where's here?'

'*Here.*' And if she hadn't burst through the bushes at that moment I don't know what I wouldn't have done next.

'What's the matter?'

'Take it,' I said. 'For God's sake take it—' I turned away because I didn't want her to see me shaking. I didn't turn back until the crying stopped.

'Where have you been, Harry? We've been looking everywhere for you.' She had it out of the pram again and was rocking it in her arms.

'It doesn't work with that one,' I said.

'What?'

'What you're doing.'

She laughed and shook her head at me. She must have been hunting under the bushes or something because there were twigs and leaves and things stuck in her hair.

I said, 'I wish we hadn't left old Alberto back there. This one's nasty.'

'Go on, don't be silly.'

'You'll see.' Suddenly I remembered where we were. 'Come on, we've got to get out of here. They've probably called the fuzz by now.'

She shook her head. 'I've just had a look at them'—she nodded at the bushes—'They're still at it on the bench. I don't think they even heard the screaming. Isn't love wonderful?'

'You went *back*? After all that fuss?'

'Well, you disappeared, didn't you? I had to try to find you. You might have been caught or anything. We couldn't leave without making sure one way or the other.' She tried to make it sound casual but I wasn't fooled.

'Thanks, anyway,' I said.

She put the kid back in the pram. I waited for it to start howling again but it didn't make a sound. Birds are great when you get them on something they know.

'This way.' Paula turned the pram around and I followed her back up the path. It didn't take us a minute to get to the villa. Morland was sitting on a bench in the shade looking very pissed off.

'You want to watch where you're going, Harry. You almost broke my leg.'

'How did I know you'd be standing there?'

131

'I wish I could be sure you didn't do it on purpose.'

'Well, don't be too sure.'

'Oh, come on, you two, for heaven's sake,' Paula said. She was off again with the pram, trotting down the asphalt path to the piazza, with me a couple of paces behind and Morland limping along in the rear like a broken-down grasshopper. We all kept looking back but there was no sign of pursuit.

Paula said, 'Quick, the pram.' She'd taken Selim out and was getting into the back of the *cinquecento*.

Morland and I heaved and strained. We got it on to the luggage-rack all right but the car was parked on a slope and the pram kept wanting to slide off the back.

'Hold it while I do up this strap,' Morland said.

'I can't hold it alone. It's slipping.'

'Hold it, Harry.'

'I can't—'

'Hurry up,' said Paula.

'*Hold it, Harry—*'

I shut my eyes. There was a crash and a horrible scream. I opened them and saw Morland flat on his back and the pram galloping down the Clivo di Scauro, gathering speed, heading straight for this *cinquecento* coming up the hill. I stood and watched—there was really nothing else I could do. The guy in the *cinquecento* held his ground pretty well, blowing his horn like a maniac and shaking his fist. But at the last moment he swerved and the pram whistled past. I watched it finish in a big bush of pink flowers at the bottom of the hill. Morland groaned.

'Jonathan, are you all right?' Paula leaned out of the car.

I bent over Morland. He opened one eye.

'Are you trying to kill me, Harry?'

'Sure,' I said. 'Only I'll make a better job of it next time. Come on.'

'I just want to know, Harry. That's all. I just want to know.'

'Are you going to lie there squawking till they catch us?'
I helped him up.

'I've got a feeling I won't see the end of this caper, Harry.'

'Don't let it worry you,' I said. 'We'll split your share.'

That did the trick.

'What are we hanging around here for?' he snarled. 'Get moving. Where's the pram? Why didn't you catch it, Harry? Sloth—that's your trouble. Sheer brute laziness—'

We drove down the hill. The guy in the *cinquecento* had got out of his car and was looking up and down the road in a dazed way. He shook his fist as we went by and I caught something about an *assassino*, or maybe it was a *cretino*. The pram had ploughed right into the middle of the bush, but it didn't seem to be damaged and we got it out and on top of the car without too much trouble. Meanwhile, Morland was getting very jumpy because we hadn't called Rifai yet. It was after four and Helen and Silvio would be going back to the car any minute. So I stopped at the first café in Viale Aventino and Morland and I went in to phone.

Now, telephone booths are pretty well non-existent in Rome and most of the public phones are in bars and cafés. Which is fine as long as you don't mind being overheard saying things like, 'What do you know, Mr Rifai? Your son has just been nicked.' The phone in this café though was in a corner which made it easier for us. While Morland made the call I stood behind him pretending I was next in line to use it: that way I kept anyone from coming too close. He had some difficulty at first since Rifai is not the sort who answers his own phones. But after he'd given them the old 'matter of life and death' bit they put him through. Naturally I only heard Morland's side of the conversation but I'll give it all to you as he gave it to me later.

Morland: Mr Rifai?

Rifai: This is Yusuf Rifai.

Morland: I have some unpleasant news for you.

Rifai: Who is speaking?

Morland: In a few minutes your son's nursemaid and bodyguard will phone from the park to tell you that Selim has disappeared. They'll say that a young couple apparently walked off with his pram by mistake.

Rifai: Indeed?

Morland: Yes. But I am calling to tell you in advance that there is no mistake. Your son has been kidnapped.

(Long pause)

Rifai: You are not from the police.

Morland: No.

Rifai: I see. How much?

Morland: A quarter of a million. Dollars, that is.

Rifai: That is a lot of money.

Morland: It depends what you are buying. Now if I were trying to sell you a new brothel, say, you'd have a point.

('Let's keep our prejudices out of this,' I hissed.)

Rifai: I do not care for your choice of example, Mr—?

Morland: Abercromby. Then let's get down to business, shall we? I want the money in small notes—nothing bigger than tens—exactly one week from today. I'll call you again before then to arrange the time, place and manner of payment.

Rifai: And if I decide to go to the police instead?

Morland: Do whatever you wish. The police will not find your son. We have taken precautions to ensure that. All that will happen is that you'll have to wait longer to get Selim back. Much longer, Mr Rifai. I think you'll find it to your advantage to keep this between ourselves.

Rifai: You don't imagine I can keep it a secret, do you?

Morland: If you can prevent the nurse and the bodyguard from talking, there should be no problem.

Rifai: I have a large staff, Mr Abercromby. How do you expect me to explain the disappearance of my only son?

Morland: You won't have to. We're providing you with a substitute. Just make sure no one gets close enough to him to spot the difference.

Rifai: A substitute baby?

Morland: That's right. We'll take him back when we return your son, which will be after you've paid us.

(Long pause)

Rifai: One week, you say?

Morland: Ample time, I should think.

Rifai: Aren't you forgetting something? The threats, I mean.

Morland: Threats?

Rifai: Against my son's life—if I refuse to pay.

Morland: Your son's life is in no danger, Mr Rifai. If you don't pay you won't get him back. That's all. One week—remember. Goodbye.

Morland put the phone down and leaned against the wall. He'd gone all pale again just as though he'd had another 'heart attack'.

'Will he call the police?' I said.

'I don't think so.'

'You shouldn't have said that bit about the kid not being in danger. You should have kept him guessing.'

'I couldn't lie about a thing like that, Harry. He'd have spotted it. And besides—' He didn't finish but I could guess what he was thinking: that telling a father—even a father like Yusuf Rifai—that his kid's life was in danger was way below the old minimum level of morality.

We went out to the car. Paula was still in the back with Selim. She looked ready to drop. 'Please can't we go home now,' she said.

135

After we'd driven some way I said, 'Aren't you going to ask what Rifai said?'

'What did he say?' She didn't sound very interested.

'Morland thinks he'll pay—isn't that so?'

Morland nodded slowly. Suddenly he didn't seem very interested either.

I thought that for three people who'd just knocked off a quarter-million-dollar baby we were about as cheerful as a trio of dummies on Guy Fawkes night.

Chapter Thirteen

'But how did he *sound*?' I asked, for about the five hundredth time.

Morland threw up his hands. 'What can I say, Harry? He sounded like—like you'd expect Yusuf Rifai to sound. Cold and matter-of-fact. Businesslike.'

'Not shocked? Not even a little?'

'There is nothing in the world that can shock men like Rifai because there's nothing in human nature that surprises them. That's their secret. They've seen it all before—in themselves.'

We were sitting on the terrace watching the sun go down behind the Janiculum, watching the light get softer and pinker until you were sure it couldn't last another second, except it stayed there, hanging in the air like fine gold dust. Paula, taking a break from pinning up nappies, was leaning on the wall, gazing out across the rooftops. Her skin picked up this soft gold tint and for a moment the strain seemed to melt away and she looked quite peaceful. It would have been a really nice moment for all of us if Selim hadn't been there in Alberto's cot under the umbrella grizzling away like a dripping tap. It was three days since we'd snatched him. It felt like three years.

Paula pegged the last nappy—Selim seemed to get through about twice the number that Alberto had used—and went over to the cot. In the shade of the umbrella her face went pale and tight again. Her hair was a mess, too, and that wasn't like her at all.

'He never stops, does he?'

'Maybe he really has got the pox,' I said.

'Oh, don't say that, please.'

I was referring to Selim's 'chicken-pox' which was Morland's brainwave for keeping people away from him. So far it was working. He'd caught it, so to speak, the minute we got back from Celimontana. Paula had raced straight upstairs from the car and Morland and I had gone into Giorgio's to break the sad news. When Morland said '*varicella*' Mrs Giorgio crossed herself three times.

'We must call a doctor immediately.'

'That will not be necessary,' said Morland. 'I am a doctor.'

Giorgio flung out his arms. 'A poet *and* a doctor. *Fantastico.*'

I thought it was pretty *fantastico* myself.

When Morland said he'd have to go up and examine the patient, Mrs Giorgio said she'd come along too.

'Impossible, signora. The danger of infection.'

'But I have had the *varicella*.'

'It is not you I am thinking of. It is all the children here in the street who will catch the germs that you bring down from the sick-room.'

That rocked her for a moment, but then she asked, what about the Signor and Signora Brighton, wouldn't they also be spreading germs and things around? Of course not, said Morland. It was well known that parents couldn't spread the children's germs.

Giorgio said, 'Of course not. It is well known. Have another brandy, *dottore.*'

It was all very well Selim having chicken-pox, but Paula was the one who was suffering. Maybe you remember Morland and me agreeing earlier that one baby was much like another. Well, forget it. Selim was no more like Alberto than a busted flush is like a royal routine. Apart from the screaming and crying and carrying on, which was just his normal daily behaviour, Selim also refused his grub as a matter of principle and peed his pants so often you'd have thought he'd sprung a permanent leak. And if he slept at all it wasn't noticeable, in fact it got to the point where I was actually glad to be sleeping out in the living-room on my own. For Paula though there was no escape, especially as she was meant to be nursing a sick kid who couldn't be left alone for a moment. She'd had to stay in the flat cooped up with him for three days. So far she'd stood it pretty well but I knew she was counting the hours.

'One week of this is all I can take, Harry, I warn you.'

'Don't worry,' I said. 'I wouldn't keep him a day longer if Rifai paid us double. Just as soon as we get the money—'

'And Alberto.'

'And Alberto.'

Obviously it wasn't the moment to point out that once we'd been paid, Alberto would be heading back to the ranch and the loving arms of Tony the Phony, Paula couldn't have forgotten that, but maybe she'd just decided not to look ahead, which is a trick birds pull when they want to. Morland was anxious to keep her that way.

'She'll be worried about Alberto, Harry. That's natural. What we have to guard against is saying anything that even suggests it may go wrong, that something may happen to Alberto, or that she won't see him again. You know how women are, Harry. You've got to play them along—gently mind you, but firmly.'

To listen to Morland you'd have thought it was just another game of marbles.

He was right about one thing though: it didn't take her long to start worrying about Alberto. The very first evening just as I was popping off she came out of her room and asked me if I thought Alberto was okay. Of course, I said, why shouldn't he be? We don't even know for sure that they took him back with them, she said. Maybe he's still there in the park. Oh, for crying out loud, I said—then I realized that all she wanted

139

was a little comfort and reassurance which I was quick to offer, only she took it wrong and went stamping back into her room, slamming the door after her.

The next day she was at it again. Were they feeding Alberto properly? Was he getting enough exercise? Did I think Rifai would pack him off to an orphanage? Having Selim to look after only made it worse for her. Every time he started screaming she'd wonder about Alberto. Was he doing the same thing up at Rifai's villa? Of course I tried to tell her that was nonsense, that Alberto was a pro who took things as they came, but she wouldn't listen. Then there were the neighbours, and especially Mrs Giorgio, always coming to the door to ask how Alberto was getting on. They'd stand there listening to this squealing coming from the next room, shaking their heads and muttering '*poverino*', crossing themselves like spastics. Alberto had become a very popular figure up and down the old Scorpion, mainly because he was bigger and fatter than the other one-year-olds but also because he had this special thing —style, I call it. The other mammas were for ever patting him and petting him and telling Paula what a *bravo puppone* he was, but you never got the feeling it was going to his head. He played it very cool. And of course there's nothing that drives women crazy quicker than that. All of which explains why there was this daily procession to the Brighton doorstep and why, whenever I managed to slip downstairs for a quick one, Mrs Giorgio would clutch her bosom and say, '*Allora?*' It was beginning to get me.

There was one particular thing, though, that was worrying all three of us. Why didn't Hermann call? It had been three days now and not a word from him. I wanted to phone him at the villa but Morland wouldn't have it. He said Rifai might suspect that one of his staff was in on the snatch and have a check kept on the phones. I also suggested calling Rifai again, just to keep the needle in, but Morland was dead against it.

'If we do that he'll know we're worried. He's the one who's supposed to be worried.'

So we waited.

Sitting up there on the terrace watching the sunset I was having one of my favourite day-dreams. This is the one where I strike it rich, win the pools, pick the spring treble—or maybe even collect sixty thousand for snatching someone's kid. This evening I was picturing myself with that sixty thousand walking into Angelo's and ordering up a whole new wardrobe: a row of suits to start with, custom-tailored with the stitches hardly showing, and then a stack of silk shirts, hand-made, smooth as cream . . . I could almost *taste* those shirts and was just beginning to really enjoy my dream when this old bat on the terrace across the way had to start waving her arms and pointing down at the street until I couldn't hold the picture any longer.

I went over to the side of the terrace and looked down. Giorgio was in the street looking up, holding one hand to his ear and making these turning motions with the other: a phone call. He shook his head when he saw me so I called Morland over. Giorgio nodded and pointed inside. Morland and I looked at each other. We were both thinking the same thing: Hermann.

Morland was gone a long time, and when he came back I saw right away it was something important.

'That was Hermann all right. He hasn't been able to call before. He says it looks as though Rifai will pay.'

'What about Alberto?' Paula said.

'He's fine.' There was something about the way he said it—just a flash of the old shifty look.

'How's fine?' I said.

Morland shrugged. It wasn't easy getting things straight from Hermann, he said, but one thing was sure: Rifai had told his secretary to get two hundred and fifty thousand dollars in cash ready before the end of the week. Hermann had got that from the secretary himself.

'That's it,' I said. 'We're home.' I could see myself walking into Angelo's, cool as you please.

'What about *Alberto*?' Paula said in this tight little voice.

'Hermann hasn't actually *seen* him—'

'*What?*'

'Now wait a minute, Paula, listen—'

It turned out that Hermann hadn't seen Alberto because Rifai was keeping him locked up in the nursery with only Helen to look after him. No one else was allowed into the room, according to Hermann, but he'd managed to have a word that morning with Helen who'd said Rifai had warned her not to tell anyone about the kidnapping. The only reason she'd told Hermann was because he'd promised to get word from her to Silvio who was locked in his room above the garage, also on Rifai's orders.

'It's all working out,' I said. 'Don't you see, Paula? He's going along with it.'

'I want to know about *Alberto*.'

Morland said, 'All Hermann knows is that these plates of food keep going up full and coming down empty.'

'What did I tell you? A real pro.'

Paula snatched up Selim's cot and stamped off downstairs without a word. Pretty soon we heard Selim start crying again.

Morland said, 'There is something that might cheer her up. Maybe you can tell her later. Apparently Rifai has taken quite a fancy to Alberto, goes up to the nursery to play with him a couple of times a day. And he's bought him a crate of new toys too, the nurse says. I mean it's not as though they were treating him as a prisoner.'

'I don't think I'll tell her that.'

We sat a big longer until it was dark.

Morland said, 'Strange the way this is all working out so perfectly. I mean after the way things have gone for us before.'

'Don't talk about it,' I said. 'It's unlucky.'

Morland shook his head. 'I don't see how it can go wrong now. We collect from Rifai at the end of this week and exchange Selim for Alberto. You and Paula stay here till the end of the following week when Tony gets back from Naples. We give Alberto back, close the flat, Hermann resigns and everyone goes his own way.'

'Paula's going to be happy, isn't she?'

Morland shot me a quick look. 'I expect you could do something about that,' he said.

'Do you now?' I said. 'Do you now? Well, for your information . . .'

'Look, Harry'—he touched my arm—'I know it isn't easy for you. But stick it out. Keep her sweet for a few days longer. It's almost in our hands now. I tell you, nothing can go wrong.'

Well, I ought to have known then. I ought to have remembered that Morland has just about the all-time record for famous last words.

The very next evening, while Paula was down in Giorgio's taking a ten-minute breather, the doorbell rang. Thinking it was another deputation of the Alberto Fan Club, I opened up. There stood Tony—and right behind him, Big Mamma.

'Okay, wise guy, what's the story?'

'Story?' I said. I stared at him. My brain had gone sort of paralysed.

He tried to slip inside but I blocked the way.

'I thought you were in Naples,' I said. It was all I could think of.

Tony opened his eyes wide. 'You thought we were in Naples,' he said in this baby voice. 'Did you hear that, Mamma?' He half turned to her, then suddenly spun round and jammed his little ferret's face right under my chin. 'Well, we're not in Naples, wise guy, like you can see. If you wanna know I ran a little short down there and I thought I'd collect another instalment on the rent. And what do I hear when I get here?—the kid has the chicken-pox. So I'm asking *what's* the story, and *where's* the kid? And I mean like *now*.'

Chapter Fourteen

'THE KID?' I said.

'What's the matter? You gone deaf?' Tony pushed past me. Mamma was right on his heels. 'Where is he?'

I opened my mouth to say something but the words wouldn't come.

Tony laughed. 'Maybe I got it wrong. Maybe it's you that's got the pox. Come on, where's the kid?' He walked towards the bedroom.

'The terrace,' I croaked.

'What about the terrace?'

'They're on the terrace. Alberto and Paula.'

'Why the hell didn't you say so? *Andiamo, Mamma.*'

They went up the stairs to the terrace. Do something, Harry, I said, for Christ's sake do something. In a few moments I heard their steps on the roof. I couldn't move. I stood there waiting for Tony to start yelling.

Selim was in the bedroom. If Tony saw him it was all over. Either he'd shout the place down and everyone would know about the switch, or else I'd have to tell him what was going on and hand him the sweetest bit of blackmail he'd ever got his nasty little paws on. The only answer was to hide Selim—but where? If I took him downstairs, everyone, starting with Mrs Giorgio, would want to know who this squealing brat was and where the hell was Alberto? I'd be lucky if they didn't lynch me. But I had to do something . . .

It was Tony's voice shouting, 'What is this?' that did the trick—snapped me out of it. I ran into the bedroom, snatched

Selim out of his cot, raced back through the living-room into the bathroom, picked up Alberto's plastic bathtub on the dead run and skidded over the tiles of the bathroom floor into the loo just as Tony and Mamma came pounding down the stairs from the roof. I dropped the tub on the floor next to the loo and stuck Selim in the tub. He lay there goggling at me with these black-currant eyes: the poor little sod was too surprised even to scream. Then I pulled the chain, locked the door of the loo and strolled back through the bathroom into the living-room.

Tony popped out of the bedroom like a cork shouting, 'There he is, there he is.' Mamma followed, spitting out a string of Italian.

'Okay, where is he? What have you done with him?'

'Who?' I said.

Tony let out a screech and grabbed the front of my shirt. 'You really want it, don't you? You really want it. Okay, you're gonna get it. *Mamma, vieni qui.*'

Mamma moved in. She had this big shopping bag in her hand. It looked full—of what I couldn't say, bricks maybe. I moved round, keeping Tony between me and the bag.

'If you'd just tell me what you're so excited about,' I said, watching Mamma. She was skipping about from side to side trying to get a clear shot.

'What am I excited about? I come here to collect the rent on my kid and the first thing I hear from some dame downstairs is that he's got the chicken-pox. And you wanna know what I'm excited about. Well, I'll tell you. I'm excited about this kid that belongs to me and is worth a lot of money picking up some cruddy limey disease from a cruddy limey bastard who doesn't know how to take care of him proper. That's what I'm excited about. Okay? You got it?'

All I'd got was a terrible itch in my cruddy limey knee from wanting to stick it in his cruddy Chicago gut.

But I managed to screw up a smile and I said, 'Well, if they're not on the roof they must have gone for a walk.'

'With the *chicken-pox*?'

'It surprised me, too. But that's what the doctor said.'

'He said you had to take Alberto for a *walk*?'

'Every day, he said, without fail.'

'I don't believe you. What's it supposed to do then, this taking him out for a walk?'

'How would I know? Maybe the germs blow away.'

Tony let go my shirt and turned to Mamma. He rattled off something in Italian of which I got only the word *varicella*. Mamma responded with a lot of head-shaking, then gave me a sneering look, slapped the side of her head and raised her eyes to heaven.

'Mamma says it's a load of crap.'

'Maybe Mamma is not familiar with all the latest advances in medical science.'

'Listen, wise guy, you start insulting my mother and—'

'No one's insulting anyone,' I said. 'Look, all I know is the kid has a very mild case of chicken-pox and the doctor said to be sure to give him plenty of fresh air in the park. Which is what we're doing. Now if you want to wait an hour or two you'll see for yourself he's okay. If you don't want to wait I'll give you the rent now and you can check him next time you come to town.' I was praying they'd take the money and go: I was praying Paula wouldn't come up from Giorgio's: I was praying Selim would keep his mouth shut for just one more minute. I was getting a headache from all that praying.

Tony consulted Mamma again. I heard something about a bus going back to Tivoli.

'Okay, I'll take the rent now. But I'm coming back in a few days and the kid had better be here. And he'd better be in good shape too, pox or no pox.'

I took out two hundred and gave it to him.

147

'I'll take two weeks this time.' He said it with a sneer like somehow he'd guessed I wouldn't refuse: that I'd give anything to get him out of there. I peeled off another two hundred. My hands were shaking and I could feel the flushes coming on.

'Thanks.' Tony snapped the notes to test them. 'Maybe I'll take Mamma to Venice for the weekend.'

I didn't say anything. The black spots were starting too.

At the door Tony said, 'Say hullo to Paula for me. Tell her I'll look her up one of these days.' He stopped at the mirror to straighten his bow tie. As he stepped back I heard it begin, just a thin wailing sound at first, but getting stronger every second. I got the door open in a hurry and Mamma on to the landing, but Tony stopped and put his head on one side.

'What's that?'

'What's what?'

'That noise. It sounds like a kid crying.'

'So it does,' I said.

Tony looked back into the living-room. The noise seemed to be coming from the bathroom but the bathroom was wide open so I couldn't be hiding anything there. From where we stood the door of the loo was hidden.

'It sounds like the baby in the next flat,' I said. 'Always yelling its head off. That's one thing I'll say for Alberto. Never a murmur out of him.'

Tony gave me a long look. 'Yeah,' he said. Then he went out and I shut the door and locked it.

It took me a few seconds to get a grip. The floor seemed to be tilting under my feet and there was this funny buzzing sound in my ears. Then things got a bit calmer and I fetched Selim out of the loo and shoved him back in his cot in the bedroom. He'd worked himself into a fair old froth by this time but I reckoned he had another ten minutes in him before he choked or whatever and I'd let him run the limit, and serve him right too. Then suddenly I thought, Christ, say they go into Giorgio's and

148

see Paula? I ran out on to the balcony and looked down. They were right below me in the street: Tony's straw Panama and Mamma's two sacks of coal, which is to say, Mamma. For maybe half a minute they stood there talking while I held my breath, not six feet from the entrance to Giorgio's. Then Tony took Mamma's arm and they started up the street. I put my head down and wondered why I didn't puke. I was still there when Paula came in a few minutes later.

'Harry, I could hear that baby screaming down in Giorgio's. What's the matter with you? Can't you do anything to help me? I told you, all you have to do is pick him up and hold him for a few minutes.'

'My problem,' I said, 'is to stop myself picking him up. Because the next time I do I'm going to drop him over this balcony.'

'Oh, don't be ridiculous.'

What I needed was a drink, several drinks.

'Where are you going? For a drink, I suppose. Anything to get out of here and leave all the dirty work to me. Well, I'm getting sick and tired of you spending all your day down in Giorgio's and furthermore—'

'Paula,' I said, 'If you want to behave like a wife, you know where to start, don't you?'

And on that cruncher I walked out.

Of course Morland had to be down in Giorgio's, and just when I wanted a few moments to myself. Giorgio was showing him how to work the espresso machine. It didn't surprise me, Morland is always ready to learn something new. He has this passion for cramming his head with all sorts of junk.

'Harry! I was just coming up to see the patient. Paula was here a moment ago.' He pulled on the handle of the machine and then bent down to watch the hot coffee trickling into the cup below.

'You're jerking, Jonathan. Smoothly, you must do it

smoothly.' Giorgio showed him, pulling the handle back with this slow easy motion. Morland watched very closely. You'd have thought they were landing a Boeing.

Giorgio wiped his hands and came over. 'A cognac, Harry?' I shook my head.

'Coffee, then. A beer?'

'No thanks.' What I meant was I didn't want company, not even Giorgio's. I was trying to work out something in my mind, a pretty complicated sum involving five weeks' rent for Alberto, the cost of renting the car, the household bills for a month and such little extras as a new aluminium luggage rack. The way it came out I reckoned I had less than a hundred dollars left. I took out my wallet and checked. There was fifty in green and maybe another fifty in lire. A month ago I'd had two thousand, give or take a hundred. It just didn't seem right or fair.

'What's wrong, Harry?' Morland said.

'Nothing. I'm going for a walk.'

'What is it?'

I turned at the door. Giorgio was listening.

I said, 'Tony and Mamma have just paid us a visit.'

Morland went white. 'They're supposed to be in Naples.'

'Yes,' I said. 'I remember you saying so.'

'Did they see . . . ?'

'No, they didn't. And it cost a lot of money to see they didn't. And I'm getting tired, Morland, sick and tired and bloody fed up with paying for your cock-ups. So I'm warning you now, fair and square, you've had your last penny out of me. Not another kopeck, Morland.'

'Harry . . . gentlemen,' Giorgio squawked as I went swishing through the string beads.

'And another thing—' I stuck my head back in—'you owe me twelve hundred for that ticket. Don't you forget it.'

Chapter Fifteen

AFTER THAT I really did need a walk, and a drink too, so I went down to the Piazza di Santa Maria intending to look in at Marzio's. It was getting dark when I reached the square and as usual the cars and scooters were zipping around the fountain like it was open season on pedestrians and double your money for the first clean knockdown. I got halfway across without any trouble, then for just a second I took my eye off the action to give this blonde the once-over.

'Cretino!' There was a screech and a clatter right behind me and I felt a blast of hot breath on my neck. *'Porco cane!'* That was enough for me. I spun round, ready to let one go, and got a very nasty shock when I found myself eyeball to eyeball with this horse. *'Cornuto!'* Of course it wasn't the horse yelling, it was this fat Ite up on the carriage behind who was waving his whip around and screaming at me to get my imbecile carcase out of his way. Since I was good and ready for a punch-up anyway, I ran round the side of the *carrozza* hoping to get a poke at him. We saw each other at the same time.

'Harry, *mi'* amico.'

'Bruno, me old mate.'

It was a very emotional scene. Bruno wept and flung his arms around me. I thumped him on the back and even gave his horse's fanny a couple of friendly slaps. The cars behind the carriage were blowing their horns like mad but Bruno paid no attention. I was really touched. Finally he dragged me into the *carrozza* beside him and we set off.

'It is a miracle, Harry.'

I thought a miracle was putting it a bit strong, but I didn't want to hurt Bruno's feelings so I said, 'Sure.'

He took me across the river to his home off Via della Scrofa. Two of his kids were told to put the horse in the stable and clean up the *carrozza*. A third was sent up the street to buy a litre of *vino rosso*. Mrs Bruno was ordered to produce *un piatto di spaghetti speciali* double-quick. Bruno is another with style.

'Harry, it *is* a miracle. Only this morning I said to myself, Bruno, if Harry Brighton does not appear this very day you will have to go ahead and sell it to Mr Schwartz.'

'Sell what to who?'

Bruno leaned over and put his lips to my ear. 'The ticket,' he said.

Ticket?

Then I remembered. Bruno had always promised to give me first refusal of anything he picked up. Again I was touched. But what the hell could I do about it with only a hundred dollars in my pocket?

'It's nice of you, Bruno, but right now I'm carrying such a heavy stock—'

He shook his head impatiently and grabbed my shoulder. There was this devilish smile in his eyes I'd never seen before. 'Forget your stock, Harry. Wait till you see *this*.'

He got up and went to the door, opened it an inch and peeped through into the kitchen. Mrs Bruno was banging away with her pots and pans. He went to the window, closed the wooden shutters, and switched on the light. Then he unlocked a small cupboard in one corner and pulled out a parcel wrapped in brown paper. He brought it to the table.

'Open it, Harry.'

All of a sudden my lips went dry. It can't be, I thought, please don't let it be, not now when I can't even afford a secondhand Nansen. I unwrapped the paper. One glance at the lettering was enough. I shut my eyes. I had to.

'Is it real?' I asked.

Bruno grunted. He was staring at it like he was hypnotized. 'I asked Fingers Goudounov to check it. He says it's genuine.'

I shut my eyes again. If Fingers said it was kosher, that was that.

'Isn't it beautiful, Harry?'

I nodded. It was worth five thousand bucks of anyone's money too. And all I had was a hundred dollars in my pocket and four tickets back at the flat which wouldn't fetch three thousand between them.

'What's the matter, Harry?'

'I can't buy it. I'm broke.'

Bruno sat down with a thump. 'Harry, it can't be true. Not you. You're too smart.'

'Well, it is true. I haven't got that kind of money. I haven't got—' Then I stopped and stared at him. What was I saying? Of course I had that kind of money. I had any kind of money. I had sixty thousand dollars! Well, almost. 'Bruno,' I said, 'can you wait, just a few days? I'll know by then if I can raise it.'

'I can't wait, Harry. I told you how I was saying to myself that if you didn't turn up today I'd have to sell it. Tomorrow's my deadline.'

'Mr Schwartz?'

'Yes.'

'C.I.A.?'

Bruno nodded. 'You know how these government types are, Harry. You can't mess them around. I must sell.'

'How much is he paying?'

'Four thousand.'

That's the C.I.A. for you. Real cheap-skates.

'I'd give you four and a half.'

'Harry, I've got to know for sure.'

'Four days,' I said. 'No more.' Morland would call Rifai in three days. If all went well we'd get the money right away.

Bruno chewed his lips. I could see he didn't want to lose that extra five hundred.

'Three days,' I said. In three days I'd know, one way or the other.

'Okay.' He grabbed my arm and gave it a squeeze. 'For you, Harry.'

'Thanks, Bruno,' I said simply.

You're probably wondering why I got so worked up about a ticket that was worth five thousand when I was all set to collect a cool sixty. The answer is pride, professional pride. I may have helped to snatch a kid, but it was under protest: at heart I was still a ticket man. I picked up this passport and looked inside. The funny writing was all Greek to me of course but I didn't need a translator to tell me what it meant. This was a real, unforged, legitimate Russian ticket. Fingers had said so. A Russian ticket! I'd never seen one before. Very few people had, except Russians I suppose. Ziggy claimed he'd got a sniff of one once, but he didn't like to talk about it. Now I'd got one right in my hands. I might even end up owning it. There aren't many moments in a man's life when he sees a dream coming true. Right then I'd have gladly given up the whole sixty thousand if I could have been sure of getting this Russky ticket in return.

Bruno saw how choked I was and when his kid brought the wine he sent him back for a bottle of cognac as well. Over dinner he told me how this squad of Russian tourists had hired six *carrozze* for a spin around Rome and how, when they'd dropped them back at their hotel, Bruno had found the ticket lying on the floor of his carriage.

'I broke down and cried, Harry.'

'Why not?'

In the end we made quite a night of it. I also had a lot to tell Bruno and he's a good listener from his days in the hotel trade. Of course I didn't mention the snatch, but I did tell him how

I'd got caught up in this business deal which was bleeding me dry. Bruno was sympathetic, but also disapproving. He held the view that it was a privilege to be in the ticket trade and if you were, you shouldn't mess around with anything else on the side. Bruno is a purist.

'Do you think I wanted to? If you only knew what I've gone through.'

'You're too trusting, Harry. That's your trouble.'

Sometime after midnight we killed the bottle of cognac and Bruno said he'd take me home. It was a fine night and the streets were nearly empty. We crossed the river at the Ponte Vittorio Emanuele and then Bruno put the horse in top for the run down the Lungotevere. We made a lot of racket clattering along the road but there was no one around to complain. It was like we had the city to ourselves—the avenue of trees, the lights on the river, the dark buildings. I couldn't help thinking how much trouble was caused just by people being around: how peaceful things would be if they weren't.

We didn't go home right away. Instead we stopped off at a little trat Bruno knew of in Via della Lungaretta and had a last one, or maybe two. I don't know what they put in the drinks but from here on I find I have a problem remembering exactly what happened.

We were both feeling pretty good, I do know that, and even the horse seemed charged up, though maybe that was because Bruno was whipping him on more than usual. Our arrival in the old Scorpion was full of style and it's a pity no one was up to see it.

'Shhhh, Harry. Everyone is asleep.'

'Good old Bruno.'

'Perhaps I had better help you upstairs, Harry.'

'Perhaps you had, Bruno.'

Four flights is a long way up and it seemed especially so that night. Bruno kept saying, 'Shhhh' as we went past each landing. He's never outgrown this bell-boy's mentality. When we got to the top he helped me unlock the door.

'Where's the bedroom, Harry?'

I must have told him, though it's something I don't remember doing. What I do remember though, and very clearly, is the light coming on suddenly and this heavy glass ashtray brushing past my ear and hitting the wall with a tremendous crash.

'*Mamma mia*,' said Bruno, backing out quickly.

She was sitting up in bed. Her arms were smooth and white and her red hair was all over the place.

'What a dish,' I said.

Then I dropped right where I was standing because I could see she was going to throw the alarm clock next.

'You're drunk.'

'Never felt better.'

'*Signora . . . signorina?*' Bruno was taking no chances. He stuck his head in the door.

'Who are you?'

'That's my chum Bruno,' I said.

They dragged me into the living-room and dumped me on the couch. Don't think I was drunk or anything, a little merry perhaps, nothing more. I'd just decided to sit this one out. Besides I could see Paula was mad and I wasn't in the mood for a punch-up any more. Bruno bent over me, tucking something into my shirt pocket.

'That's my number, Harry. Remember, three days. After that I must sell to Mr Schwartz.'

'Good old Bruno,' I said.

Paula stood with folded arms tapping her foot on the floor. It was making Bruno nervous. He bent down again. 'Harry,' he whispered, 'you didn't tell me you were married.'

'Who's married?' I said. 'This is Paula. Paula—Bruno.'

Paula made a hissing noise. Bruno got the message and beat

it very quickly. 'Remember, Harry, three days,' he called out from the door.

Paula stood over me. She was swaying from side to side, or maybe it was the couch.

'There's something I have to tell you, Harry.'

'Good old Paula,' I said. Things were really going round.

'I can't stand this any longer. I'm going to phone Rifai in the morning and—'

'Phone Rifai in the morning?' I was trying hard to concentrate. But it just wasn't my night. She was bending right over me, her hair almost touching my face. 'Paula,' I said, 'you're a dish.'

And that's the last thing I remember.

Until the next morning—boy, did I remember then!

Phone Rifai!

I sat straight without thinking and almost died in that position. The pain was something awful.

Phone Rifai?

I looked around. There was no sign of her, and no noise coming from the kitchen either. I tried to call 'Paula', but a horrible croaking sound was all that came out. Right then I knew what the trouble was: I'd got a touch of the old malaria. But it was no time to feel sorry for myself. I stood up and grabbed my head quickly before it rolled off. Terrace, I thought, terrace. That meant I had to tackle the steps. To be on the safe side I went up on my knees. The worst part came at the top when I stuck my face out into the sunlight without thinking. After the waves of pain had died down I opened my eyes again, but this time just a fraction. She was there, digging away in a flower-pot. The cot was under the umbrella. I croaked again.

'Harry! What are you doing on your knees?'

'A touch of malaria,' I said.

She snorted. 'Malaria,' she said. 'You've got a hangover, that's all.'

'I never get hangovers,' I said, which happens to be true.

'I'll get some coffee anyway—for your malaria.'

'Wait,' I said. 'What about this phoning Rifai bit? I seem to remember you saying something last night—'

Paula stabbed her trowel into the flower-pot, dusted off her hands and stood up. 'That's right, Harry. I'm going to phone Rifai. I was just waiting for you to wake up to tell you.'

'But why—? What—?' There are some mornings when speaking just isn't on.

Paula came over and stood looking down at me. I saw something I hadn't noticed before: she was upset, really worked up, I mean. It wasn't the sort of thing that showed unless you knew her: it was in her eyes and her lips, and in the way she kept her fingers gripping tightly on nothing. She said in this small choked voice, 'I have to find out how Alberto is.'

'But we'll know in two days. Morland's going to call—'

'I don't want to know in two days. I want to know now.' Her hands were shaking.

'Now just stop and think,' I said with a smile. 'What could possibly be wrong—?'

'That's what I want to *know*,' she said furiously. 'I want to know if they're looking after him. I want to know what they're doing to him, whether he's sick. Maybe that's why Rifai is keeping him locked up away from everyone. I want to know if he's eating and sleeping, if he's cutting any more teeth, I want —I want—'

'All right, all right.' I got up quickly and took her hand. It was rough on the old skull, but anything to stop a bird crying.

'Oh, Harry—'

'It's okay. I understand.' I had my arms around her for the first time: a fat lot of good it was doing me.

'Harry—?'

'Sure,' I said. 'I'll do it. I'll call Rifai for you.'

She'd got me on my soft spot, see, with this crying bit, and just when I had malaria too, which as everyone knows lowers the resistance.

I phoned Rifai after lunch. Paula had wanted me to do it right away and come and listen herself. I said 'no' to both: to the first because Giorgio's would be full of customers all morning, to the second because the last thing I needed during a delicate chat with brother Yusuf was to have Paula hanging over my shoulder. She didn't argue. And why should she? She'd got me nailed to the floor as it was.

I waited till the street was quiet and the shutters were down on the windows before I went down to Giorgio's. I had it all worked out in my mind what I'd say: the trouble was I also had it worked out what he'd say: if he didn't, I was going to look pretty stupid. And if Morland ever found out what I'd done, looking stupid would be the least of my worries.

Mrs Giorgio was alone in the bar. When I said I was going to telephone she clapped her hands to her face and said, '*Il piccolo sta peggio.*'

'*Non—piu bene.*'

'*Grazie al Dio!*'

When she'd finished crossing herself with my *gettone* I dialled Rifai's number.

'Mr. Abercromby for Mr Rifai.'

There was a click and then this soft oily voice said, 'Mr Abercromby?'

'Mr Abercromby is detained on other business. I represent him.'

There was a chuckle. 'He sounds like a very busy man.'

'You know how it is in the season.'

'What is it, Mr—?'

'Nothing much,' I said, ignoring the 'Mr' bit. 'I'm just calling

159

to tell you that Selim is in good health and eating like a two-year-old.'

'Thank you. I'm surprised you take the trouble.'

'All part of the Abercromby service.'

'Is that all, Mr—?'

Right here I'd like to say that Morland's description of Rifai's voice as 'cool' and 'businesslike' was about as imaginative as saying the Venus de Milo is physically handicapped. To me, Rifai's voice sounded the way a snake would sound if a snake could talk: soft, smooth and wriggly. And somewhere down at the bottom of it was a laugh you couldn't hear. That sounds crazy I know but it's true. It was as if he'd spotted something very funny right at the heart of everything, of the world if you like, and he couldn't stop laughing at it, only he had to keep his laughter quiet because the joke wasn't one for sharing.

'Yes, that's all,' I said. Then, very casually, like I'd just thought of it: 'Oh, by the way, I suppose our kid's okay?'

There was a long pause. Then a chuckle. 'Why do you ask?''

I managed a laugh, more like a cackle. 'Mr. Abercromby likes to know that his staff are happy in their work.'

'A remarkable employer, your Mr Abercromby.'

'That's what we all say.'

'Well, if there's nothing else, Mr Fitch—'

'Mr *who?*' Then I caught myself and thought, watch it, Harry, he's getting to you. 'No, there's nothing else,' I said.

'Don't you want to hear about the baby?'

'What about him?'

'I'm not sure, really, the doctor says—'

'What do you mean? What doctor? What's the matter with Alberto?' I could have bitten my tongue clean off.

'Alberto?' He laughed. 'Yes, well, as I was saying, the doctor thinks—'

'Sure, Mr Rifai,' I said. 'Good try. You'd better have that money on Tuesday.'

I slammed down the phone. These Arab bastards will take you every time.

I had a couple of cognacs while I tried to think what I could tell Paula. Then I went upstairs.

'Harry—?'

'He's fine, in the pink. I don't know why you worried.'

'What did he say?—and about the new teeth?'

'We didn't get to the teeth,' I said. 'But Rifai said Alberto was in top form and eating like a two-year-old. He says he's never seen a baby look so fit.'

'That's funny, him being so friendly all of a sudden.'

I coughed with embarrassment. 'It wasn't a case of being friendly exactly. He was more scared than anything else. You see, I sort of hinted that Selim wasn't doing too well and that put him into a panic and he kept on wanting to tell me that Alberto was getting the best of everything and Selim ought to have the same.'

'You said *that*? To a *father*? That's the most horrible thing I've ever heard of. You're a monster. I hate you.'

Bang. Crash. Slam.

There are days, I know, when nothing goes right. But whatever happened to the other kind?

Chapter Sixteen

MORLAND looked so pale and peaky I was worried he might have another 'attack' before we got it finished. My own heart wasn't exactly jogging along what with the thought of that two hundred and fifty thousand dollars coming closer and closer . . . a quarter of a million . . . I couldn't believe it, not really. But I drove extra carefully just the same.

We'd worked out a plan for collecting the money. Rifai would have to bring it himself, alone, to the Excelsior. I'd be there in the lobby waiting. As soon as I saw him I'd call Morland at Giorgio's. Morland would ring back right away, have Rifai paged and tell him what to do next. The Excelsior bit was to throw off the fuzz in case they were staked out at the hotel. When he'd got his orders, Rifai would go back to his car and I'd be watching to see whether he spoke to anyone on the way out, and also whether he was followed. The actual pick-up would be on the Isola Tiberina which was where Morland would be waiting for Rifai, out of sight. It was a perfect spot for what we had in mind. From the middle of the island you could keep an eye on both bridges which meant, among other things, that the coppers couldn't come sneaking up on you without you knowing it. Rifai would leave the money in a side chapel of the church of San Bartolomeo and Morland would collect it as soon as he was sure it wasn't a trap. All in all it was a lovely little plan: the only thing it needed was for Rifai to agree to it.

The problem of switching the babies again was somewhat

tougher: in fact, to be honest, we hadn't actually come up with a solution to that yet. But as Morland said, once we'd got the money we'd be able to think a lot more clearly. I felt the same way. Paula didn't indicate what she felt which was probably just as well. We had enough to worry about as it was.

Morland's breathing was getting rougher.

'You feeling okay?'

'Fine, Harry, fine.'

I wasn't convinced but I thought, maybe it's nerves. Morland is a very nervous guy.

'There it is, Harry, that café over there.'

I parked and we walked across the road. We were in Viale Trastevere, a block or so from Piazza Ippolito Nievo. Morland didn't want to call from Giorgio's in case Rifai had the coppers tracing the call. It goes without saying that I hadn't told him about *my* call. If he ever found out—but I didn't like to think about it.

The trouble women can get you into . . . and the worst part is, it's not worth it. Just a door slammed in your face. Monster! I hate you! I wasn't sure that even a quarter of a million would make up for that.

Morland had chosen this particular café because the phone was in a small room at the back, almost a private booth, and it had an extra earpiece on an extension cord.

'I thought you'd like to listen in, Harry. After all, this is the big moment.'

'Thanks,' I said. 'It'll be something to tell my kids.' Actually, one little chat with Rifai had been more than enough for me, but it wouldn't have done to say so. All I hoped was that Morland didn't start inquiring after Alberto's health.

Morland gave his face a last wipe with a handkerchief and took out a *gettone*.

'All clear, Harry?'

I peeped out of the door. It was two in the afternoon. The

padrone was leaning on the bar gazing into the street. Otherwise the place was empty. 'All clear.'

I watched Morland dial the number. Two hundred and fifty thousand dollars . . . He pointed at the earpiece and I took it off the hook.

'Mr. Abercromby for Mr Rifai.'

There was the same click as before and then the same soft, slippery voice.

'Is that Mr Abercromby himself?'

'Yes,' Morland said, looking a bit baffled.

'Excellent. I prefer not to deal with subordinates. I'm sure you feel the same.'

'Yes.' Morland gave me a puzzled look.

I shrugged.

'I suppose you're calling about the money.'

'That's right.'

I wet my lips. Morland swallowed.

'Well, I've got it here. Two hundred and fifty thousand dollars in cash. A quarter of a million. That is correct, is it not?'

I felt the tears coming and I had to turn away. It couldn't be true. I blinked and shook my head. Morland was opening and shutting his mouth like a fish: nothing was coming out. I jabbed him in the ribs and pointed at the phone.

'Yes, yes—that's correct.' He was swaying about like a punchbag and I thought, please, let his ticker keep going just a few more minutes.

'And nothing bigger than tens? You did say that, didn't you?'

Morland nodded dreamily. 'Nothing bigger than tens,' he said. 'Nothing bigger than tens.'

Rifai made a grunting, satisfied noise. 'Good. I just wanted to make sure.' There was a pause. 'You know, I've got the money here on the table in front of me—' We heard a crackling sound and Morland licked his lips. 'It's quite a sight, believe me. Would you guess, Mr Abercromby, that not even I, Yusuf Rifai, have ever seen two hundred and fifty thousand dollars—in the flesh, that is. Frankly, I'm overwhelmed.'

'Yes,' Morland said. 'Now about the arrangements for—'

'I was thinking only this morning, Mr Abercromby, that for so great a sum of money a crime such as yours becomes understandable, even justifiable. When both crime and reward are on such an enormous scale, ordinary standards of morality seem grossly inadequate, don't you think? I speak from experience since this line of reasoning is one which I have applied to my own activities from time to time. Indeed, I think we can safely say, Mr. Abercromby, that with this coup you have lifted yourself clear of the common ruck of criminals and are now among the giants of your profession. I congratulate you. But a word of warning. Up here, where we live, the air is cold and thin, as you will soon discover, if you have not done so already. It takes a strong constitution, a special type of toughness to survive. Are you sure you have that constitution, Mr Abercromby? Are you tough in that special way?'

Poor old Morland looked fit to collapse as it was, never mind all that cold thin air, but he made a good try all the same. 'I'd be happy to discuss the climatological perils of the criminal conscience some other time, Mr Rifai, but could we confine ourselves today to arranging how you are going to pay us?'

'Pay?' Rifai gave his snake-chuckle. 'I said nothing about paying you.'

I shut my eyes and heard Morland take a deep breath.

'I don't follow you, Mr Rifai. If you don't pay us, you won't get your son back. I explained that to you.'

'And I understood you.'

'But—'

'Let me explain, Mr Abercromby. I must first of all say that indirectly you have done me a great favour. By kidnapping my son and providing me with a substitute you have given me the basis for a comparison which I have never been able to make before. Frankly, until these last few days, I had considered all babies indistinguishable, with the possible qualification that my own appeared to be more noisy and disagreeable than most others, in which respect, I might add, he resembles his late mother. Now I find that I have been wrong. Babies are not all the same. And more to the point, they are not all disagreeable. I have discovered that equally they can be pleasant, well-behaved, amusing and reasonably clean companions. All of which qualities, needless to say, have come to light in the person of Alberto—the admirable Alberto. So much for that. Now, on a more practical level, I should tell you that I fully intended to pay the ransom. I even had the money drawn from the bank and brought to the house. I will not pretend that I love my son, for already you will have guessed otherwise. But the obligations of a father are sacrosanct. Or are they? This intriguing thought occurred to me only yesterday, Mr Abercromby, while I was upstairs in the nursery playing with Alberto. What is life, I thought, but a slow process of casting off received ideas, beliefs, morals, customs, behaviour, and all the rest. We are like snakes, shedding one skin after another. It is a pity we die when we do for it is only after fifty years of adult life that we begin to understand our true selves. I am perhaps a little ahead of most other people in this respect—it's that cold, thin air I spoke of, Mr Abercromby—and I have long since realized that there is very little we can believe in and absolutely nothing we should be sentimental about. And so, with this in mind, I asked myself what my true feelings as a father were. You will be very disappointed to hear, Mr Abercromby, that they were precisely nil. When I came right down to the root of the matter I realized that through an external act beyond my power to predict or prevent, my sickly squealing, unhappy little wretch of a son had been exchanged for a healthy, vigorous, entirely delightful male child. Fortune does not show us her favours so often that we can afford to spurn even her most unlikely advances. I am offered what few men have ever been offered: a choice of sons. I do not hesitate for a moment. I choose Alberto. And so, may I make a suggestion. You keep the baby you've got, I'll keep the baby I've got, and we'll call it quits.'

'UNNATURAL FATHER!' Morland shrieked.

It was too late. Rifai had hung up.

Chapter Seventeen

MORLAND stood there, pale as a plucked chicken, staring straight ahead. He still had the receiver screwed to his ear. His lips were moving but he wasn't saying anything. I wondered if you could have heart attacks standing up.

'Take it easy,' I said. 'Don't move.' I ran out and got a glass of water from the *padrone*. Morland hadn't budged. 'Here, drink this.' I had to unlock each finger to get the phone away from him.

'Harry—?' At least he could still talk.

'Sure,' I said. 'Take it easy.'

He shook his head slowly. 'Did you hear him?'

'Yes. Come on. Let's go.' I took his arm.

'But his own son— Wouldn't you think he'd—?'

'I wouldn't know,' I said. 'I've never had a son. Come on, we have to go.'

It's not that I didn't feel sorry for him—him? what about me?—but the thing that was really worrying me was what was I going to tell Paula? We drove back without a word. Morland acted like he was in shock, and to tell the truth I wasn't anxious to alter the condition. There were certain little things Rifai had said which seemed to have slipped his mind in the general confusion. I was praying they'd stay slipped.

We stopped off in Giorgio's for a shot, mainly for Morland's benefit.

'Are you going to tell her or am I?'

'Please, Harry. I couldn't.'

'All right,' I said. In a way it was my responsibility, I

suppose. But as it happened I didn't have to in the end. Paula was waiting for us at the top of the stairs. She'd seen us arrive from the balcony. She only needed one look at our faces.

'Oh, no. Oh, *no*.'

So there I was with a hysterical bird on one hand and a semi-stretcher case on the other. And pretty soon Selim joined in, too, so that I was running from one to the other and back again until I was ready to throw a small fit myself, except there was no one around to notice. In the end I just poured everyone a shot of brandy. Except Selim of course. Him I picked up and shook a few times.

After a couple of drinks I told Paula what Rifai had said. She sat there, holding her glass, swaying a little, hardly seeming to hear me. Morland was stretched out on the couch with his eyes shut.

'That's how it is,' I said. 'And I don't see what we can do about it. He's got us by the——'

'Aagghh!' Morland let out this strangled scream and sat up like a jack-in-the-box. 'I knew there was something. I knew——'

I rushed the brandy over. 'Have another shot.' He pushed the bottle away and gave me a really blistering look.

'Tell me, Harry, how did Rifai know his name was Alberto? *How did Rifai know his name was Alberto?*'

I gazed up at the ceiling. 'Why,' I said, 'I expect Paula sewed it on his clothes or something. Didn't you, Paula?—— And I gave *her* a really blistering look so she'd get the point.

I should have saved my breath.

She dropped her glass on the floor, burst into tears and said, 'It's all our fault.'

'Yes,' I said quickly. 'We're all to blame.'

'Just a minute.' Morland stood up.

'Whose fault is it, Paula?'

'It's our fault, Harry's and mine. No, that's not fair. It's mine. I made Harry do it.'

I didn't say anything. I just went over to the couch and lay down. I reckoned it was my turn.

Morland stood over me looking very tense. 'All right, Harry. Let's have it.'

So I gave it to him, word for word, what I'd said to Rifai and what he'd said to me, the lot. Morland listened carefully. Then he poured himself a double, tossed it back and went out on to the balcony. I couldn't believe my eyes. I'd been expecting an epileptic fit at the very least.

'Oh, Harry—'

'It's not your fault,' I said. 'It's no one's fault. It's just the way it goes.' That was the truth, too, I reckoned. It was that old Roman emperor's auction all over again—and guess who'd got the shoe?

Paula said, 'If we hadn't shown Rifai what Alberto meant to us, if we hadn't shown him we love him, he'd have paid the ransom. I know it. Rifai doesn't want Alberto, or poor little Selim either, I expect. He just wants to win. We showed him we were weak and he knew he could beat us. I can't bear to think of Alberto there with that dreadful man. Say he really does keep him. Just think of it.'

'Oh, I don't know. He'll have a pretty soft life. Yachts and villas and caviar, and think of all the birds he'll have when he gets a little older.'

That was meant to cheer her up but all it did was start her crying again. You can never tell with women.

Don't think, by the way, that I was unsympathetic to all this emotion that was being flung around. But with a hot baby on our hands and no way of getting rid of it that I could see, someone had to keep cool. Meaning me. I remembered a little talk Ziggy had given me once on economic theory. One thing had always stuck in my memory: the law of diminishing returns. That had really made an impression, mainly, I think, because it applied to just about everything I'd done up till then. I thought about it now. Our returns hadn't exactly diminished, it was true. They'd just never existed. I wondered whether there was a law to cover that. All I knew was that however I looked at it, it was time to cut and run.

I started making a quick inventory of the flat: kitchenware, curtains, carpet, couch—I wouldn't be sorry to see that go. Paula's chair? I wondered—I wasn't sure exactly what she and Morland had bought. I was going to ask her, then I thought, no, not now. Over in the corner was the pram. That certainly ought to fetch a nice little sum, though I couldn't think who'd want to buy it. I went into the bedroom. The bed? It was a beauty, no question about it. I bounced up and down a couple of times. It's funny how you can miss things you've never had. I looked in the cupboard. All of Alberto's gear was stacked there: playpen, toys and rattles, a set of wooden blocks and that damn rubber duck. I remembered checking Morland's list and being surprised at how little they had cost. Looking at it from another point of view though, the gear wasn't going to fetch much either. Last of all I went to the cot. Selim was lying the way I'd stuck him, on his stomach, with his face on one side, making soft drizzling sounds into the pillow. He was lucky. He'd never miss all those yachts and villas. He'd never even know about them.

'But what, Gamal Abdel, are we going to do with you?' I said.

I wondered if we could give him back to Tony and say this was how Alberto looked after the pox. I didn't think Tony would swallow it. I was sure Big Mamma wouldn't. What was really hysterical was that there was every chance we'd end up getting charged with kidnapping the baby we hadn't snatched. And then the coppers would say, 'But if this is not Alberto, who is he?' It was definitely time to move on.

'What are we going to do, Harry?'—I hadn't heard her come in.

'The first thing is to get out, and quick.'

'And leave Alberto—?' She began, then she smiled, a very sad little smile I hadn't seen before. 'Poor Harry. You've had a bad time, haven't you?'

'I wouldn't say that.'

'All your money gone and nothing to show for it.'

'There are some things that don't show.'

'What things, Harry?'

Birds can be very dense sometimes.

'Well, living here with you and Alberto. That sort of thing.'

'You didn't get much out of it.'

I thought about that for a while. In some ways it was true, I hadn't got a thing, not even—but then in other ways I wasn't so sure.

'I suppose I didn't if you look at it that way,' I said, wishing I knew what the hell I was talking about.

She sat down on the bed and looked up at me. Her nose was red and her eyes were swollen. But she was still a dish. 'I got a lot out of it,' she said.

I smiled. 'Alberto's going to miss you, too, I know, never mind all the yachts and the caviar and stuff.'

'It wasn't only Alberto.'

I smiled again and looked away. Birds can go soft all of a sudden and then feel sorry for it later. No one ever got anything out of Harry Brighton.

'It wasn't only Alberto, Harry.'

I laughed. 'You could have fooled me.' I tried to walk past her but she caught my hand.

'Stop fighting for just a moment.'

That's the moment when they get you, I thought. But I stopped all the same. It was a very ordinary sort of kiss, bumped noses and all that sort of thing, and her tasting more of salt than anything else. But I liked it. So much, in fact, that I wanted another and was just moving in for it when that damn Morland had to come bursting in.

'Harry—Paula.' He looked really wild, eyes blazing, hair sticking up, arms waving around.

'Not now, Morland.'

'I've got it,' he said. 'I've got it.'

'Got what?'

'So Mr Rifai has a special constitution, has he? He's tough, is he? We'll see. We'll see. Cold thin air, eh? We'll see about that too.' He was marching up and down at the foot of the bed, waving his fists around, really raving.

'Look, Morland—'

'Oh, it's perfect. So absolutely perfect. Why didn't I think of it before? Oh, Mr Yusuf Rifai, are you going to catch it? You're going to wish you'd never set eyes on Alberto. Before I'm finished with you, Mr Rifai, you'll be begging me, begging me, do you hear—'

We got hold of him, Paula on one arm, me on the other. We made him sit down on the bed.

'Now, Jonathan. Calm down. What are you going to do to Rifai?'

'Do?' He looked stunned. 'Isn't it obvious?'

'No,' I said. 'It's not obvious.'

He threw back his head and laughed. 'Why,' he said, 'we're going to snatch Alberto, too!'

'Oh, no,' I said.

'Oh, *yes*,' Paula shouted and flung her arms around him. 'Oh, yes. Oh, yes. Oh, yes.'

Oh God, I thought. It was starting again, the same old nightmare with the same old ending, only each time it got worse.

'But Harry, don't you see—'

I said, 'I see all right. I see we have to get out of here, and not just out of Via dello Scorpione either. Out of Rome—out of Italy! And that's not all I see. I see we're lucky even to have the *choice* of getting out. Morland, if you'd come back to earth for just two seconds—'

'Coward,' Paula said.

'I beg your pardon.'

'I said "coward". You're afraid. You don't care about Alberto, or me, or anything except yourself. You just want to make sure that no harm comes to Harry Brighton.'

And what was wrong with that? Who else was going to make sure that no harm came to Harry Brighton? Batman?

'Don't worry, Jonathan,' Paula said. 'You and I can do it.'

Oh, sure. With a little help from U.N.C.L.E. maybe!

Morland said, 'Listen, Harry, we *can* do it. It's the last thing in the world Rifai would expect now. He thinks we're going to call him in a day or two and beg him to take Selim back. And of course he means to keep Alberto, too. He thinks he's got us on the spot. And so he has, except that we're going to turn the tables on him—now don't get excited, just listen a minute. Suppose we *can* snatch Alberto, and suppose we *do*, where does that leave Rifai?'

'Laughing,' I said.

'Maybe, but not when the word gets out about the kidnapping. Not even Rifai would dare tell the world he doesn't care about his own son.'

'But who's going to put the word out? Rifai won't.'

'We will, Harry. After we've snatched Alberto we're going to tip off the press that *Selim* has been kidnapped. We're going to say that a ransom of two hundred and fifty thousand dollars has been asked. Rifai won't be able to deny the kidnapping. He'll have lost his substitute baby, and anyway, the police will be around asking questions as soon as the story breaks. And unless I'm much mistaken Rifai won't want to tell them about the switch. It would raise too many awkward questions for him.'

Paula said, 'He may admit to the kidnapping, but I don't see how we can make him pay. Why don't we simply switch the babies around again and leave it at that?'

Morland and I stared at her. At least she had the decency to blush. 'Well, it was only a suggestion.'

Morland said, 'We don't have to do anything. He'll pay.'

'Just like that?'

Morland nodded. 'Just like that.'

'Elementary psychology, I suppose.'

It was Morland's turn to blush. 'I admit I misjudged Rifai before. But not this time. Just think: a man worth a hundred million dollars is asked to pay a measly quarter of a million for his only son. The story is splashed across the front pages of every newspaper in the world. Television commentators weep, old widows offer their life savings. Can't you just see it all?' Morland held up his hands. 'With that sort of pressure Rifai wouldn't dare refuse. He's got a public image, remember. He can behave like a bastard as much as he likes in private, but in public he's Yusuf Rifai, millionaire philanthropist, friend of kings, adviser to governments and all that stuff. Public opinion is something he cares about. And in this little caper, Harry, public opinion is on *our* side. He'll have to pay.'

'What about the police?'

'What about them? They'll look for Selim of course but they won't find him. We've kept people out of this flat for a week with the chicken-pox story. We can keep them out for another week.'

'Including Tony and Mamma?'

We all looked at each other.

'That settles it,' Morland said. 'We've got to get Alberto back right away.'

'Oh, yes, right away,' Paula said.

I asked her, 'Have you any idea what it will be like looking after two babies and pretending they're one?'

'I can do it,' she snapped. Then she smiled at Morland. '*We* can do it, can't we, Jonathan?'

'Well, go and do it then.' I was halfway to the door before Morland stopped me.

'We need you, Harry. We can't do it without you.'

That was more like it. I looked at Paula, but she was sulking. Typical.

I said to Morland, 'There's just one thing. You said yourself we couldn't pull that pram trick more than once. And anyway, I can't see Alberto being taken for any walks in the park. Just how do you propose to snatch him?'

'We'll have to break into Rifai's villa.'

'Break into—?' I was speechless. 'You really have lost your marbles.'

'Not at all.' He had this smug, cat-with-the-cream look again, just dying for me to ask him how it could be done. As far as I was concerned he could go ahead and die.

Paula squeezed his hand. 'I can't *imagine* how we can do it.'

Morland smirked. 'It's simple really. You've just forgotten one thing.'

'What?' Paula and I said together.

'Hermann,' he said. 'You've forgotten Hermann.'

Chapter Eighteen

THE NEXT MORNING Morland and I drove out along the Appia Antica to have a look at Rifai's villa. We'd taken a chance and phoned Hermann before we left. He was pretty shocked when we told him about Rifai deciding not to pay the ransom.

'That is not good,' he whispered into the phone. 'What are we going to do, Jonathan?'

'I'll tell you when we see you.'

I wondered what the kraut would say when he found out we wanted him to help us break into his boss's villa. I knew what I'd say if I was in his shoes. I'd say, Morland, go stuff yourself.

The Appia Antica, in case you don't know it, is a road which the ancient Romans built a couple of thousand years ago. It runs south from the city straight as an arrow and for several miles is lined with old tombs and catacombs and crumbling ruins just as if there'd been a war there and no one had bothered to clean up afterwards. Naturally the tourists love it. Apart from the ruins the road is also lined with villas, and not just ordinary villas either, but the biggest and plushest in Rome. With all that junk lying around—bits of broken statues, chewed-up walls, crumbling aqueducts—only millionaires can afford to live there. Most of the villas are hidden from the road by high stone walls and hedges. As you go by the gates you get a glimpse of long curving drives: sometimes you can even see the houses in the distance, though usually they're too far away for that.

We'd gone about two miles beyond Porta San Sebastiano when Morland clutched my arm and said, 'Here it is.' He'd said it like he'd got a shock and when I looked I saw why. Rifai's villa had the same high stone walls as everyone else's—with one small difference: along the top of the wall was a mat of iron spikes nearly a foot high. Morland shook his head. 'I'm sure they weren't there before.'

'You're right,' I said. 'Look.'

Farther on, beyond the iron gates, a couple of workmen were sitting astride the wall hammering away. They were fitting six-foot sections of the matted spikes to the top of the wall. The sections were being handed up to them from below. The guy doing the handing was Hermann.

I pulled off the road and parked under one of a row of cypresses growing between the wall of the villa and the road. The villa was bordered on one side by a neighbour's garden, on the other by an open field where a couple of legs of an aqueduct were still standing. We walked into the field out of sight of Hermann and the workmen. The side wall of Rifai's villa ran back from the road for more than a hundred yards. Iron spikes covered every inch of it.

After a minute or two Hermann strolled around the corner, smoking a cigarette and staring up at the spikes like he was inspecting the defences. We moved closer and Morland said, 'Hermann, why are you putting up these spikes?'

'Mr Rifai's orders.' Hermann spoke to the wall. 'We started putting them up soon after the kidnapping. We are nearly finished.'

'How much longer will you take?'

'Maybe we finish today.'

'You mustn't finish today, Hermann. You must leave part of the wall clear. Just a little.'

Hermann dropped his cigarette and turned round slowly. Here it comes, I thought, the old kiss-off. Hermann knows when to cut his losses. I wished to hell I did.

'You mean—?' His blue eyes bulged.

'We're coming in tonight, Hermann.' Tonight! No one had told *me*. 'We're coming for Alberto.'

Hermann opened his mouth, then shut it again.

Morland went on quickly, 'There's no time to explain now, but we have to do it. It's the only way to make Rifai pay. Can we count on you?'

'*Ja*, but—'

'Good. We need a plan for getting into the house and the nursery. Who guards Alberto?'

'The nurse, Helen, but—'

'Only Helen?'

'No. I sleep in the next room. I am not allowed to see the baby though. Only Mr Rifai and Helen go into the nursery. No one else must go in, not even me. Those are my orders. But Jonathan—'

'Helen,' Morland said, sucking his teeth. 'Helen.' He stared at Hermann, who was getting very nervous and kept glancing over his shoulder like he was hoping someone would come and rescue him. I knew exactly how he felt. 'Helen,' Morland said again, then he snapped his fingers. 'Of course—Silvio. Where's Silvio?'

'Locked in his room in the stables—the garage.'

'Who has the key?'

'I have the key.'

'Is Helen worried about him?'

'Is she worried? *Mein Gott!*' Hermann slapped his forehead. I was glad it wasn't mine. 'I hear nothing else all day. "Please! tell Silvio this, please tell Silvio that." And now I have to tell *her* that Silvio is being sent back to Beirut. Mr Rifai has told three of the boys in Beirut to fly here. They are coming tomorrow.'

'All the more reason why we must do it tonight,' Morland said. 'Now listen. Tonight you must give Helen the key to Silvio's room—and tell her he's leaving tomorrow. Say you'll keep an eye on the baby while she's with Silvio. I don't suppose you'll have much trouble persuading her.'

Hermann frowned. 'Why?'

Morland and I groaned.

'She's in love with him, that's why,' I said. 'She'll want to see him for sure, maybe have it off with him. Doesn't he get a nibble now and then?' I was curious to know whether Silvio was doing any better than me.

Hermann just shook his head like it was all too confusing for him. But he said, 'I think she will want to see him—*ja*.'

'That's good enough,' Morland said. 'Now how can we get in? Into the house and into the nursery? Time, place, method? You're the only one who knows the villa. Think, Hermann, *think*.'

Hermann's eyes bulged a little further. You could see it was pure agony.

'Pssst.' I spotted one of the workmen coming round the corner. Hermann turned and waved. '*Vengo subito*,' he called out. He stood there, biting his lips, staring at us.

'There must be a way, Hermann.'

Hermann scratched his crew-cut. He looked very unhappy.

'All right, don't worry.' Morland patted him on the shoulder. 'Can you phone me at Giorgio's this afternoon?'

'*Ja*, I think so.'

'Good—and Hermann, try to work something out.'

'I will try.' He shook his head. He looked dazed.

As we turned to leave I had a brainwave.

'Just think of it as an operation, Hermann.'

'An operation?'

'In the war. You're an officer. Captain Hermann—*Major* Hermann. We're your men and we're depending on you. You can't let us down.'

'War.' Hermann's face lit up.

'That's right—biff, biff, biff.'

'War.' Hermann drew himself up. '*Mein Gott,* I will do it.'
He slammed a fist into his palm. Morland and I winced. 'We
will do it just like in the war. Like Alamein, *ja.*'

'Not exactly like Alamein—' I began, then I thought, what
the hell, we all remember things the way we want to, and I
expect that goes double for krauts.

Back at the flat Paula had bad news. Bruno had come round
in his *carrozza* looking for me.

'He said to tell you he couldn't wait any longer and was
going to sell whatever it was you wanted to buy from him to
someone else.' She said it with a thin little smile like she knew
it was going to hurt. She hadn't forgiven me for last night.

I rushed downstairs and rang Bruno's number. He was there,
having lunch.

'*Please*, Bruno.'

'It is too late, Harry. I sold it to Mr Schwartz an hour ago.
You promised to call, remember?'

'If only you knew what I've been through.'

'I am sorry for you, Harry. But I think maybe you should
give up the business. I think maybe you have your mind on
other things.'

I knew he meant Paula. Besides being a purist Bruno is also
something of a prune.

I slumped on the bar. Giorgio brought me a double.

'Bad news from the publishers?'

'Very bad news from the publishers.'

'Ah, well, an artist must persevere. Now I myself have
struggled for many years and even today my poetry is not
recognized or appreciated. I think the main trouble is that I
spend too much time working in the bar and not enough on
my poems. What do you think, Harry?'

'I agree.' When you want them to shut up, agree.

'Do you really, Harry? Do you really?'

He was staring at me: big bushy moustache and wet brown eyes. It was pathetic. He was actually hanging on my answer, me, the big author.

'I don't know, Giorgio. Honestly. Morland says your poems are good, but maybe they could be better.'

'With more work?'

I shrugged.

'Thank you, Harry.' He blinked and reached across the bar to squeeze my arm. 'Thank you.'

I shrugged again. Any time.

When I got back upstairs I found Paula looking pale and upset.

'Jonathan says you're going to do it tonight.'

'Aren't you pleased?'

'I don't know.'

I followed her into the kitchen.

'Was it bad news—from that Bruno person?'

'Yes.'

I told her about it, about the Russian ticket and what it meant to me. There aren't many who would understand, but she seemed to.

'It's like the time I found out I was too big to be a ballet dancer.'

Well, maybe she did.

'Harry, be careful tonight. Please.'

'Aren't I always? Harry Brighton takes care of himself, remember?'

'Don't.' She turned away. For a few seconds she stood like that, staring at the wall. Then she swung round. 'I want to come with you.'

'Well, you can't.'

'But it's all my fault—'

'And that's final. Anyway, who'd look after Selim?'

'I thought we could find a babysitter or something.'

I just looked at her.

Half an hour later, while digging into a bowl of *fettucine al ragu'*, Morland collapsed. This time I knew he wasn't putting it on. Not even Morland could make his own face turn such a nasty blue colour. We got him on to the bed, and Paula was on her way out to call a doctor when he stopped her.

'I'll be all right,' he gasped.

'Don't be ridiculous.'

'In a few minutes. Really. Look, I'm getting better already.'

It was true. The blue colour was fading a little and his breathing was easier.

'Harry, we must get him to a doctor.'

I looked at Morland, and then at Selim lying in his cot. If the doctor sent for an ambulance we'd have the whole of Scorpion Street on our doorstep to find out what was wrong. 'How do you feel?' I said. 'Honestly.'

'Fine, Harry, fine.' He smiled weakly. He was wearing his old black jacket with the cuffs frayed and the buttons missing and he made me think of a piece of dead wood with the bark beginning to peel. 'Just let me rest for a few minutes.'

A few minutes! A few months, more like it.

'Well, there goes the snatch, anyway.'

'No,' Paula and Morland said together.

'I'll be all right—'

'No you won't,' Paula said. 'And you're not moving off this bed. I'll go with Harry.'

'No,' I shouted. Morland almost choked.

'Don't argue, either of you, or I'll call a doctor this minute. And an ambulance, too. I mean it.'

Morland and I looked at each other.

'I can do it alone,' I said. 'Alberto doesn't weigh that much.'

'I said I was coming with you, and that's final.' She flashed her green eyes at me. I could see it was hopeless to argue.

'What about Selim?'

183

'I'll feed him before we go. And I'll put his cot close to the bed where Jonathan can reach it. If he cries, Jonathan, all you have to do is rock the cot. See?' She showed him.

'What if he doesn't stop crying? What if he chokes?'

Paula said coldly, 'Let him choke.'

Inside, the car was like an oven: outside wasn't much better. It was one of those steamy nights you get in Rome in the summer when the air feels like hot towels and the sweat springs up from nowhere like dew. Paula lit her third cigarette. I checked my watch. Still twenty minutes to go.

We'd got out to the villa more than half an hour early because Paula had suddenly had a fit of nerves and started imagining all the things that might go wrong—'Say we have a puncture, Harry?'—'What if we run out of petrol?'—'Suppose we're stopped for speeding'—and when a bird gets like that there's nothing to do except humour her. So there we were, sitting in the car, parked up against the wall of the villa, twiddling our thumbs and counting the minutes.

I said Paula was nervous. Well, frankly I was petrified. I'd never done anything like this before, not remotely. The furthest I'd gone in what you might call the field of active larceny was a spot of hotel roulette. (You know the game? Open a door and say, 'Oops, sorry, wrong room,' and keep trying until you hit the *right* room.) But that was a long time ago when I was a kid and just getting started. I thought I'd left that sort of stuff far behind. Now here I was, my ticket business gone to hell, waiting to do my first-ever bit of breaking and entering. Whichever way I looked at it, my career just wasn't advancing.

'I'm getting out for some air.'

Paula grabbed my arm. 'No, Harry. We're supposed to look like a courting couple, remember.'

'Oh, all right.'

'Not *now*, Harry.'

184

A courting couple! That was Morland's idea. At night the Appia Antica is a sort of no-man's-land for all except snoggers. If you go there after dark it has to be for one thing—and if you're not doing it you're likely to be regarded as highly suspicious by any passing fuzz. Paula and I were parked under the branches of a big tree that hung over the garden wall. It would have been tough for anyone on the road to say what, if anything, we were up to, but they would certainly guess.

Paula said, 'Do you think it'll work?'

'It's a fine time to ask.'

She meant Hermann's plan. The kraut had phoned us at Giorgio's that afternoon half out of his mind with excitement— 'I haf the plan, I haf the plan'—and it was some time before I got him calmed down and semi-coherent. I thought he'd be really upset when I told him Morland had blown a fuse but he just grunted and muttered something about the 'fortunes of war'. He didn't seem particularly surprised either to hear that Paula was coming instead. Maybe in Germany birds are expected to do their bit.

First, he gave me some good news. Rifai would be out for the evening: a dinner at the Lebanese Embassy which wasn't expected to finish before midnight. Then he told me he'd sent the workmen home early and that a small section of the wall, including the bit under the tree, was still uncovered. He'd also seen to it that the ladder had been left lying outside, so all we had to do was lean it against the wall and pop over. With luck the branches of the tree and our *cinquecento* would hide the ladder from people driving by. From the top of the wall we'd have to jump down into the garden, a drop of nearly fifteen feet. I asked Paula whether she could make it. She just sniffed and then looked me up and down like it had occurred to her to ask me the same question. On the way back we'd have to collect a stepladder from a shed at the bottom of the garden to get back over the wall.

All this came from Hermann, so you can see that the old kraut brain had been fairly buzzing. And there was more, a lot more, a whole plan of operations in fact, which, since I was the one who had to take it down over the phone and put it into English, I'll reproduce, *in toto*.

Operation 'Alberto'.

Objective: to snatch Alberto.

Method: Commando night raid.

('Hermann, you've got to be kidding.'

'What do you mean, Harry—kidding?')

2130. Rifai leaves villa for Lebanese Embassy accompanied by bodyguard Hamid.

2135. Harry and Paula cross over the wall and advance up garden towards left side of house.

2145. Hermann gives key to Helen and suggests a visit to Silvio.

2150. Hermann lets Helen out of side door so that she will not be seen either by servants in kitchen or by bodyguard Abdul, on duty in entrance hall.

2155. Harry and Paula reach shrubbery at side of house underneath nursery window on first floor.

2200. Hermann opens window and flicks light on and off. This is signal for Harry to start climbing vine.

('Hermann, you've *got* to be kidding.'

'It is a strong vine.'

'Maybe. But I'm not a strong Harry.'

'Please?'

'Why can't I come in by the side door?'

'Because they will look at the vine later and see that someone climbed up it. Then they will know how you got in.'

'Couldn't *you* nip up it once when no one's looking?'

'It is not *that* strong.')

2205. Harry comes in through nursery window. Hermann and Harry prepare Alberto for departure. Paula

186

keeps watch on the stables in case Helen returns suddenly.

2215. Hermann goes downstairs to take Abdul's place in entrance hall while Abdul goes to kitchen for his evening meal.

2220. Harry goes downstairs with Alberto. He ties up Hermann with curtain cord and gags him. Hermann's story is that three armed men surprised him. Investigation will show they climbed up vine to nursery. Hermann will admit to having given Helen permission to visit Silvio. Hermann will certainly be fired.

2230. Harry and Paula with Alberto withdraw to bottom of garden, get stepladder from shed, cross wall.

2245. Abdul returns to post in entrance hall and finds Hermann.

Operation 'Alberto' concluded.

'It is a good plan?'

'Bloody brilliant, Hermann. I don't know how you boys lost.'

'Please?'

Morland perked up a little when I read it to him. He said it had 'the virtue of extreme simplicity,' which I suppose is another way of saying even a bird-brain could have thought it up. What I didn't like about it was that it only needed one little thing to go wrong—Helen to come back suddenly, say, or Abdul to decide he wasn't hungry—and we'd be rumbled. There was also the question of what would happen to Hermann.

'You don't think Rifai's going to believe his story, do you?' I said. 'He's going to be very suspicious.'

'Let him be. I'm not worried. I know Hermann won't crack.'

That's nice, I was going to say, only let's make sure Hermann knows too. But then I looked at this starved scarecrow

187

figure lying on the bed and I thought, give the old boy a break for once. That's my trouble, see, I'm soft.

Paula said, 'He's late.'

I looked at my watch: nine thirty-three. If Rifai didn't leave soon the whole plan would be thrown out of gear and we'd have to scrub it. I didn't think we'd be that lucky, but I said a small prayer just the same.

Paula lit another cigarette. She caught my eye for a moment and smiled in the darkness.

'We'll look a prize pair of charlies if they catch us.'

A prize pair of charlies! If that's all she thought we'd look, good luck to her. It reminded me of something Morland was fond of saying: happiness is just another word for ignorance.

I took out a handkerchief and mopped my face. It didn't help. The sweat broke out again like water squeezed from a sponge. My shirt was drenched, the backs of my knees were dripping wet.

Nine thirty-five.

'It's too late, I thought—I'll never forget that feeling of relief—we'll have to call it off. I shut my eyes for a moment and said a small word of thanks.

'There he is.' Paula clutched my arm.

I opened my eyes. The Rolls was coming slowly out of the gateway. It stopped and the driver got out and shut the gates behind them. Then it swung on to the main road, heading for the city.

You should never be too quick to thank anyone.

Chapter Nineteen

'COME ON.' Paula was out first, hunting around in the dark for the ladder. Hermann said he'd left it under the tree but we had to go down on our hands and knees before we found it, tucked up against the bottom of the wall. Lifting it into position wasn't easy either: the top kept getting tangled in the branches hanging over the wall and by the time we'd shaken it loose it sounded like half the tree had come down.

Paula went up it before I could stop her. 'Come on, Harry, we're late.' She was wearing jeans and a dark sweater. I saw a pair of legs pause at the top of the ladder: then they disappeared. Next thing I heard was the sound of branches snapping, then a thud.

I took a last look around. A long way down the wall, past the gates, a car pulled off the road and cut its lights. A 'courting couple' probably. They were too far away to see the ladder. Otherwise the road was empty. My foot found the bottom rung of the ladder and I went up carefully, feeling my way, so as not to have an eye poked out by all the twigs and stuff jabbing into me.

'Why are you so *slow*?' A dim white face was peering up at me. 'Come on, jump, it's not very high.'

There was more snapping of branches and then another, louder thud. Not very high! Then why was I sitting there with a fractured pelvis?

'For heaven's sake, Harry, come *on*.'

'Wait a minute.' I got up and had a quick scout around to get my bearings. To the left of us were the gates which would stay locked until Rifai returned. The drive ran from the gates up to the house in two slowly curving arms which met at the front door. Inside the arms was a long terraced lawn with fountains at each end. Between the drive and the outer wall there were shrubs and flower-beds and a few trees dotted here and there. The idea had been for us to work our way up the garden to the house, getting what cover we could from the trees and shrubs. Which would have been fine if we'd had the twenty minutes which Hermann had given us in his plan. I looked at my watch: nine fifty-seven. In exactly three minutes Hermann would open the nursery window and flick the lights: the signal for me to start climbing.

'Harry, if we stand here a second longer—'

'Shut up,' I said. I grabbed her hand. 'Come on.'

We cut straight through the shrubs and flower-beds to the drive. When we got to the edge I pulled her down behind a bush.

'Don't say a word. Just do what I tell you. Understand?'

'Yes, Harry.'

I peeped over the bush. The villa was maybe sixty yards away. The only light I could see was over the front door. But if anyone was watching from those darkened windows . . . well, it was too late to worry now. I pulled her up.

'Run,' I said. And then we were off.

Sixty yards may not seem a long way. But on a loose gravel drive, under a clear night sky, with the thought of twenty years running merrily through your mind, it can feel like for ever. We stuck to it right up to the point where the drive turned in sharply towards the front of the house. Then I dragged Paula off to the side and we collapsed behind a bush. For a few seconds there was only our breathing and the smell of grass and earth. I was listening for another sound: a shout, a door opening, footsteps. But all we heard was the splash of the fountain.

Very slowly I got up on one knee. The house, still in darkness, was less than thirty feet away. From the bottom of the garden it had looked long and low, sort of ranch-style, with the windows of the upper floor hardly more than a jump above ground level. Now that I'd got closer I saw that it wasn't like that at all. A stone terrace running the length of the house cut off nearly a third of its real height. Along the side, where there was no terrace, the windows on the ground floor were out of reach: and the windows on the floor above that were practically out of sight! I made a note to take it up with Hermann if I ever got the chance.

The spot where we'd gone to ground was opposite the corner of the house. To get beneath the nursery window, second from the corner on the upper floor, we had to move to the right and then cross a spur of the drive that ran along the side of the house to the stables at the back. Once we'd crossed the drive we could hide in a bed of thick shrubs growing against the side of the house and wait for Hermann's signal. I squeezed Paula's hand. She squeezed back and smiled. It was all a game to her.

Half crouching, we moved from one bush to the next until we were almost on the drive. I looked left, to the front of the house, then right to the stables. There was a light showing in a window above the garage. It had to be Silvio's room. Helen would be with him by now. Lucky old Silvio! I pointed at the clump of shrubs and Paula nodded. As we stood up to cross the drive a door opened in the side of the house straight in front of us and a bright light burst in our eyes.

I dropped like a stone and Paula came down on top of me. Who—? Then I heard Hermann's rumble and a girl's voice whispering. It was Helen. Hermann was also running late. We heard the door shut and Helen's footsteps growing fainter. Paula rolled off me, giggling. I would have asked her what was so funny if I hadn't known it just wasn't my night for jokes.

'Now,' I whispered, and we shot across the drive and into the shrubbery like a pair of whippets.

Crouching, I looked up. There was just enough angle to see the nursery window. It was still dark. I tested the vine. It made a nasty creaking sound. If Hermann knew the vine wouldn't carry him, how did he know it would carry me? Paula tugged at my sleeve. She was pointing through the shrubs at the stables. The light had gone out.

'It didn't take them long,' I whispered. I felt a little pissed off at the thought of Silvio holing out in one.

'These Italian boys are fast workers.'

'Are they?'

'Don't be clever.'

'Well, I'm glad to see someone's getting it.'

That got *me* a punch in the kidneys.

Paula whispered, 'If Helen comes back suddenly, I'll have to warn you somehow.'

'Don't worry. Not even the Ites are that quick.'

'Listen for this'—she whistled a few notes—'that'll mean, look out.'

The light came so suddenly, falling flat on the drive like a spotlight, that I thought we'd been rumbled. Then it went off. A couple of seconds later it came on again, then off. Hermann was signalling. I looked up and saw a head lean out of the darkened window.

'Harry?' Hermann's whisper came floating down to us.

I stood up straight and waved. Hermann motioned me to go up.

'Take care, Harry.' She squeezed my fingers.

The first few feet were okay. The vine seemed solid as a rock. Then I put my foot on what felt like a good strong branch and practically dislocated my neck when it snapped clean through without warning. A hand touched my leg.

'Harry, are you all right?'

192

'Get down,' I hissed. If there's one thing I can't stand it's being watched.

I started up more carefully this time, testing each branch before I put my full weight on it. The vine did a lot of creaking and groaning but seemed to be holding up okay. Directly below the nursery was another window, barred like all the ground-floor windows. I had to climb up the wall beside it and then move across a couple of feet to get in line with the nursery. After what seemed like an hour at least but was maybe five minutes I looked down. I could see Paula's white face among the leaves. She waved.

'Harry, come on. We are late.'

Hermann's head was still a long way away. I got moving again, but it was getting tougher. Vines are like trees: the higher you go the thinner they get. After I'd broken three branches in a row looking for a firm foothold I found something deep in the vine, a pipe sticking out of the wall maybe, that seemed solid enough. The moment I put my weight on it and reached up for another handhold I knew I'd made a mistake: my weight wasn't pressing *down* any longer, it was hanging *out*, away from the wall. I'll never forget that tearing sound as the vine slowly came away from the wall. I stretched up, up, up. It was no use. I was grabbing at air. As the vine and I keeled over slowly I remember thinking quite calmly that this was it. In the morning they'd scrape poor Harry off the drive. All I hoped was that Ziggy never heard about it. Then suddenly the vine stopped moving. I reached up again: a hand gripped mine. Next thing I knew I was being hauled up like a sack of potatoes in a shower of twigs and leaves. Good old Hermann!

He pulled me clean through the window and on to the floor. I lay there for a few moments, kissing the carpet.

'That was good, Harry. Now they will know for sure you came up the vine.'

Me and an army!

Hermann helped me up. 'We must hurry. Abdul will go to eat in five minutes.' He drew the curtains and switched on the light.

'Alberto—?'

He pointed. The cot was in the corner, a really plush job, carved walnut or something, all polished and old-looking. I went over. The little bugger was flat on his stomach, head on one side, fists clenched, out like a light. His hair had grown a bit, I noticed. I touched his cheek with one finger. Just lightly.

'Quick, Harry, put him in this.'

Hermann was dragging what looked like a shopping bag out of a cupboard. It turned out to be a carry-cot and Alberto fitted in very nicely, bedclothes and all. I stuck him on his back and that woke him up. He blinked a couple of times and made his gurgling sound. I took it for hullo.

Hermann put his finger to his lips, opened the door and went out on tiptoe. I looked around. There was a bed in the other corner: Helen's. The walls were papered with blue flowers and silver bells and little frisking lambs. The carpet was thick and spongy. Inside the cupboard, which Hermann had left open, there were shelves packed with fluffy toys and rubber balls and all kinds of other stuff which I'd never even seen before but which obviously was baby's gear. I thought of the terraced lawn and the fountains.

'You've got it pretty soft here, haven't you?' I said. That was the first time I realized that being a baby wasn't all coconuts. I mean no one was asking Alberto whether *he* wanted to be snatched.

Hermann came back, still on tiptoe. He shut the door.

'Abdul is in the hall. I will go down now. In five minutes you come. When you are at the top of the stairs, listen. If you hear me whistling or humming, it means Abdul is still there, and you must wait. It is clear?'

'As crystal, Hermann. You're the greatest.'

He went all bashful. 'Well, it is a good plan.'

'The best, Hermann, the best.' I was going to shake his hand too but I thought, no, I still have to use mine.

As he turned to leave I heard Paula's whistle.

'Wait.'

I ran to the window and parted the curtains a fraction. She was down in the shrubbery, waving. I waved back and then leaned out as far as I could to check the stable window. Silvio's light was still out. Paula whistled again, a bit hysterically I thought.

'What is it?' I hissed.

There was no reply, only a lot of thrashing about in the undergrowth. Then suddenly Paula burst out of the shrubs into the middle of the drive, looked up at me and pointed frantically: not at the stables—the other way, towards the front gates!

I leaned out again. Away down the drive I saw lights: they seemed to be moving, coming up towards the house. Hermann pushed me aside and stuck his head out. He shot back immediately like a spring, reached the door in two steps and switched off the light.

'Who—?'

'Rifai.'

'It can't be.'

'No one else has a key to the gates.'

'Do you think he saw the light?'

'Maybe.'

The car's headlights flashed through the drawn curtains for a second as it swept up the curving drive. We heard the crunch of tyres on gravel.

'Will he come up here?'

'Maybe.'

A door slammed. Footsteps sounded on the gravel. Hermann opened the door softly.

'Wait here.'

I looked out of the window. The drive was empty: Paula had vanished. From downstairs came the sound of the front door being unlocked: a nasty wet click, like a gun being cocked. I heard voices in the hall. Then it hit me: there I was, alone in the nursery, with the stuff all wrapped up and ready to go: a perfect cop. If Hermann had an ounce of sense in his thick kraut skull he'd come bursting back into the room, grab me and shout copper before I could get away down the vine. That way he'd save his own skin at least, and I can't say I would have blamed him. I didn't blame myself either for deciding to get out quick. I had my leg over the window-ledge feeling around for a foothold when the door opened.

'Harry, what are you doing?' He was just a dark shadow in the doorway.

'I thought—' What could I say?

'Listen.' He shut the door softly and came over. 'I heard Rifai saying something about the ambassador being sick and the dinner being cancelled. He is very angry because they did not tell him. He has gone to do some work in his study. Look.' He pointed out of the window: the light in the room below had been switched on: it fell on the drive in a big square of gold cut into smaller squares by the bars criss-crossing the window. As we watched, a man's shadow appeared in the patch of light: he stood, either looking out or with his back to the window. All we could see was the silhouette.

'Rifai,' Hermann whispered.

Then the shadow reached out an arm and the curtains were drawn together, cutting off the light except for a thin strip of gold where they met. We heard the car being started.

'Hamid will park it in the garage,' Hermann said. 'Then he will go to the kitchen for his supper. Abdul has to stay on duty in the hall. He is too afraid to tell Rifai that he hasn't had his food. Unless I go down to take his place he will stay there.'

The headlights of the Rolls lit up the drive below. I hoped Paula was good and deep in the shrubbery.

'What about Helen?'

I felt Hermann's shrug.

'She and Silvio'll hear the car being parked in the garage,' I said. 'She'll panic. She'll come rushing back.'

'Maybe.'

'Well, what are we going to *do*?' All this Teutonic calm was beginning to get me. 'You're in command, Hermann, remember?'

'*Ja*,' he said briskly, like it was just another desert patrol. 'Listen. First we get Alberto outside.'

'How?'

'Sheets.'

'I beg your pardon?'

'Sheets. Bed sheets. See.' He started dragging the sheets off Helen's bed. 'Tie these, Harry. Quick.' He went out again and I did what I was told. He was back in a second with more sheets. 'These are mine. Tie them too.' I did what I was told.

'Is it long enough?' He looked out of the window. '*Ja*, I think so.'

This time I didn't need to be told. I tied the end of one of the sheets to the handles of Alberto's carry-cot. It was too dark to see his face but his little eyes were gleaming: he wasn't missing a thing. Poor little bleeder, I thought: swung down the wall like a bunch of bananas.

'Maybe he will cry,' Hermann said.

'What do you mean, cry? This is no squealing Arab. This is Alberto. He's a pro.' All the same, as I took him over to the window, I whispered, 'Just keep your mouth shut this once, sport, and I'll see you right, I promise.'

As we pushed him over the side he gave a gurgle and started waving his fists around. I couldn't tell whether it was because he was enjoying it or was just pissed off.

'Slowly, Hermann, slowly.'

We inched it down. I hoped Paula was watching. If not, she was going to get a hell of a shock when Alberto suddenly came swinging through the branches. The strip of light from between the curtains fell on the cot as it went past. I saw that Alberto was still waving his fists around furiously. If Rifai chose this moment to open his curtains he was going to have a lot of trouble believing his eyes. The cot disappeared into the top of the shrubs and then hit something solid. I prayed it was Paula. After a few seconds we felt a sharp tug on the sheets. We tugged back and found the weight gone. At least Alberto was sprung.

'Now what? Should I tie you up?'

'We have no time,' Hermann said. 'And no rope.' He reached into his jacket and pulled out a nasty looking Lüger. 'You will have to use this.'

I knew these krauts were fanatic and all but this was ridiculous.

'I couldn't, Hermann.'

'Here.' He pointed at the back of his skull.

'Think of the mess.'

'You hold it like this, see?'

'Oh, you mean *hit* you?'

'And make it hard, Harry. My head is very thick.'

'Hermann, I don't like this—'

'You must do it, Harry. Now. Rifai may come up at any minute, and the nurse too. I will say I heard a noise in the nursery and came in to investigate. That is all I remember.'

I took the gun, though it wasn't easy. Personally I never touch the things.

'Bend down a little, Hermann, I can't reach.'

Hermann knelt on the bed. I remembered how I'd almost run out on him and felt ashamed. I'm telling you that because it's not something I feel very often.

'Hermann,' I said, 'I just want you to know that your plan was great'—I took aim—'and when everything went wrong, you did even better improvising'—Just pretend it's ping-pong, I told myself—'I want you to know that in my book, Hermann, you'll always be an officer—'

'It's true, Harry?'

'—and a gentleman,' I said.

Then I socked him good and hard—for old times' sake. He went over like a log and he stayed down.

I'd already decided I wasn't going to trust that vine again, so I spent a minute tying one end of the knotted sheets to the foot of Helen's bed. Hermann was flat out on the floor and seemed comfortable enough. The last thing I did was lock the door.

Going down the sheets was a lot easier than coming up the vine, but I took it slowly all the same, letting myself down a few inches at a time so as not to make a noise. I wondered if Paula had got to the car yet. I knew the cot was heavy but I hoped she'd reached the wall at least. I'd got as far as the window of Rifai's study—the light was still on inside—when I heard footsteps: hurried, nervous sort of steps, stopping suddenly and then starting again as if the person, whoever it was, didn't want to be seen. Paula! I thought—but she wouldn't have come back, she couldn't be that stupid. I hung there like a constipated spider, swinging slowly around, pouring sweat, trying to see who it was, not daring to move any lower for the noise it would make. The footsteps sounded again, much closer. And then I spotted her, less than a dozen feet away, half-crouching, running from one bush to the next, coming down the drive from the stables. It was Helen!

I don't know how she didn't see me, dangling up there a few feet above her. Maybe she had her eyes as well as her mind on the side door and couldn't think of anything else. Whatever it was, she reached the door without seeing either the knotted shcets or me hanging on them, and popped inside. The strain was too much. I just slid down the rest of the way like a peeled banana and crashed through the shrubs.

'Harry, is that you?' The shock was something awful: and coming on top of everything else it was the last straw.

'No, it's flipping Father Christmas. What the hell are you doing here?'

'Waiting for you.'

Jesus! I was speechless. In thirty seconds Helen would reach the nursery door, find it locked, go into Hermann's room, find it empty, and then more than likely go into hysterics. We'd have to run for it again.

I dragged Paula out of the shrubbery, still hanging on to Alberto's cot. I took one handle myself, gave her the other, and said, 'Just keep running till I tell you to stop.'

And then we were off, belting down the drive, me panting like a leaky old bellows, Paula with her hair flying and Alberto bouncing about between us, shaking his fists and squeaking like a teddy bear. Every second I was expecting to hear a shout —or even a shot. There was no telling what Rifai would do when he found another baby had been nicked, and this one right under his nose. I hoped for Hermann's sake that I'd put him out for a good long spell.

'Left,' I gasped, and we cut off the drive, dodged a couple of bushes, stumbled through two flower-beds and almost ploughed straight into the wall before we spotted it.

Shed! I thought. Shed! It was near the corner of the wall. The door was unlocked, just as Hermann had promised.

I set up the stepladder under the tree.

'You go up first and get on to the ladder on the other side. I'll hand him up to you.'

She went up like a squirrel and was over the wall in two seconds. I carried the cot up carefully. Alberto was muttering away to himself and generally threatening to throw a small fit:

and who could blame him? I laid the cot on top of the wall: Paula picked it up by the ends and started backing down the ladder. Suddenly she stopped and stared over my shoulder.

'Look.'

Through the trees we could see lights springing on all over the house. The front door was flung open and a tiny figure appeared in the lighted doorway. It didn't move, just stood there silhouetted against the light, staring out into the garden, helpless. I had a feeling it was Rifai. I hoped he was doing his nut.

Chapter Twenty

'WASN'T THAT *exciting*? And weren't you brave? Swinging down the wall like that, hiding in the bushes. What *will* you be up to next?'

No, you're right, it wasn't me she was talking to.

'We're not even sleepy, are we? We're ready for more. What shall we do now? Stick up a bank?'

Alberto sneezed.

'Oh, well, perhaps we'll just go home and have a nice hot bath.'

We were back in the city, whipping along the Lungotevere, almost home. Paula had Alberto on her lap. She was chatting away to him, pretending it was all a great lark, but I'd heard her sniff a couple of times, and once she wiped her eyes quickly. Alberto on the other hand was quite his old self again. He hadn't even thrown that fit I'd been expecting. Once we'd got him over the wall and into the car he settled down immediately and probably would have gone back to sleep if Paula had only let him. I had to hand it to him. Not many would put up with being tossed around like an old cement bag, and still come up smiling.

I swung left on to the Ponte Garibaldi. In a few minutes we'd be home and then I'd have to call the newspapers and 'announce' the snatch. I wondered if Morland knew what he was talking about. On the basis of past experience, the answer to that was easy.

Alberto sneezed again. I passed her my handkerchief. 'Here, blow his nose. And yours too.'

'Do you think he's caught a cold?'

'He'll be lucky if that's all he's caught after what he's been through tonight.'

'Nonsense.' She bounced him up and down on her knee. 'We're tough, aren't we? We can take it.'

It reminded me of what the fight managers say when their boys are carried out on stretchers.

Via dello Scorpione was locked and shuttered for the night. Only Giorgio's was still showing a light. I drove past slowly and saw him leaning across the bar chatting with a customer.

'You run upstairs with Alberto. I'll bring the cot.'

'Can't we show him to Giorgio now? We can say he's better.' She was dying to tell the world she'd got her boy back.

'And when Selim starts crying tomorrow morning?'

'Oh, all right. When are we going to get rid of him?'

'Get *rid* of him. He's the one that's going to get us our quarter of a million dollars. Just remember that.'

'Well, he hasn't done much about getting it yet.' She slammed the door.

I pulled the cot out of the back and followed her up the stairs. When we reached the second floor she stopped and said, 'Listen.'

'What?'

'It sounds like Selim crying.'

We looked at each other, both thinking the same thing.

'Harry, quick!'

I tore up the steps three at a time, but she kept right on my heels. Selim's crying rose and fell like an air-raid siren. I ran across the living-room into the bedroom. Then I stopped. Morland lay on his back, hands folded, nose pointed at the ceiling, stiff as a rod.

'He's croaked,' I said.

'Oh, *no*.' Paula rushed past me. 'Jonathan, Jonathan.' She

dumped Alberto on the bed and bent over Morland. 'Harry, do something.'

What could I do? It was a typical Morland performance, croaking on us at the worst possible moment.

'We should never have left him alone.' She bent lower and put her ear to his chest. Selim, who was in the cot right behind her, got his second wind and really started bellowing. 'Wait!' She took the 'corpse' by the shoulders and gave it a little shake. It groaned.

'He's alive, Harry, he's alive.'

I might have guessed.

'Call a doctor, quick, and an ambulance too.'

'Wait a minute.' I bent over the bed. 'Morland, can you hear me?' There was another groan. 'Well, if you can hear me you can open your eyes, for God's sake—'

'Harry, what's the matter with you? This man's dying—well, if you won't go, I will.'

I grabbed her arm. 'Call an ambulance now and half the street will come in to see what's going on. There are two babies in this flat, I'd like to remind you, and neither of them belongs to us.'

She went as white as a sheet.

'Trust Harry Brighton to keep his wits about him,' she said. I'd never seen her eyes so cold and angry. 'I will say this for you though, you never stop thinking, not for a second. Ice-cold Harry, they call him, always one step ahead of the game. All right, we'll just let him die—'

Then I hit her, good and hard, smack across the face, and she sat down with a bump.

I said, 'I'm pretty sick of hearing you tell me about Harry Brighton, but you're right about one thing. I'm still thinking, and it's lucky I am because otherwise you'd have the fuzz up here in five minutes and that wouldn't be very nice, either for you or me, but particularly for Morland. Twenty years, dear, that's the name of the game. Your Jonathan is going to be deeply touched when he finds out we whipped him off to hospital in an ambulance to save his life. The fact that it cost him twenty years is probably something he'll overlook. Twenty years? What am I saying? He won't have to spend more than six months in the nick, because that's how long he'll last if they stick him inside. I'm thinking all right, you can bet on that. And what's more I'm going to go on thinking. And if thinking is something that's beyond you right now, then do me one small favour. Belt up.'

I bent over Morland again. 'Did you hear that?' I said. He opened his eyes and nodded. 'Any comments?' He shook his head. 'Right.' I turned to Paula. 'Bring me a blanket, quick.' She stared at me. There was a nasty red mark on her cheek. I clapped my hands. 'Come on, snap out of it.' She got up slowly and went to the cupboard. 'And for God's sake do something about that screaming kid.'

I gave Morland a shot of brandy and then wrapped him in the blanket. He was very pale and breathing in short gasps, but he seemed to be getting stronger. There's nothing like a mention of the nick to pump life into a creaky ticker. Alberto, who was still on the bed, got up on his hands and knees to watch us. Morland spotted him for the first time and gripped my hand.

'You did it, Harry.' It came out in a gasp.

I nodded.

'I always knew you had it in you.'

'Thanks.'

Morland stretched out his other hand and touched Alberto's hair. 'It's good to have him back, isn't it?'

I shrugged. Right at that moment two babies were just double trouble.

'I'm taking you to hospital.'

'It's not necessary, Harry. I'll be all right.'

'I know,' I said, 'except you may croak at any minute, and if you do, I want it to happen in hospital.'

That shook him. 'I wouldn't make any bets on it if I were you,' he snarled. 'I'm not finished yet.'

'That's what I thought.'

Now he was looking much better, there was even a spot of colour in his cheeks. I reckoned he was strong enough to be moved, so I wrapped the blanket round him tightly, stuck another cognac into him so as to keep at least one cylinder firing, and picked him up. He didn't weigh a thing.

Paula opened the front door for us. She hadn't said a word since I'd socked her, but she'd been looking at me in a very funny way, rubbing her cheek. Probably plotting revenge, I thought.

'Don't wait up,' I said coolly, and I didn't look back.

I took Morland across the river to a big clinic in Aventino. It was the only place I knew in Rome apart from the public hospitals, and I didn't think it was fair to stick old Morland in a public ward with a lot of jabbering Ites. A doctor came out of the emergency reception centre to have a look at him and sent for a stretcher right away.

'Be sure and call the newspapers tonight, Harry.'

'Don't try to talk now.'

'Once the story gets into the papers the police will be round to see Rifai and he'll have to admit it.'

'Yes, but will he pay?'

'Just tell me how he can refuse.'

'It won't be easy collecting, not with the fuzz tipped off.'

'That's true.' Morland blew a big sigh. 'I'll have to think of something.' He said it like the whole world was resting on his shoulders, and him sick and maybe dying. As they rolled him away he lifted his fingers just a fraction.

206

I waved back. 'Good luck. I'll come and see you tomorrow.'

I went inside to give the details to the nurse at the reception desk. It's funny how little you know about people, even those you think you know well. Age? Nationality? Place of birth? Father's name? Home address? The first three were easy, I took them out of his ticket—out of Mr Robert Browning's ticket, that is. For the others I made up answers.

'Religion?'

I shrugged.

The nurse said, 'Protestant,' with a little sneer, and wrote it down.

'Next of kin?'

I shrugged again.

'We must have the next of kin.'

'I'm his cousin.'

'That will do. Sign here.' I signed. 'Thank you. That will be thirty thousand lire.'

'What for?'

'A deposit against medical expenses. It is a rule of the clinic. You can pay the rest later.'

'I've only got fifty dollars on me.'

'I will take it.' She took it and gave me a receipt. 'Next time bring lire please.'

I don't remember driving away. In fact I don't remember anything until after I'd stopped in a little trat off the Piazza di Santa Maria and had a double cognac. When I'd paid for it I had exactly one thousand six hundred and twenty lire left. It's times like that when your training shows. I took out the list of newspapers Morland had given me to phone ... *Il Messagero, La Stampa, Il Corriere della Sera* ... I didn't bother to go on. If there was one thing I wasn't up to doing that night it was speaking Italian, by intuition or any other way. At the bottom of the list there was a section headed 'English-speaking.'

I rang the first name, which was the Associated Press.

'Yeah?' For a moment I thought our Tony had joined the fourth estate.

'Listen,' I said, 'I've got some hot news for you'—this is how you have to talk to these people—'Yusuf Rifai's baby son has just been kidnapped.'

'Come again.'

I gave it to him slowly.

'And they're asking a ransom of two hundred and fifty thousand dollars,' I said.

'You're kidding.'

'Of course, I do this every evening just for kicks.'

'How do you know about this kidnapping?'

'Because I'm the one that did it.'

'Oh, sure, and my name's Ho Chi Minh.'

'It may very well be,' I said, and hung up. Screw the A.P.

The next one was United Press International. This time I got an Italian who took it all down in longhand and kept asking me to spell words for him. 'Millionaire—it has two ells, no?' He was really impressed though when I told him the tip was coming straight from the horse's mouth.

'*Davvero? Duecentocinquantamila dollari! Bravo, signore, e buona fortuna.*'

Your Ite has a great respect for easy money.

The last name on the list was Reuters, and I got this really chintzy English voice on the line. He didn't want to listen at first but in the end he took it down, muttering something about 'not the kind of thing we usually handle.' When I said I was the boy who'd done the dirty deed, he perked up a bit and said, 'Oh, really, could we have your name and telephone number?'

After that I needed another double, so it was well after two before I got home. And to tell the truth I wasn't exactly hurrying. For one thing, I was still pretty dazed from having had to cough up my last dollars to keep Morland's ticker running.

For another, I was remembering the punch-up I'd had with Paula earlier and thinking how things between us kept on getting worse. It came to me suddenly as I was walking up the stairs that I'd had just about enough of them all, Alberto included. I was even sick of that lousy two hundred and fifty thousand dollars which somehow never appeared. If I had my choice, I said to myself, I'd just as soon pack my bag when no one's looking and do a quick fade. Let them have the money, if they ever got it. Well, I did have a choice, you're probably thinking, so why didn't I go? The answer is, it wasn't that easy. I mean choices are not really choices, are they? They're just another word for day-dreams. What I would have done if—it's the 'if' that stops it being a choice. Most of us have only one choice at a time, and what sort of choice is that? With Morland in hospital and Paula on her own with two kids, what sort of choice did I have?

A light was showing under the bedroom door. I guessed she was waiting for round two to begin. Then I saw that the couch hadn't even been made up—a clear provocation. But I'd had enough for one night. I'd make my own bed. I went to the cupboard where she kept the bedclothes: they weren't there. That did it. I wasn't going to sleep in my clothes on a bare couch, even if it meant having another go with Paula. I barged into the bedroom without knocking. She was lying in bed, propped up, reading. She peeped over the top of her book but didn't say anything. I noticed Alberto was stowed away in the carry-cot on a wooden chest under the window. Selim still had possession of the master cot.

'Where are my sheets?'

Paula pointed at the wardrobe. She watched me open it.

'There aren't any here.'

She shrugged.

I closed the wardrobe. 'Look,' I said, 'I don't want to get nasty—'

'Then don't.' She smiled. The mark on her cheek had gone all blue.

'It's just that I happen to like sleeping between sheets. And furthermore I think I'm entitled to sleep between sheets.'

She put the book on the bedside table, tossed one of the pillows on to the floor, settled down on her back, switched off the light and said, 'These are the only sheets there are.'

Later on, much later, I said, 'And all it took was a sock on the jaw.'

She giggled. 'Don't be silly. Women don't fall for that sort of thing.'

Maybe, but I'm passing it on to you anyway for what it's worth.

Chapter Twenty-one

'WOULD YOU like a boiled egg?'

Would I like a boiled egg?

'Or toast. We've got honey and strawberry jam. And one peach. Would you like a peach?'

'I'd like a kiss.'

'What? In front of the children? She rolled away off the bed and ran out laughing. I lay back and stretched. It had been a long time since I'd had breakfast in bed, any bed.

Alberto was sitting in his high chair by the window watching me. He'd got his old rubber duck on the little table across the arms and he was pulling its beak and twisting its tail and generally getting the feel of it again. He'd put on weight, even I could see that, and with his long black curls and toasty brown skin he looked a real devil. What a time he was going to give the birds, I thought, and I sighed. It made me feel old.

Paula called out from the kitchen, 'Do you think it's in the papers?'

'What?'

'What we did last night.'

'All of it.'

There was silence. Then her face appeared in the doorway and a bit of peach skin flew by. I sighed again. She was even peeling it for me. What a morning! Then Alberto dropped his duck on the floor and gurgled politely to me to pick it up. I wasn't fooled. He just didn't like being left out.

Breakfast took a long time and was a pretty messy business. First Alberto joined us on the bed and soon had himself smeared in jam and egg shells and I don't know what else. Then Paula said it was a shame to leave Selim out of it so she fetched him from the cot. He didn't really take to it though and you couldn't blame him since it probably wasn't the sort of thing he was used to. He spat out the spoonful of strawberry jam I gave him and wouldn't even taste the honey. The only thing he seemed to want was Alberto's rubber duck, which wasn't very smart of him. Alberto let him have it for a few minutes, then reached over, yanked it away and gave poor old Selim a shove which sent him arse over tip. If I hadn't caught him he'd have rolled clean off the bed.

'Naughty boy,' said Paula, beaming.

Alberto gurgled and thumped the duck on the bed a couple of times in case anyone had missed the point. Selim started crying.

I'll remember that morning for a long time. Not because anything special happened, the contrary in fact. I'll remember it because all the little unimportant things which happen every day and which you forget because they're always the same were just a little different that day. The morning sun on the Janiculum, which I'd seen a dozen times before but never quite like it was that day, all fresh and sparkling. Our old bat across the way waving through the lines of washing and shouting something about *varicella*, the same thing she shouted every morning, and me giving the same answer, a shrug, only knowing that things were different this time. Mostly I remember Paula running up to the terrace between bits of housework to see how the babies were getting on, just like she'd always done when one or the other had been there alone: and this time stopping to smile at me, a new smile I hadn't seen before, the one you only get from a bird when you've—well, a private smile. Once she ran her fingers through my hair as she went by and once she stopped behind me and bit me on the neck. Little things like that.

To start with we put Selim and Alberto into the playpen together, but it didn't work. Alberto had pretty definite ideas about what belonged to him and it included all the toys and about nine-tenths of the space in the pen. Selim just crouched in one corner looking very nervous. Now and then Alberto would come rolling across to have a closer look at him, thinking maybe he was just a bigger duck, but there was no more rough stuff. They both seemed to know who was boss. After a bit I took Alberto out of the pen to give Selim a go at the toys. Alberto didn't like that at all. He crawled back to the pen, grabbed the bars and shook them. Selim almost pissed himself. I could see that if this sort of thing went on we'd have a neurotic baby on our hands, so I carted Alberto off to the other side of the terrace, gave him the old broken flower-pot and told him to get on with his gardening. He sat there for a few minutes looking at the pot and then at the pen and then back at the pot. Finally he gave a gurgle as if to say, what the hell, and got down to his digging.

'Of course he doesn't like Selim taking what's his,' Paula said. 'You forget, he's never had anything of his own. No parents to speak of, then adopted by Tony and offered out for rent. Poor little fellow. How do you expect him to behave?'

'I don't know, but all I can say is that for an underprivileged orphan he seems to live in pretty high style.'

'That's because he's a professional. You said so yourself. He has to be. He'd never have survived otherwise, would you, darling—?'

'I know exactly what you mean,' I said. 'My own childhood was somewhat the same.' But she laughed and put out her tongue.

That morning lasted a long time and was full of sun and laughter and that's why I remember it.

Just before lunch Paula went downstairs to do some shopping. I was going to ask her to buy a paper but I couldn't bring myself to spoil the mood. Another couple of hours wouldn't matter, I thought. Five minutes later she was back, panting.

'Harry, I heard it on the radio—in Giorgio's—couldn't understand it all—heard Rifai's name though, and something about the two hundred and fifty thousand dollars. Oh, Harry, I'm afraid.'

Me too, I thought, as I held her tight. 'There's nothing to worry about,' I said. Not half.

'It was awful. They're all sitting around listening to it, Giorgio and Mrs Giorgio and the others, saying how horrible it is and who could do such a thing. Oh, Harry, why did we do it?'

'We were conned,' I said.

'No,' She jerked away. 'That's not true. We were—oh, I don't know, stupid and greedy, I suppose. I'm always doing stupid things with my life, I told you.'

I wondered if that included me. Probably, I thought. I made her sit down and dry her eyes.

'Listen,' I said, 'whatever you think about it now, we're caught. Morland's in hospital, maybe dying. God knows what's happened to poor old Hermann. It's up to us and we have to go through with it. We can't stop now. We can't say, sorry, Mr Rifai, here's your baby back, we didn't really mean it.'

'We needn't take his money.'

'Now none of that,' I said quickly. 'You thought you knew about Rifai before. Well, now you know what he's really like. Can you think of anyone in the world who deserves to be separated from a quarter of a million more than Yusuf Rifai? What we're doing is practically a public service.'

'I don't mind making him pay. I just don't think we should —Couldn't we make him give it to a charity or something?'

'A *charity*! I'm a charity,' I said. 'I'm a charity that's been supporting you and Morland and Alberto and Selim, and I've

214

now got exactly one thousand lire and some loose change left. You don't understand. We are broke—and I mean skint.'

She looked at me, the tears starting again.

'Anyway,' I said, 'who's going to pay Morland's hospital bills?'

That did it. She broke up. I held her again and stroked her hair because you have to be soft with birds when they get like that. But don't think I was going soft myself, not for a moment. It's true I never wanted to do the snatch, but I'd done it, and I was going to get paid for it, and that was that. It was the professional approach. Alberto would have understood.

Morland lay propped up on a heap of fat pillows staring across the room at a blank wall. There was a soft, deep smile on his lips. He had on a pair of white pyjamas a shade darker than his skin, his hair was neatly combed, his nails were spotless. Everything about him had a scrubbed and polished look. Frankly, I'd never seen him so clean.

He didn't look round when I came in. He just went on staring at the wall. What with this funny smile and all it looked like he really had died this time, and I was just thinking that at least he'd died happy when suddenly he clapped his hands twice, gave a short barking laugh, and then went back to staring at the wall. Not died, I thought. Just flipped.

They'd given him a nice room with only one other bed in it, and that was empty. There was a jug of orange juice beside the bed and a bowl of flowers on the white dressing-table. The sound of water splashing in a fountain came through the open window. Morland had probably never had it so good, I thought. It seemed a pity he'd had to almost croak in order to get it, but that's the way things are. Coffins are what they line with satin.

I walked to the foot of the bed. His eyes bulged. 'Harry,' he squawked, and fished something out of his ear. It was a small plastic earphone connected to a radio dial set in the wall above the bed. 'Have you heard?'

'About the snatch?' I nodded.

'No, no. About the press conference Rifai gave this morning?'

'No. What about it?'

'Oh, Harry.' He shut his eyes and sighed. 'I heard it on the news first an hour ago. I was listening to it again when you came in. I've memorized his exact words. He said, "Gentlemen, at a moment such as this a father does not ask himself questions. He does not wonder whether he has chosen the wisest course. He does not listen to the prudent counsels of those who caution that attempts at extortion in any form are best met with a firm refusal. He acts, gentlemen. A father acts. I have already given instructions for a sum of two hundred and fifty thousand dollars to be prepared. I shall pay it to these men when and how and where they demand it. I despise them for the crime they have committed. But I would grovel at their feet for the life of my son." ' Morland opened his eyes. 'What do you think of that?'

I wasn't sure what I thought of it. I wasn't sure at all.

'It means he's going to pay, Harry. He can't get out of it now. Think of it. A quarter of a million.' His eyes were shining like he'd seen a vision.

'We haven't got it yet.'

'We will, don't worry. I'm working on a plan now, something absolutely foolproof, something that can't go wrong—'

Well, I knew all about those. But I let him ramble on for a while. It was his big moment after all, and from the way his ticker was behaving he might never have another.

'. . . all the same I think we ought to call him right away.'

'How's that?'

'I was saying we ought to ring Rifai now, strike while the iron's hot.'

'But you haven't worked out a plan for collecting yet.'

'We'll do that later. What you should do now is tell him we've got both babies and that we don't want any more nonsense out of him. Be tough. I was too polite before. Force is the only thing Rifai's kind understands. Tell him that he's got to be ready to leave the villa with the money at a moment's notice, day or night. Tell him to sit by his phone, that'll keep him on edge. And of course warn him to keep the police out of it from now on.' Morland rubbed his hands. 'Yes, in fact a few threats about what could happen to Selim might be in order at this stage.'

I sneered. 'So much for the old minimum level of morality.'

Morland flushed. 'What's the matter, Harry, going soft?'

'Don't worry about me. Just see you don't croak before you've thought up a way of collecting.'

'Charming, charming. What a colleague, what a friend!'

'Watch your language, Morland.'

'The trouble with you, Harry Brighton—'

But I never found out what it was because a nurse came in just then with a copy of the *Corriere della Sera* for Morland.

'It's in here too, Harry. Look.'

There was a big piece on the front page headed '*Delitto Barbaro*' and a picture of Rifai standing with a guy in uniform who turned out to be the chief of police. He had his arm around Rifai's shoulders. It was a very touching scene.

'. . . police searching every inch of villa grounds . . . crime believed committed by band of armed men . . . German bodyguard brutally beaten . . . mysterious telephone calls . . .' Morland read out bits of it. 'They've also got his press conference. It's definite, Harry. He's going to pay.'

'We'll see,' I said, but I couldn't help feeling he was right. It looked as though we'd screwed the Arab a treat. 'Shall I call him now?'

'Yes. Tell him to stand by for orders. You'd better not ring from the clinic. They may be tracing calls to the villa. Come back when you've talked to him.'

'What about the threats?' I asked, watching him closely. 'Any ideas? Let's have something nice and juicy.'

'Oh, for God's sake, Harry.' He stared out of the window. 'Use your imagination.'

I went to the door.

'And Harry'—I turned, he was grinning from ear to ear—'be sure to ask him how the air is up there today.'

I walked down the hill to Viale Aventino to make the call: to the same café in fact from where we'd phoned Rifai the first time right after we'd snatched Selim. It seemed such a long time ago now. I was thinking about what the paper had said— 'Delitto Barbaro'—and of Giorgio and his missus asking who could do such a thing. But then I remembered Rifai's press conference and all that crap about being a father. I'd have said he didn't deserve to have a son if I hadn't learned by then that kids are not prizes for good behaviour. But there was something else he definitely didn't deserve to have and that was what I kept in my mind. I mean the two hundred and fifty thousand.

'Mr Abercromby?'

'No, it's me.'

'Ah, the estimable Mr Fitch. How you two keep dodging about! Well, I'm glad you called. I wanted to say that your exploit last night was superb. Really, I mean it. To hit back like that without a moment's hesitation. It takes nerve, my friend. I know.'

'Thanks,' I said.

'In fact, I was wondering if, by any chance, well—I don't know quite how to say this.' He gave his little hissing laugh. 'What I mean is, would you be available for a little contract work on the side? I pay well, I assure you, and—'

218

'Mr Rifai,' I said. 'Has anyone ever told you that you have a very childish sense of humour?'

He laughed again. 'No, Mr Fitch. No one has ever told me that.' His voice didn't shake exactly, it just came over a little tighter than before. I wondered what it felt like to be worth a hundred million and to be able to break people like little sticks whenever you fancied it, and to have someone on the end of a telephone line just out of reach.

I said, 'We'll let you know when we want the money, so keep it at the house.'

'Ah, then you've heard about my press conference already.'

'Yes, and don't worry, it's not likely you'll have to grovel at our feet.'

'I am relieved to hear that, Mr Fitch. All the same, you know, you shouldn't believe everything you read in the newspapers.'

'Oh?'

'In fact some of the reports you see are nothing but fiction, pure fiction, from start to finish.'

It didn't come as a shock this time. In a way I'd been expecting it. In a way it was almost a relief. 'What a tricky little devil you are,' I said.

'My dear Mr Fitch, in a discussion of this nature the amateur invariably reveals himself by a tendency to resort to personal insult.'

'So you don't want your son back after all.'

'On the contrary, I want him back unharmed and in good health within twenty-four hours.'

'You'll get him when you've paid us.'

'But I have paid, Mr Fitch—that is to say, I have announced my intention of paying, and by tomorrow morning the trans-action will have been completed. For the benefit of the public, that is, which, like you, tends to believe what it reads in the newspapers. It was a good idea of yours to use public opinion against me but like other—and better—men than yourselves, you will soon discover that it is a sword with two edges. You thought that public opinion would be outraged at the prospect of a millionaire refusing to pay a ransom for his son. How right you were. And now consider for a moment how doubly enraged that same beast will be when it learns that even after the ransom has been paid the kidnappers refuse to disgorge their prey. That can mean only one thing. They have destroyed it. My friend, I would advise you for your own good, your own health and your own safety to return my son to me before tomorrow morning. If you do not you will be branded not merely as kidnappers but as murderers as well. Surely you don't think you can escape detection indefinitely. There is only one way you can do that, but I know you haven't the stomach for it. You told me so in that first call, or was it Mr Abercromby? In any case, when you said no harm would come to my son you told me all I needed to know. And then ringing up to inquire about Alberto's health. Really, Mr Fitch. Frankly, this whole affair has given me more cause for laughter than concern.'

It was the last chance to put the screws on him, the last chance to tell him we might have just a little more stomach than he thought. To tell him that old Selim's health hadn't exactly improved and might just keep on getting worse. To tell him that babies were easily disposable. It would have been easy to say all those things. Too easy maybe.

'Well, Mr Fitch, are you thinking?'

'Yes,' I said. 'I'm thinking.'

'Let me give you something more to think about. I have just brought some members of my organization here from Beirut. I have instructed them to conduct an investigation of this affair independently of the police. As you might imagine there are certain sources of information available to me which the authorities are not aware of. The person of Hermann Schmidt, for example. It is possible that these people of mine will find you before the police do. I hope for your sake they do not. It would be very unpleasant for all of you, but particularly for the girl.'

It was like a knife in the gut.

'What girl?'

Rifai chuckled. 'I believe you have enough to think about now.' I swallowed and swallowed again but my throat stayed dry. Hermann, I thought. But he wouldn't talk, or if he did, Paula would be the last person he'd mention.

'You have been thinking a long time, Mr Fitch.'

'I'm finished thinking,' I said. 'Goodbye—'

'Wait, please, just a moment. There is something else.'

'What?'—We'd have to get Selim out of the flat before tomorrow morning, I thought.

'There is still some business we can do.'

'Business?'—And what about Hermann? We couldn't just leave him.

'You have something I want, Mr Fitch. I am willing to pay to get it.'

'Pay? What for? Selim?' I couldn't think with all this chatter going on.

'You are not paying attention, Mr Fitch. Selim is my son. I don't buy what already belongs to me. I am referring to Alberto.'

'Oh, yes.' It didn't register for a moment.

'Yes, Mr Fitch. And since you deal in this rare commodity—babies—I thought that an offer for Alberto would not be out of place.'

Alberto! But of course. I'd never thought of that. I couldn't help laughing.

'Have I said something funny?'

'Oh, no, not at all. It's just that here I've been sweating to try and sell you back Selim and all the time you were ready to buy Alberto.'

'We can do business then?'

'Why not? How much?'

'Shall we say—ten thousand?'

'Please, Mr Rifai. That hardly covers our expenses.'

He laughed. 'Yes, you must have put a lot of planning into it. It was a good job. I meant it when I said you could work for me. Well, let's double that. Twenty thousand, say.'

'Don't think me rude, Mr Rifai, but I must point out that you're the one who's given himself away this time.'

'What do you mean?'

'I know what you said to Mr Abercromby about Alberto, how he'd opened your eyes to the better side of babies, so to speak. How you'd been given a choice of sons and how you'd chosen Alberto. You showed your hand there, Mr Rifai, and you're going to have to pay for it.'

At first I thought a hose had burst on the other end of the line, then I realized it was only Rifai laughing. 'Mr Fitch!' he gasped. 'Oh, Mr Fitch, what a character you are. And also a shrewd businessman, I can see that. Take my advice and stick to business from now on. Crime requires narrower and more specialized talents. Well, you have caught me fairly. I admit it And you are quite right, I value Alberto very highly. Perhaps higher than you think. I'll tell you what I'll pay for him, Mr Fitch. Two hundred and fifty thousand dollars'—he spluttered with laughter—'and not a penny more.'

'In cash?'

'Nothing bigger than tens, Mr Fitch.'

I whistled. I couldn't help it. Our quarter of a million—and not a ransom either. A straight sale. Legal!—Well, almost. The thing was I knew we were going to have to give up Alberto anyway. We'd hardly be doing him a favour by handing him back to Tony rather than Rifai. Of course, Tony would certainly squawk at Alberto being sold without a by-your-leave. But I didn't think for a moment we couldn't square him, not

222

with a kitty of two hundred and fifty thousand dollars to draw on. It all came together so beautifully. Rifai got his son back, Alberto got a fancy home, and we got our quarter of a million. For the first time in my life I felt that fairy godmother I'd always been looking for sitting on my shoulder. It taught me a lot about fairy godmothers.

'Well, Mr Fitch, is it a deal?'

I paused a few seconds longer, thinking. Then I said, 'I'd do it like a shot, Mr Rifai, believe me, but there's just one thing worrying me.'

'What's that?'

'Alberto's health. I'd have to be sure I wasn't sending him somewhere where he might get sick.'

'My dear man, what sort of treatment do you imagine he's going to receive in my home?'

'Oh, the best,' I said. 'Nothing but the best. I'm sure of that. It's not the treatment I'm worried about. It's—how shall I put it?—the general living conditions, the climate if you like.'

'The *climate*?'

'The altitude then.'

'The *altitude*?'

'The air, Mr Rifai. The cold thin air.'

I don't know whether he tore his hair, or ground his teeth, or tied his guts in a knot, or simply did his nut. But I imagined them all happening at once. And it was very nice. But I'll never know for sure because that's when I hung up.

Chapter Twenty-two

Do you ever feel the need for an hour or so to yourself? Time to catch your breath, I mean, time to stop for a moment and try to work out where it all went wrong? Time to pick up the pieces? I do, quite often. In fact, on looking back over my life, I'd say I've probably spent as much time as anyone picking up the pieces. You could even call me an expert at it.

Well, when I came out of that café after phoning Rifai I could see nothing *but* pieces. My head was spinning with them. There was Paula and me with two kids, one of them costing us two hundred a week, the other liable to cost us twenty years—if we were lucky, that is, if Rifai's meatballs didn't find us first. There was Morland at the hospital racking up medical bills he couldn't hope to pay. And there was Hermann. That was a piece I didn't want to even think about.

As I said, you need an hour or so to yourself to sort these things out. I had about ten minutes, which was the time it took me to walk up the hill to the clinic, so it won't surprise you to learn that the only answer I'd come up with was a rather simple one: we had to get out. Quick, quick, quick.

First we had to get Selim back to Rifai. Then Paula and I had to move out of the flat. And finally, Alberto had to go. The first two were easy, but how was I going to tell Paula about the third? I didn't waste time wondering. When the moment came I'd tell her the truth, that I hadn't a penny. She'd have to swallow it. Tough, I know, but what can you do? It's not that I didn't like the little bugger. But two hundred dollars a week! That kind of money could sour any affection.

So much for Alberto.

Then there was Morland. I couldn't see any solution to his problem apart from the obvious one. Him croaking, I mean. And I didn't set much store by that. Morland would never croak to suit anyone. And I didn't think he'd take too kindly to any suggestions from me on the subject. Still, as I walked up the stairs to his room I was thinking that what I had to tell him about Rifai might well do the trick. I was all set to let him have it too—both barrels—when I opened the door and saw his face light up suddenly like a kid's. Poor old Morland, I thought. Picking up the pieces was something he knew a fair bit about too. I just shook my head, and ten years rolled over his face like a shadow.

'What went wrong?'

I shrugged. Morland stared at his feet.

'All that stuff about paying, just for public consumption, I suppose?'

I nodded. Morland sighed. He started picking at a loose thread on the bedspread, picking, picking away. I don't think he feels really comfortable unless everything around him is worn and frayed because that's how he is himself, and I don't mean that in a nasty way. I told him what Rifai had said, most of it, anyway. I left out the bit about Alberto. I couldn't see that knowing about that would do him the slightest good. When I'd finished he gave me a little smile and nodded.

'He was right, you know. What he said to me. We're out of his class.'

'Don't you believe it. We were unlucky, that's all. If you'd been fit you'd have taken him. I'm sure of it.'

'Thanks, Harry.' He patted my hand. 'But I think it's time I packed up.'

'Now none of that,' I said sharply. 'You'll be on your feet in a couple of weeks.' I didn't add that even if he was, I couldn't see him walking out of there, not with all those bills unpaid.

'Maybe.' He blew another big sigh and stared out of the window. I wanted to get back to Paula but I couldn't leave him like this.

'I'm worried about Hermann,' I said.

He nodded vaguely. *He* wasn't worried, I could see that. Morland has a great capacity for not worrying about other people. After a couple of minutes he said in this same vague way, 'What did he say when you threatened Selim?'

Trust Morland to remember that.

'I didn't.'

He frowned. 'Didn't what?'

'Make any threats.'

'Well, for God's sake, why not?'

'What was the point?'

'What was the point?' He laughed, a nasty sneering laugh. 'She really has turned you soft, hasn't she?'

'It's nothing to do with her. It's just—'

'Yes?'

'It's just—' I didn't know how to say it, I wasn't even sure what I meant. 'Put it this way,' I said. 'Granted we'd never actually hurt Selim, no matter what, but I think we shouldn't even talk about it because that's the first step towards doing it. Never mind that *we* know we're not going any further, I think we shouldn't even take that first step. I don't want us—that's you and me—to get used to even *talking* about hurting a kid. I don't want even the idea to occur. Got it?'

Morland stared at me like he couldn't believe his ears. 'Harry Brighton, are you feeling all right?'

'And don't get cute either.'

A snigger turned into a chuckle and then slowly, like a seam splitting, into hysterical laughter. Eyes screwed up, tears streaming down his face, he rolled around, hugging himself and thumping the mattress with his fist, laughing in great gulps and half-choking in between. It was a disgusting performance.

226

'Oh, oh, oh, this is going to kill me.'

'Please,' I said. 'Oh, please.'

'Harry Brighton joins the human race. What a day! Are those bells I hear? Where are the flags, the cannon? Summon the young men, bid the maidens dance, let the trumpeters sound forth—' and so on, really disgusting. I was just wondering whether I could risk clocking him one, when the door opened and this strange-looking character staggered in. He had bandages and plaster all over his face except for one eye and his right arm was in a plaster cast. He stopped when he saw us and stood by the door swaying a little.

'Yes?' Morland said nervously. He started reaching for the bell-push above his bed.

'Jonathan. Harry. It's me.'

'*Hermann!*'

'*Ja*, Hermann,' the muffled voice said. You couldn't see the lips, only the bandages moving. The swaying was getting worse so I led him over to the spare bed and made him lie down.

'What happened?' I said—as if I needed to ask.

A funny sound came out of the blob of bandages. It sounded like a growl.

'Rifai?' I said.

The blob nodded.

'Bastard.'

Rifai hadn't believed a word of his story, he said, even with the lump I'd left him on the back of the head. Abdul and Hamid had worked him over during the night, and when the three new meatballs arrived from Beirut, the fun had really started. They'd also questioned the nurse but as far as Hermann knew they hadn't hurt her.

'Bastards,' I said. I felt really sorry for poor old Hermann and I didn't want to ask whether he'd let anything out, about Paula for instance.

'It must have been pretty bad,' Morland said, looking at the cast on Hermann's arm.

Hermann did his best to snort. 'They are not so tough,' he said. 'In the desert things were worse.'

Good old Hermann! I should have known he wouldn't talk. But then how had Rifai known about Paula? Of course, he might simply have guessed that we'd need a girl to look after the kids.

Hermann told us he was lucky to have got off with only his arm busted and his face rearranged. Rifai had told Abdul to take him out of the city and dump him, but Abdul was an old chum of Hermann's and he'd taken him to a hospital instead. Hermann had called Giorgio's bar from the hospital and talked to Paula. She'd told him about Morland being in the clinic.

'Why didn't you stay in hospital, Hermann?' I said. 'I'd have come to see you there.'

'Stay in hospital?' Hermann sounded puzzled. 'But they fix me up. See.' He showed me the plaster cast.

'I see,' I said, and I shook my head. There just wasn't anything I could say. 'What about Rifai?'

Hermann shrugged. 'He thinks I am dead. Maybe that is good.'

Maybe was right. I wished I could say the same for me and Paula.

Morland groaned and buried his face in the pillow. 'It's all my fault,' he said. It was the first time I'd ever heard him admit it—and no one has had more opportunities.

Hermann said, 'Jonathan, you must not worry. It will make you sick. Remember, in war there are always casualties. Next time we will win, I promise. Next time—'

If you're a kraut I suppose you get used to thinking about next time. But I wasn't having any of it, so I cut in right there and said goodbye to both of them.

'You'll look in again tomorrow?' Morland asked.

'Sure.' It wasn't the moment to tell him that the time had come to part. In fact the longer it took him to realize it, the more time his ticker would have to recover. And it would certainly need to recover if he was going to find the money to pay the clinic.

'Hermann,' I said, 'it's been a pleasure.' And I meant it.

'*Ja*, Harry, me too. You are a good boy.'

'Just remember—biff, biff, biff.'

'*Ja*—biff, biff, biff.' Hermann shook his fist. It was the one with the plaster cast on. You have to hand it to these krauts. They just never get enough.

On the way out I ran into Giorgio coming up the steps.

'I have just heard about Jonathan. I was coming to see him. Is he very bad?'

'Not too good,' I said. 'He could do with some cheering up.'

'Perhaps I shall read him one of my poems.'

'Yes,' I said, 'you do that.'

Poor old Morland, one way or another we'd finish him off.

When I got back to the flat I found Alberto sitting alone in his playpen on the living-room floor. There were splashing noises coming from the bathroom so I supposed Selim was having his bath.

Alberto was looking a little pinker than usual. He'd obviously had his tub already. And from the way he was gurgling and shaking the bars of his pen I could see that he thought his grub was overdue. Well, at least I can get him ready, I thought, so I fetched his chair from the bedroom and set it up by the window where he liked to eat. Then I hauled him up out of the pen. What a lump!

'You've been over-eating, my boy. And no exercise either, locked up in that nursery for a week. We're going to have to get you slimmed down.'

I started to put him in the chair but he hung on tight,

229

gurgling away like mad until I got the message. He didn't want to eat, he wanted to play our game! Our game was nothing much, just me holding Alberto up in the air above my head, pretending to drop him, and then catching him again a second later. Not much of a game, I know, but he'd got quite used to it before he went away and I was tickled to see he'd remembered it. We got down to business right away and soon he was squealing and kicking and carrying on just like in the old days.

'Once more,' I said, and up and down he went, letting out a really good yell. Then I stopped for a breather: we both needed it.

'What are you doing? Where are you taking him?'

I looked round. She was standing right behind me with a saucepan in her hand, holding it in a funny way that wasn't entirely unfamiliar.

'I'm not taking him anywhere.'

'Put him down.'

Since she had the saucepan and I had Alberto, there wasn't much choice about it. I stuck him in his chair and pried his fingers loose from my shirt. 'Look, it was just a game. It won't do him any harm.'

She looked very hard at me for a moment, then went back to the bathroom taking the saucepan with her. Now I know that birds can get upset over nothing when a kid is involved, but this was going too far. I followed her. Selim was lying in the plastic tub looking half-drowned and very pissed off.

'What's all this?' I said, pointing at the saucepan.

She shook her head and turned away. But she put it down.

I went back to the living-room and did some thinking. It didn't take me long, about two minutes in fact. I went charging back into the bathroom, picked up the pot, threw it on the floor, grabbed her by the arm and shouted, 'Come out here, I want to speak to you.'

'But Selim—' she said, very nervous all of a sudden.

'Let him drown.' I pulled her along until she was standing in front of Alberto, who was watching it all with great interest.

'All right,' I said, 'now tell me about your chat with Rifai.'

Of course she burst into tears. What else?

'None of that,' I said. 'When did you talk to him?'

'After lunch . . . I rang him.'

'Why?'

She sniffed. 'Have you got a handkerchief?'

'Don't change the subject.'

'I wanted to tell him'—sniff—'that he could have Selim back'—sniff—'for nothing'—sniff. I gave her a handkerchief. 'All we wanted was to be left alone.'

'And what did he say to that?'

'He said we were going to have to give Selim back anyway and he wasn't worried about that and what he wanted was *Alberto*.' She looked at me accusingly. 'He said he'd give us ten thousand dollars for him. I just slammed down the phone.'

'But you knew I'd be phoning him later?'

'Yes.'

'And that he'd make the same offer to me?'

'Yes.'

'And you thought I'd accept.'

She stared at her toes.

'Well, for your information, he did make the same offer to me.'

'Oh.' She peeped up through her hair.

'But I did better than you, I pushed up the price. Would you like to guess how high he went?'

'No.' It was just a whimper.

'He offered me two hundred and fifty thousand. A quarter of a million. What do you think of that?'

Apparently she didn't think anything of it.

'Knowing me as you do, of course, you don't have to ask whether I accepted. Do you?'

Mumble, mumble.

'What?'

'I said, no, I don't have to ask.' She started reaching out a hand to me and edging closer, but I moved away.

'I want Selim bathed and fed in half an hour. Understand?'

'Yes.'

'I'll be down at Giorgio's if you need me.' I stopped at the door. I didn't want to say it, really I didn't, but sometimes you can't stop yourself. 'Anyway,' I said, 'you don't really imagine you're going to keep him, do you?'

She just looked at me.

Chapter Twenty-three

IT WAS STILL LIGHT when I took Selim downstairs in the carry-cot. The car was parked a few feet from the doorway and I don't think anyone saw us get in. Even if they did, it didn't matter. I could always say afterwards that the cot had been empty, that I was taking it to be repaired.

Driving through the city was something else though. Each time I stopped for a traffic light I felt all these eyes peering into the back of the car where Selim's cot lay on the seat. It seemed like everyone had suddenly become very conscious of babies, which wasn't surprising, what with the newspapers and the radio still going on about this 'barbaric crime'. To tell the truth I was beginning to get a little pissed off with all the fuss since the one real barbarian in the whole business was sitting up there in his 'palatial villa' acting like a popped virgin.

I drove up the river to the Borghese Gardens and parked under the trees near the Piazza di Siena. When it was dark I took Selim out of the back and carried him into the piazza, which is not really a piazza at all but a place where they have horse-jumping and stuff like that. It's oval-shaped and looks like a small race track, only prettier, with cypresses and tall pine trees all around it. There's a gravel track at the outer edge of the ring and inside that a big patch of grass. During the day you find a lot of kids playing on the grass, but at night the whole place is deserted except for a few benches on the embankment above the ring which are generally occupied by what Morland calls 'courting couples'.

I carried Selim to the middle of the ring and put him down.

In the darkness I could just make out the lighter shade of the gravel where the grass ended. Even Selim couldn't hurt himself here. He might manage to climb out of his cot, true, but he'd have to crawl the best part of a hundred yards across grass and gravel to reach the road, and I couldn't see our little Arab working up that kind of energy. I pulled back the veil and had a last look at him. He lay on his stomach, head on one side, both fists clenched, asleep for once but still fighting. Poor little devil, I thought, and for the first time I felt really sorry for him. One day he'd be worth a hundred million and have all the yachts and birds and caviar he could manage. Yet I had a feeling that sending him back to Rifai was the only really cruel thing we'd done to him. That was a barbaric crime all right.

I tucked the veil in carefully so as to keep the mosquitoes off him and then walked back to the car. I wondered what the 'courting couples' were making of it. Pretty soon one of them would come down the bank to see what it was that was lying there in the middle of the ring. Maybe someone had even been alert enough to notice a man driving away in a *cinquecento*. There are about a million *cinquecentos* in Italy.

On the way back I stopped at a café and phoned the gentlemen of the press. This time I got a lot of respectful attention.

'And you say you definitely haven't been paid the ransom?' said the Associated Press.

'No. We just changed our minds.' At least it might stop Rifai claiming that quarter of a million as a tax deduction.

United Press International offered me ten thousand for an exclusive series, to be signed A. Kidnapper. I declined with real regret.

Reuters said, 'Can we quote you on all this?'

Afterwards I had a cognac and then spent my last four hundred and twenty lire on petrol. It was the first time in my life I could ever remember being completely cleaned out, not having even the price of a paper on me. It was a weird feeling, unnatural you might say, certainly not one I'd recommend to anyone.

A different kind of weird feeling came over me when I got back to Via dello Scorpione. The street looked different somehow, well, not different exactly, what I meant was . . . and then.it clicked. There was no one I knew on the street, that was it, just people walking up and down I'd never seen before. It gave me a nasty turn. I'd got used to driving along slowly, waving to Toto, the *barbiere*, who always stayed open late, and old Signora Whatsit outside the *macelleria*, and Guido, who flogged lottery tickets from his wheelchair, and all the others. I poked my head through the string beads of Giorgio's. There was an old bird behind the cash desk I'd never seen before, and no sign of Giorgio himself. I was just beginning to think I'd flipped when I spotted this familiar figure, all in white, striding down the road towards me. It was Marcello, the copper. He seemed to be in a hurry to get somewhere. Normally I never speak to coppers on principle, but this was an emergency, so I waved and said, 'Where is everyone?'

'*Scusi?*'

'*Dove sono tutti?*'

He scratched his head, so I waved my hands around a bit, which always helps when you're talking to an Ite, and said, '*Tutti.*'

'*Ah.*' He beamed under his white helmet. '*Ma, in casa sua, naturalmente.*'

'*In casa—?* Whose *casa?*'

'*La sua.*' He tapped me on the chest and grinned.

'*Ma, ma, ma*'—what the hell was that word?—'*perchè?*'

'*Perchè?*' Marcello threw up his arms. '*Ma per la festa di Alberto, certo.*'

235

He slapped me on the back and trotted up the stairs—our stairs!

La festa di Alberto?—Alberto's feast?

I shot up the stairs after him like a bullet. We heard the racket long before we got to the fourth floor, mainly because the door of the flat was standing wide open. As we went in Toto came staggering out of the kitchen carrying a huge bowl of spaghetti.

'*Ecco il padre*,' he squawked when he saw me, but he didn't stop, he went straight up the steps to the terrace. We followed him, since that's where the noise was coming from.

'*Magnifico*,' said Marcello, and plunged right in.

I just stood there speechless. Every inch of the terrace was packed. It looked like the whole population of the Scorpion was up there including the kids and the old bats, and even the cats, for all I knew. They were all shouting except for a few who were screaming. Everyone had a glass of wine and some had plates of spaghetti as well. Over in one corner Guido sat in his wheelchair squeezing away at an accordion. The noise, all put together, was about ten degrees higher than the human ear could bear. I couldn't see Paula anywhere but I did spot Alberto, right in the middle of the terrace, in his chair, surrounded by a pack of jabbering women who were at their old game of poking and patting and petting and also stuffing spoonfuls of spaghetti down him. He looked pretty desperate, I thought, but as far as I was concerned he was on his own.

'Harry.' It was Paula standing behind me with another big bowl of spaghetti. 'I'm so pleased you're back. I was so worried.'

'Yes, it looks like it. Who's paying for all this?'

'Oh, Harry.' She put her head on one side. 'We're celebrating Alberto's recovery from chicken-pox. It was Mrs Giorgio's idea. She said we'd have a *festa*, just like they have for saints. Isn't it lovely?'

'Lovely,' I agreed. 'We can take the collection next Sunday.'

Over at the side of the terrace where the crowd was a little thinner I found a glass of wine standing on the wall. I took it and turned my back on the noise, leaning out over the wall, trying to get a breath of fresh air. Something caught my eye across the street: a figure standing in a lighted window, waving. I looked harder and recognized our own old bat, the one who waved to me every morning and asked about Alberto's *varicella*. I made signals telling her to go downstairs and come up to our flat, but she shook her head. Maybe she never went downstairs any more; maybe she was just too old. I raised my glass, pointed at her and drank. She smiled and made little clapping signs. What a nice old bat, I thought. And what a perfect relationship we had. It just showed how well two people could get on together as long as they kept the width of a street and a four-storey drop between them.

'Harry.' It was Paula again, touching my shoulder. I turned slowly, then froze. Standing beside her, grinning all over his ugly little puss, was Tony.

'You're early,' I said. 'The rent isn't due for a week.'

'Tony just dropped in to see whether Alberto was over the chicken-pox.' She was smiling, just as if nothing had happened between us.

'He looks great,' said Tony. 'I gotta hand it to you.'

'It's all those walks we took him for. Very good for the pox. You'd better make sure Mamma knows in case you catch it next.'

Tony blinked and Paula said quickly, 'I've asked Tony and his mother to stay for the party.'

At that moment the crowd behind them heaved and Mamma burst into view with a plate of spaghetti in each paw. She stopped when she saw me and curled her lip. Tony took one of the plates from her and fished a fork out of his pocket. 'How much longer do you need him anyway?' he asked.

Paula caught her breath and looked at me. 'It's not that I'm pushing, mind you.'

I glanced at Paula. Her eyes were begging me, but it was no good. I hadn't got the money: I hadn't got *any* money.

'As it happens,' I said, 'the job is just about finished, so you can—'

'Tony, can I have a word with you?' Paula cut in quickly. 'In private.'

Tony looked at her, then at me, grinned, stuck the plate of spaghetti into my hands and said, 'Sure. Any time.'

'Now.'

I watched them go. They went downstairs. Downstairs! I started after them and ran smack into Mamma. She grinned and shook her head. Obviously I wasn't going anywhere, except backwards maybe, and that was four storeys down. Oh well, what the hell. I poured her a glass of wine and said, '*Salute.*' She sniffed it, tested it with the tip of her tongue and then drank it. There were no flies on Big Mamma.

Someone rapped on the table for silence and after a bit of shuffling this figure climbed on to a chair. It was Giorgio. He started off with a twenty-minute warm-up all about Alberto, the general drift of which I didn't catch except that it was obviously complimentary. Then he switched to something else which I didn't get at all, not a word of it, though I could see that it was a big thing for him and maybe the main reason for his speech—always assuming your Ite needs a reason. He was clutching his chest and rolling his eyes and flinging his hands around and the crowd was going 'ooh' and 'aah'. A couple of the women started crying, but when he'd finished there was a burst of clapping. Mrs Giorgio did both and then collapsed into a chair.

I was just starting to work my way through the crowd to the steps when I caught sight of Paula. She must have heard the speech because she was looking at Giorgio in a funny way, biting her lip, puzzled. Then Giorgio spotted me and came barrelling through the crowd, eyes shining, moustache bristling.

'Well, Harry, what do you say now?' He saw me looking baffled and slapped his forehead. 'I forgot, you don't speak Italian. I was announcing my decision to sell the bar. From now on I am no longer a publican. I am a poet.'

'That's very nice,' I said.

'Of course you approve?'

What could I say? 'Of course.' Actually I thought he was nuts.

'In a few weeks I shall return to my own village in the Abruzzi. I shall never leave it again. A man should stay with his roots. Don't you agree?'

I said, 'We'll be sorry to see you go, Giorgio.' I didn't think I'd mention our own departure quite yet as it was bound to be pretty sudden when it came.

'Never mind, Harry, you will have your friend Jonathan instead.'

I thought about that for a while. Then I said. 'Just what do you mean exactly?'

Giorgio looked surprised. He said, 'But don't you know? The bar?'

'What about the bar?'

'Why, Jonathan has bought it, of course.'

'Morland has bought—*with what?*'

Giorgio's eyes popped. 'With . . . with money.'

'*Whose money?*'

He backed away. 'Harry, I don't understand. Jonathan and I have been discussing this for weeks. I thought you knew. Jonathan says he wants to settle down, and he's always wanted a bar or a café. How does he put it?—a place where—'

'—kindred spirits can gather?'

'That's right. Well, when I went to the hospital to see him

239

this afternoon we settled the whole thing. He'd told me before he had some money put away. He's been saving, he says, a little bit each year for many years. It's something we all do, Harry. Now he has enough to buy a bar—my bar. Or at any rate, enough to make a first payment. See?'

I took the cheque from him and held it up to the light. I had a funny choking feeling and the figures on the piece of paper were jumping up and down. I shut my eyes tight for a moment, then opened them again. The figures had stopped moving and they came to three million four hundred thousand lire, which, in case you don't know, is about two thousand quid. It was a real cheque too: not even Morland would have the nerve to sign a bouncer when he was laid up in hospital next to dead. I went on staring at it for a long time.

'Harry, why are your hands shaking? Do you feel all right?'

I looked around, trying to focus. If Tony was still there I'd start with him. One good stiff kick up that little runt's backside just to get the ball rolling—

'Harry, you look so flushed. Please, sit down.'

—and then there'd be Big Mamma to deal with. Good, I thought. Bring on Big Mamma! I wished Hermann hadn't been bashed about like that. I wouldn't have minded a crack at him too. Suddenly I noticed Giorgio's moustache bobbing up and down in front of me. Why not start with him? I thought. He's part of it, he and the rest of them, everyone, the world—

'Harry, here, drink this.'

I sat down hard and for a few seconds everything was spinning. Then I took a deep breath, and another, and the world settled down. It's moments like that when a man could push the button, no problem.

'Stay here, Harry. I'll call Paula.'

As soon as he'd gone I got up and went downstairs to the living-room. My pins still felt pretty shaky and I wanted to lie down, but there were too many people walking in and out, so I took a chair on to the balcony and sat there alone in the dark, thinking. I'd been had again, well and truly, but that wasn't the worst of it. I'd been had by *Morland*. That was the worst of it. Six weeks of whining that he hadn't a penny, six weeks of making me pay for everything out of sheer sympathy, wearing that old ragged jacket, looking twice as starved as before, and all the time sitting on top of a fat bank account, all the time knowing he had that cushion to come down on if the snatch didn't work out. It was disgusting, worse, it was dishonest. I began to tot up what he owed me. There was twelve hundred for the ticket, but I'd bump that up to fifteen hundred just to teach him. Then there was the rent for the car and the flat, most of the food bills, the fifty dollars I'd put down on his hospital bill—I'd say a hundred and fix the receipt —the cost of the aluminium luggage-rack—

'Harry, are you all right?' I hadn't heard her open the windows behind me.

'Fine, just fine.' Wasn't that what Morland always said?

'Giorgio said you were upset about Jonathan buying the bar.'

'I suppose you knew. You knew he had all that money.'

'No, I didn't. I promise. I even asked him once if he couldn't help with some of the expenses of the flat.'

'What did he say?'

'He said he couldn't and—' She stopped.

'And what?'

'And anyway that you owed it to him for something that happened in Tangiers. What did happen in Tangiers, Harry?'

'Morland got what was coming to him, that's what. And I wish I could think of a way of seeing he got it again.'

'Oh.' There was silence for a moment. 'Well, why don't you come back and join the party? Everyone's asking where you are.'

'I'm not in the mood.'

There was another silence. Then she said, 'Someone's just heard on the radio that they've found Selim in the Borghese Gardens. So we don't have to worry about that any longer.' The window creaked and she came out on to the balcony. 'Harry, I'm sorry for what I said before, for what I thought.'

'Forget it.'

'Harry, what are we going to do about Alberto?'

Then I turned and looked at her. With the light at her back all I saw was the dark outline of her head and the sweep of her long hair. 'Nothing,' I said quietly.

'You mean you're going to send him back?'

'Yes, that's what I mean.'

'We can find the money somehow.'

'I doubt it. But even if I can raise two hundred a week I've got better things to do with it than spend it on renting a kid.' She put her hand to her face quickly and I thought, why, why, why did I say it? But I'd said it, and that was that.

'Do you mean it?' Her voice had changed like something had broken in it.

I just stared out over the balcony. She must have stood there for nearly a minute waiting for me to answer before she went back inside. I sat in the dark, listening to the sounds coming from the terrace, to the shouting and laughter and the glasses breaking. I started remembering the past few weeks and thinking what a lot of effort we all put into getting nowhere. Especially me. For six weeks I'd been turning cartwheels, trying to do Morland, trying to get that quarter of a million, trying to buy the Russian ticket, and now, at the end of it, just trying to get out. However I looked at it it didn't make sense. Yet maybe sense is the last thing you should look for. Maybe all you should do is try to catch the balls when they're tossed at you, and if you drop one, *tant pis*, as Morland would say. The thing is though that there are some balls, and only

242

a few really, that you *have* to catch, and those are the ones I'm always missing. What I couldn't forgive was her thinking that I'd flog Alberto to Rifai. That really hurt. I sat there for a long time, until the noise up above had stopped, until the lights in the windows across the streets had gone on, and then gone off again.

A clock was striking two somewhere in the night when I heard the windows behind me open again. She was in her nightdress with her long hair hanging loose on her white shoulders, I waited for it. I knew I'd gone too far. Once you've dropped the ball, the game's over.

'Aren't you coming to bed?'

I almost fell over the balcony. Aren't you coming to bed! I couldn't believe it. That was the moment when I learned that a generous bird is really the only sort worth having. She could have spat in my eye for what I'd said before and I wouldn't have blamed her. But there she was just saying, 'Come to bed.' That's what I call generosity. And generosity lasts. So I forgot about Morland and the money, I forgot about Tony, I even forgot that she'd ever thought I might sell Alberto for a quarter of a million. I just looked at her and saw her smile and followed her inside like a lamb.

Chapter Twenty-four

THERE WAS no breakfast in bed for me the next morning. Paula was up and out of the flat on some business of her own before I was even awake. She left a note.

'Back before lunch. Give Alberto something at eleven. Love.'

Love? Love! *Love*.

I went back to bed so that I could smell the scent of her on the pillow, got my toes nicely tangled in her nightdress at the bottom of the bed and was just dozing off when the gurgling started. Alberto was in his chair by the window as usual, getting a bit of sun. Obviously he didn't like the idea of me drifting off to sleep again and he showed it by hammering his duck on the table a couple of times. It made me uncomfortable, not the duck getting thumped but having him staring at me all the time, and I knew why. It was because of what I'd said the night before about not spending two hundred dollars a week just for the pleasure of his company. From the way he was glaring at me with his little black eyes I'd almost have guessed he knew.

'Well, that's life, Alberto,' I said. 'And the sooner you learn it, the better.'

All the same, I got up.

It was lovely on the terrace, a real spring morning in mid-summer. The lines of washing strung across the street were flapping in a cool breeze that smelled like it had come straight from the sea. Down below the young birds in their bright colours were tripping up and down the old Scorpion with extra bounce. My old bat came out on the terrace opposite and started waving. I picked up Alberto and held him above my head so she could get a good look at him.

'*Bello, bello puppone,*' she squealed.

'Did you hear that, *puppone*?' I said, putting him back in the pen. But he wasn't having it, not after I'd held him up like that, so for the next ten minutes we played The Game while the old bat cackled with laughter and shouted, '*Basta, basta,*' till you'd have thought it was her being tossed up and down. After that I settled down to some thinking.

Money, that's what I was thinking about. And how to get it.

The first place to go was obviously the clinic. But I had a pretty good idea what would happen there. I'd tell Morland to pay up unless he wanted his ticker stopped permanently, and he'd say, 'Yes, Harry, as soon as I have the money,' and I'd say, 'Don't give me that, you've just paid Giorgio two thousand quid on his bar,' and he'd say, 'Yes, Harry, but that was all I had and I'll be paying the rest out of profits,' and if I pushed him he'd even have a bank statement to prove it. I know Morland, you see.

Still, I reckoned that if I really put the squeeze on him I could probably get a couple of hundred quid and that would be better than nothing. We'd be able to rent Alberto for another week at least, maybe two, and that'd make it easier— to give him up, I mean, doing it slow and gradual like so it wouldn't hurt her too much. First I had to get her *used* to the idea.

But that was only a stop-gap. For real money I'd have to look elsewhere.

Now you're probably wondering how I could possibly have forgotten those four tickets sitting in my suitcase downstairs which were worth maybe three thousand dollars between them. Well, I hadn't forgotten them, not for a moment. But they didn't represent cash to me—not money I could use for renting Alberto, say, or for paying the food bills and so on. They were my business, all that was left of it. A man doesn't go flogging his whole business just because things get a little tight. He sticks it out, starts building again and pulls in his belt if he has to. It looked as if we'd all have to pull in our belts for a while.

'And that includes you, *puppone*,' I said. After all, we could always give him back to Tony until I'd got on my feet, and then rent him again. For the summer holidays, say.

The first thing to do was to get cracking on the ticket business. It's like any other trade, if you lose touch, you're in trouble, and I'd been neglecting it far too long. I still had those two French tickets which were worth about twelve hundred apiece, say two thousand five hundred for the pair. With that kind of money I could probably buy half a dozen assorted Middle Easts—Syrian, Jordanian, Lebanese and so on—which you might not think were a good line but in fact move quite nicely in the right circles. I knew a Jewish boy in Athens who'd give me two hundred quid each for them, say six hundred dollars times six, making three thousand six hundred dollars and a very nice profit too. Thinking about the Middle East made me remember that gyppo ticket with the Israeli stamp. I wondered if it was possible to doctor the stamp so it would come up gyppo. That way I'd get another two hundred quid, maybe more, gyppo tickets being somewhat superior as Middle Easts go. I decided to go downstairs and look at it again.

A minute later I was sitting on the couch with my heart going thump, thump, thump, and my hands shaking like leaves and the black spots buzzing around thicker than ever before. The suitcase was on the couch beside me, open. The hidden compartment at the back was also open. It was empty.

Morland, I thought, because that's the first thing I always think.

But I knew it wasn't Morland. He'd be the last person I'd

ever tell about that hidden compartment. In fact, I'd only ever told one person.

I left the suitcase lying open on the floor and went up to the terrace. It was eleven o'clock. Time to give Alberto something. I went downstairs and fixed some milk. Then I stuck him on the pot, because I'd remembered that too, and then I changed his nappy. And all that time I wasn't really thinking, not about anything except heating milk and changing nappies, and there was this funny buzzing in my ears.

She didn't come back till after one o'clock and Alberto was starting to shake the bars of his pen from sheer hunger. I heard the front door open and knew that she'd see the suitcase lying open on the floor. After a minute or so I heard her coming up the steps to the terrace, slowly.

'Hullo.'

'Hullo.'

'I've had a busy morning.' She wouldn't look at me.

'I'm not surprised.'

She went over to the pen, picked up Alberto, felt his bottom to see if it was dry and then put him down again.

'First I had to find Bruno.'

I swallowed. 'How did you manage that?'

'Well, I got his phone number off that piece of paper he left with you and his wife told me he'd either be in Piazza Navona or somewhere around the Fontane di Trevi, but he wasn't at either of them. So I asked some of the other drivers and in the end I found him waiting outside the Colosseum.'

'And how is Bruno?'

'Oh, very well. He says he's giving up his *carrozza* soon to go into the passport business. He sent you his regards and said he was sorry.'

'That was nice of him.'

'And he said if you ever come across any loose tickets he'd appreciate having first refusal.'

247

I swallowed twice and remembered I couldn't afford even a small cognac. I said, 'How much did you get for them?'

She looked at me for the first time, just a quick peep through her hair. 'Three thousand five hundred dollars.'

'In cash?'

She nodded. 'It must have been the money he got for selling that Russian passport.'

I took a deep breath. I'd reckoned on only three thousand.

'I remembered you saying the French passports were worth twelve hundred dollars each so I made Bruno pay that. I hadn't any idea what the Liberian one was worth but he said no one would pay more than a hundred dollars for it, so I had to take that. But I had a feeling he was cheating me, so when it came to that funny Egyptian one I just said, "A thousand dollars," as cool as you please. Of course he moaned and said, "impossible", but I stuck it out. In the end I told him it was all or nothing. So he paid.'

'You made him pay a thousand dollars for a crooked ticket?'

'Yes.'

'That's dishonest.'

'I know.' There was a touch of defiance in her voice, but something else too, a sort of eagerness like she was keeping the important news back.

'Really dishonest,' I said. There's nothing like rubbing it in when you get the chance.

'I know. But he's a crook, so it doesn't matter.'

'So am I.'

'So are we all,' she said, looking at Alberto.

Suddenly I felt much better. Things were looking up.

I said, 'I'll overlook the fact that you nicked my tickets and didn't even ask my advice. Just don't do it again. We could have got a better price, but I'll overlook that too. Three and a half thousand's not bad and I know just how to use it.' I was thinking of those assorted Middle Easts.

She shook her head.

'What?'

'I haven't got it.'

'*What?*'

'Well, only five hundred of it.' She took out a bundle of notes and put them in my hand. 'That's for us to live on. Until you find a job.' When she saw I was having trouble with my breathing she said, 'I drove out to Tivoli after I'd seen Bruno. I arranged it all last night with Tony.'

'Arranged?' I whispered.

'About Alberto.' She looked me straight in the eye. 'I told Tony last night we'd pay him. When you said you wouldn't I just decided to go ahead and do it myself.'

I counted up to ten slowly. When I finally spoke I was calm and restrained. I said, 'Am I to understand that we now have a long-term lease with this little bugger?'

'No, we haven't,' she said, glaring at me.

'Well—?'

'We've bought him.'

'Oh Christ,' I said, and felt my knees going. 'For three thousand dollars?'

'Not exactly.'

'Not *exactly?*'

'That was the first payment.'

My knees did go then. Luckily there was a chair right behind me. 'First payment,' I said hoarsely.

'We can pay the rest over six months, Tony says.'

'The rest—'

'Another two thousand, that's all. Tony wanted five thousand for him. Wouldn't he be furious if he knew Rifai had offered a quarter of a million?' She stood there looking down at me, still tense, half-smiling, not quite sure whether I was going to break down and howl or stand up and sock her. When she saw I wasn't up to doing anything for the moment, she fished around in her bag and pulled out a piece of paper. 'This is Alberto's adoption certificate. It's made out to Tony.' She put it in my other hand.

'What do you want me to do with it?'

'Forge it,' she said. Then she bent down quickly and before I could stop her she'd kissed me. 'Mr. and Mrs Harry Brighton.'

I watched her pick up Alberto and carry him off downstairs, saying, 'Poor darling, you must be starving.'

'Is that a proposal?' I shouted after her. 'Because it if is—' But she'd disappeared down the steps.

Well, how about that for the shoe? How about that for the Emperor's filthy old sandal? Three thousand dollars! Now you see it, now you don't. And my whole career ruined too, though that was something I was used to. Do you ever get tired? Really tired, I mean, so tired you think you'll never get on your feet again? Well, that's how I felt then for just a moment. But only for a moment. One thing I'll say for myself, I've got bounce. I followed her downstairs.

'Just think'—I heard her voice in the kitchen—'he'd have paid a quarter of a million dollars for you. What do you think of that?' Alberto went into a fit of gurgling and Paula laughed. 'So that's what you think of it, do you?'

'He's not thinking of anything,' I said from the door. 'He's hungry, that's all, like any baby who's not fed when he ought to be.'

She pushed back the hair from her face and started peeling a carrot.

I went out, but in a minute I heard her again.

'You'll be having a little brother or sister one of these days. Won't that be nice? Which would you rather?'

I went charging back in. 'Any decisions,' I said, 'about little brothers and sisters will be taken by me. Got it? And the decision at this moment, and as far ahead as I can see, is *no*.'

Mumble, mumble.

'What was that?'

'I said you didn't behave like that last night.' She peeped round her hair.

What could I say? I was turning to go out again when she said, 'What sort of job are you going to get?'

'That,' I said clearly, 'is none of your business. Understand?'

'Yes, Harry.'

'Maybe I'll go back into the import business. That's smuggling to you.'

'Yes, Harry.'

'Or open a cat house right here on Scorpion Street.'

'Yes, Harry.'

'But whatever it is, I don't want to hear the word "job" again.'

'Yes, Harry.'

That was better. I'm pretty patient, as you may have guessed by now, and adaptable too, but I have my limits: taking a job is one of them. In the circles I move in that's the same as surrendering, running up the old white flag, tossing in your bit with the rest of the peasants. There are a billion or so people in the world with jobs. Good luck to them. They probably need it. There's only one Harry Brighton. He's on his own, and he likes it that way.

Still, she had a point. I couldn't go back to the ticket business again, not after word got around that this red-headed dish had showed up at the Colosseum one fine morning and flogged my entire stock to Bruno. What a humiliation! I'd never live it down, not in the trade. I wondered if Ziggy would ever hear about it in Knokke-le-Zoute. I hoped not. The shock might very well prove fatal to the old gent.

What I needed was something totally new, something quite different from anything I'd tried before, something that needed next to no capital to start, something artistic . . . Artistic! I dragged the pram out of the corner into the middle of the room.

What had that bearded geezer in Via Margutta said? Where was I going to exhibit it? As it stood it was worth at least a hundred quid. But as a work of art, who could say? For a few minutes it seemed like a great idea. Then I thought, what next? One masterpiece like the pram wasn't enough to get me a reputation and I couldn't see anything else lying around that looked to be in that line, except maybe Alberto's duck, and I didn't think he'd take kindly to that turning into an art object overnight. No, the art racket might be a good one like Morland said, but you needed some stock on hand just like in any other business.

Stock. Capital. Resources. Raw material. Call it what you like, it's what you start with, and if you haven't got it, you can't start, and if you can't start, you get a job. It's as easy as that, I thought, and I shuddered.

But what stock did I have, I asked myself. In six weeks I'd lost the lot. And all I'd got in return were a lot of memories, and not ones I wanted to have either. Like letting Morland con me right at the start when I thought I was conning him. And all that crap I had to put up with from Tony and Mamma and even from Paula, and worst of all, the fiasco with Rifai. Of course there were some nice memories too. A couple of evenings with Paula, some moments with Alberto, a drink or two with Giorgio. And breaking into Rifai's villa. That was my favourite memory, maybe because it was something I'd never have thought I had the nerve to do. Maybe that was what Morland meant when he said that everyone had to go for the big time at least once in his life. Maybe the big time is what you think is too big for *you*.

I certainly had memories, nothing but.

Over by the window the Olivetti was still on the table with the same sheet of paper that Morland had stuck in it the afternoon we moved in. Crafty old Morland. 'Just stick a piece of paper in . . . now anyone who calls will take your word for it you're writing a book.' The only one who'd ever asked me was Giorgio. *Professore*, he'd called me that first evening. *Professor* Harry Brighton. That was something I wished Ziggy could have heard.

Why not? I asked myself. What have I got to lose?

Only the rest of your marbles, I thought. That gave me a laugh. If there was anything I could afford to lose it was certainly my marbles. Judging by the past few weeks' performance they weren't worth a kopeck.

Yes, why not? I thought. There must be money in it or people wouldn't do it, and prestige too. Of course it would mean going straight for a while, but I couldn't see any harm in that. We all need a change from time to time. I've often thought that a little larceny would do the average geezer a world of good: tone up his muscles, get the blood circulating, put some pink in his cheeks. There's nothing like it, believe me . . . *Professor* Harry Brighton. I couldn't get it out of my mind. What a giggle it would be, I thought. And what a shot in the eye for Morland! That was all I needed. I went over to the table, stuck a fresh sheet of paper in the Olivetti, sharpened a couple of pencils and put half a bottle of *vino rosso* within easy reach.

For a while I sat there thinking, half listening to Paula humming to herself in the kitchen, with the noise of the street coming up through the open window and the afternoon sun making patterns on the balcony wall.

Then I started to write.

PS.

Now that it's finished there's something I have to tell you which I've been keeping back. It's this. All that stuff I gave you before about me being a ticket man at heart and having found my vocation and all, well, it's not true, not any longer. Now I've really found my mark. I'm a *writer*, let's face it.

At least once a day I go downstairs to remind Morland of it. Leaning on the bar, sipping a cognac, watching him sweat over the espresso machine, I make some remark like, 'You never told me this creative work was so exhausting, Morland,' or, 'Just fancy, all those years spent messing around at this and that, and all the time I had this talent locked up inside me waiting to get out. Didn't you ever notice it, Morland?' His replies are not the sort of things you'd want to see in cold print. I think that one of these days he's going to blow his top once and for all and then it'll be goodbye Morland.

We had a couple of very nasty scenes when he came out of the clinic. Finally I said I'd settle for him supporting me and Paula and Alberto on the proceeds of the bar until my royalties started rolling in. He didn't take it lying down but Paula fixed him in the end by bringing Alberto downstairs, propping him up on the bar and saying, 'Jonathan Morland, are you going to let this child starve?' Poor old Morland. He just went to pieces and next thing I knew he was offering me a partnership. But I'd learned better by then. 'A weekly allowance will be fine,' I said. Then I pushed Alberto over the bar and said, 'Kiss your Uncle Jonathan for both of us.'

The bar seems to be doing quite nicely still and I'm glad to report no sign to date of anything resembling a 'kindred spirit' among the customers. But I'm watching. Morland is still complaining that he's bankrupt and he may even be telling the truth this time, since besides supporting the Brighton clan, he's also got Hermann on the payroll. The kraut now sits behind the cash register where Mrs Giorgio used to sit and rings up the sales with his one good arm. I don't think he adds up very well because Morland is always screaming at him and saying he'll be ruined if this goes on, etc., etc. Hermann is not too happy in his work. The other day I caught him muttering something about joining the mercenaries. I don't blame him. Fighting the fuzzies will seem like a picnic after working for Morland.

There's not much more to tell you except that Alberto is still getting fatter by the day and shows every sign of developing into another Hermann—size-wise, that is. He's almost all paid up now and if I can screw another hundred quid out of Morland we'll be home. The big thing now is when is he going to say his first word? Paula can't wait for it. I can. I reckon he's going to have a lot to say when he finally gets around to it, including some things we may not want to hear. Like, what the hell did we mean by dragging him away from that plush villa and that carved walnut cot, and just when he had it made, too?

'Don't be silly,' Paula said. 'We've given him love and that's much more important.'

You see what we writers are up against?

As you'll have gathered we didn't bother to move out of the Scorpion in the end in spite of Rifai's threats to find us and do us. The only way he could trace us was through Alberto, Paula said, and in a couple of months Alberto wouldn't look anything like the baby Rifai had known. For a while I was worried about Hermann moving in downstairs in case Rifai found us through him. But maybe the kraut is considered officially dead or something, because we've had no trouble. I saw a picture of Rifai in *Oggi* the other day, smiling his oily smile, with Selim sitting in a baby chair next to him looking just the same as ever —miserable. They were on the lawn in front of the house. I could just make out the nursery window on the upper floor. 'MILLIONAIRE SELLS ROMAN RESIDENCE', the caption said. It gave Morland a good chuckle, which is something he can always do with after a day of pulling on the old espresso machine.

'The air didn't agree with him, I assume.'

And that's it, except for one last note. This book isn't exactly the way I wrote it. There were a couple of nice juicy sex scenes which I took a lot of trouble over and which were very stimulating, particularly for the author. Those have gone. Paula just tore them out without a word and from the look in her hard

255

green eyes I could see the point wasn't worth arguing. She also tried to make me show the book to Morland before I sent it to a publisher because she said a lot of the grammar and stuff looked pretty queer to her and Morland could correct it. Correct it! That gave me a laugh. I didn't need three guesses to know where he'd start his 'correcting'. So I put my foot down and said no true artist would let other people play around with his work.

'It may be a mess,' I said, 'but it's mine.'